Jim Henson's SONG OF THE Dark Crystal

PENGUIN WORKSHOP
An Imprint of Penguin Random House LLC, New York

If you purchased this book without a cover, you should be aware that this book is stolen property. It was reported as "unsold and destroyed" to the publisher, and neither the author nor the publisher has received any payment for this "stripped book."

Penguin supports copyright. Copyright fuels creativity, encourages diverse voices, promotes free speech, and creates a vibrant culture. Thank you for buying an authorized edition of this book and for complying with copyright laws by not reproducing, scanning, or distributing any part of it in any form without permission. You are supporting writers and allowing Penguin to continue to publish books for every reader.

The publisher does not have any control over and does not assume any responsibility for author or third-party websites or their content.

TM and © 2017 The Jim Henson Company. JIM HENSON's mark and logo, THE DARK CRYSTAL mark and logo, characters, and elements are trademarks of The Jim Henson Company. All rights reserved. First published in hardcover in 2017 by Grosset & Dunlap. This paperback edition published in 2019 by Penguin Workshop, an imprint of Penguin Random House LLC, New York. PENGUIN and PENGUIN WORKSHOP are trademarks of Penguin Books Ltd, and the W colophon is a registered trademark of Penguin Random House LLC.
Printed in the USA.

Visit us online at www.penguinrandomhouse.com.

Library of Congress Control Number: 2017950974

ISBN 9780593095379   10 9 8 7 6 5 4 3 2 1

Jim Henson's

SONG OF THE DARK CRYSTAL

BY J. M. LEE

ILLUSTRATED BY
CORY GODBEY

Penguin Workshop

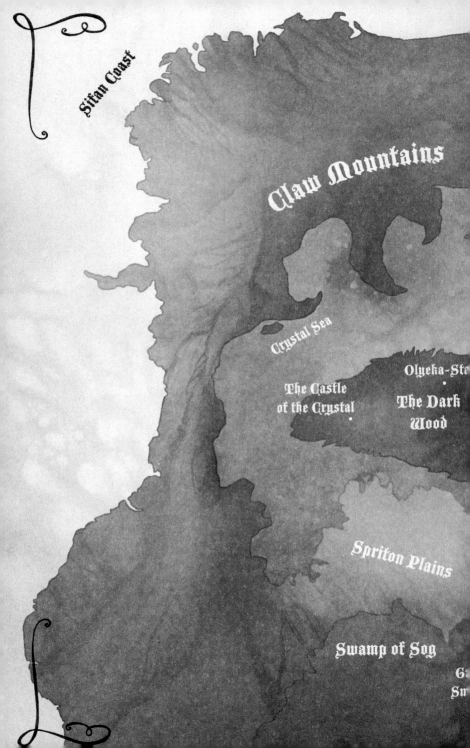

To make a sound is to trouble the roots of silence.
The Dark Crystal: The Novelization

CHAPTER 1

"This way. Almost there."

Kylan pointed to where the path forked. One way led back to the village behind them while the other twisted down and away, under arched branches and beyond. He followed the latter, trusting Naia to keep up. All around them, the air was full of morning song.

The Stonewood girl was waiting for them at the very edge of the village, where the trail changed from a row of flat stones to dirt and moss. She was young, still without her wings, and perched atop one of the many gray rocks that populated the wood. Hopping down when they arrived, she grabbed Naia's hand.

"Naia, you're awake! I'm Mythra. We met when you were asleep. Did you rest well? Is it true you fought skekMal? Kylan told me you did. And escaped from the Castle of the Crystal! That's so amazing and brave!"

Naia rubbed her cheek. She said nothing, but Kylan could tell that they shared thought. Their flight from the Skeksis in the Dark Wood had hardly felt amazing or brave. Really, they were just lucky to be alive, but there was no point in frightening the youngling.

"We nearly trampled Mythra on the Landstrider when we

found Stone-in-the-Wood last night," Kylan explained. "She brought us to her home for you to recover."

"So . . . you know about the Skeksis?" Naia asked. "And you believe Rian's stories, even though the Skeksis have told everyone he's a lying traitor?"

Mythra was already skipping down the path, disappearing into the curtains of hanging foliage. Her voice echoed back as they followed her.

"Of course I believe Rian. He's my brother!"

Kylan followed the girl through the Dark Wood, losing track of the path after one too many twists. Was this where they had come through on their flight from the castle? He probably wouldn't even know the place if he saw it. Mythra stopped when they reached a small clearing overgrown with shrubs.

"Rian!" she called. "It's me—I've brought the others I told you about. Gurjin's sister, and her friend!"

There was no one in sight, and Mythra tried Rian's name again. Naia stepped forward when no one answered, ears twisting about and eyes sharp. When Mythra went to call a third time, Naia covered the younger girl's mouth.

"Shh," she hissed. "Listen."

Kylan perked up his ears. Naia's instincts in the wild were strong, crafted and honed from growing up in the Swamp of Sog, where everything from the trees to the mud could be a danger. Sure enough, when he held his breath and listened, he heard a far-off *snap* and *crash!* followed by curses in a Gelfling tongue.

"Rian," Mythra gasped.

"This way!"

Kylan and Mythra followed Naia as she darted into the wood, hand on the hilt of the knife that was sheathed on her belt. Kylan lost track of the clearing as they hurried through the trees, bounding over rocks and thorned shrubs.

Another loud crash sent birds into flight as they mounted an outcrop of rocks. Below them, a green-furred beast with whorled horns and a clubbed tail grappled with something much smaller. When the horned creature reared and let out a broken roar, Kylan saw massive flat teeth—and under its hooved front legs, a Gelfling boy armed with a stick. Lying uselessly on the other side of the glade sat a spear, likely his usual weapon.

"Rian!" Mythra cried.

The boy rolled away, out from under the beast, looking for the one who had called him.

"Mythra! Stay back! This horner has seen the Crystal!"

"A darkened creature?" Kylan asked, heart still pounding from their flight. "Like the ruffnaw?"

"And the Nebrie," Naia agreed. "But . . ."

The last time they had come across darkened creatures, Naia had been able to heal them with dreamfasting, pushing the darkness from their hearts. It was something Kylan had never seen before. But despite her remarkable ability, dreamfasting with beasts still meant connecting with the mind and the heart. After all she'd suffered through so recently, Kylan worried. It might be dangerous for Naia to try healing a darkened creature if she was not yet healed herself.

The horner bucked, uprooting a sapling in warning. It would not be long before it tried to do the same to Rian. Kylan caught Naia's sleeve as she readied for a fight.

"Don't push yourself," he said. "Please. I know you want to fix it, but you shouldn't hurt yourself in the process."

She grimaced and hopped up onto a rock and drew her dagger.

"At least I can help get him out of there."

Before Kylan could stop her, she leaped, wings unfolding just enough to slow her fall as she landed between Rian and the green horner. The creature plowed its hooves into the earth again, swinging its head and narrowly missing the two Gelfling that stood before it.

"I don't need your help!" Rian shouted. Then he saw her clothing, her green skin and dark locs. "Wait, are you—"

"Introductions later!"

Naia and Rian dove to either side when the horner charged. Unlike the thrashing, maddened beasts Kylan had seen before, it did not seem wholly out of control. When the creature saw Naia, it paused before lowering its horns, almost as though it recognized her. It snorted, pawing the ground and unearthing rocks and roots.

"Get out of here," Naia ordered. "While I have its attention!"

"I said I don't need your help!" Rian spat back, though he took the opportunity to move closer to his spear. "This one's different than the others—I don't know how, but it's different!"

Kylan's fingertips hurt where he gripped the stone in front of him. Naia stepped steadily, drawing the horner's red gaze away from Rian. If he went down to try to help, he would only get in the way. His fingers found the rope of his *bola*, and he pulled it from his belt.

"I know you're full of darkness now," Naia said to the beast, holding out her empty hand. "But please, remember! Remember what you were before!"

Rian reached his spear and with only a moment's pause to aim, he threw it toward the beast. It sank into the horner's exposed flank, but the beast barely reacted. It was fixed on Naia, and with thundering hooves, it charged. The breadth of its horns was so wide, there was no way she could escape in time and at such close range. Rian shouted after the horner in dismay, and Kylan let his *bola* loose. It nearly missed, bouncing off the horner's back like a pebble.

Naia didn't need saving. As the horner neared, she sprang, grabbing one of the beast's horns as it swung toward her. There she clung, stubborn eyes bright with determination while the horner wailed in anger. Kylan's breath rushed out in relief just in time to be caught again. The horner was clever, even in its rage, and instead of being lost in confusion, it changed its attack. It sighted a tree and headed for it, angling its head to strike as soon as it was in range. If Naia dropped to the ground, she would be trampled, but if she didn't get out of the way, she would soon be crushed between the horn and bark.

"Naia," Kylan shouted, because it was the only thing left he could do. "Naia, hurry!"

She scrambled along the beast's horn as the others watched. She had almost made it along the horn to the beast's head when she slipped, her shoes sliding against the rough bone. She nearly lost her grip, dangling from the spiraled horn as it swung through the air and brambles toward the tree that would be the end of her.

Something dark and serpentine shot out from under Naia's hair, diving into the thick green mane at the nape of the horner's neck. Startled, the horner jerked. Instead of striking the tree full-on, only the tip of its horn glanced off the trunk, throwing the beast off balance. Naia yelped and let go, flying through the air and tumbling into the brush. Kylan watched with her as the horner stumbled, nearly toppling, then screeched and thrashed.

"A muski?" Mythra asked, eyes wide.

The black eel that had come to Naia's rescue darted in and out of the horner's fur like a water serpent leaping through ocean waves. The horner threw itself against the tree, trying to squash the little flying eel, but Neech was too agile. Naia and Rian regrouped, readying their weapons, knowing it was only a matter of time before Neech's distraction wore off. There was no way the little eel's teeth, as sharp as they might be, could penetrate the horner's thick hide.

Just as Naia and Rian were about to renew their attack, the horner's thrashing stopped. Its cries and bellowing ceased, and the glade was quiet as the great creature's knees buckled and bowed. Then it fell, bloodshot eyes closing. At first Kylan thought it had passed on, but as Neech surfaced from its mane, he saw the beast's side rise and fall. It was unconscious. He and Mythra climbed the rocky hill to meet the other two below.

"What happened?" Kylan asked.

Naia wiped her forehead and tossed her locs behind her shoulder.

"I don't know. Maybe it heard my plea without dreamfasting and let go of the darkness . . . I can only hope. Oh, Neech. To the rescue again. Did you find a snack in there?"

The flying eel drifted through the air and alighted on Naia's shoulder. A black, arthropodic leg stuck out of the eel's weasel-like mouth, still twitching. Kylan didn't want to know how many other bugs lived within the horner's dense coat. With a last few crunches, Neech finished his victory treat with an audible gulp.

"You're Naia. Gurjin's twin."

The hardened voice was Rian's. He was tall for a Gelfling, with olive skin and dark eyes. His thick dark brown hair was tousled and wild, broken by a single streak of blue above his right eye. His face was young and kind, though his eyes were weary and his lips were pressed in a tired line.

"And you're Rian," Naia said.

They had heard his name so often since they had begun their journey. In fact, at many times, his name was almost all they'd had for guidance. To finally meet him in person had seemed impossible, yet here they were.

"Another darkened horner!" he said. "They dig where the Crystal's veins are buried, and they're too dim-witted to look away when they uncover it."

"It was certainly darkened, but something felt different," Kylan said.

Naia agreed.

"It was focused. Like it recognized Rian and me..."

Rian watched the sleeping horner, brow drawn tight.

"If you've seen the darkened creatures, then the darkness is spreading. Maybe it's changing, too. Just last season we saw our first glimpse of it in the wood. At this rate it won't be long before all of Thra is gazing into the shadows and turning on itself."

Rian shook the thought off and pulled his spear from the poor horner's hide. Mythra climbed up with a bundle of forest moss and pressed it against the bleeding wound as Rian hopped down.

"You look just like Gurjin... Is he with you?"

"He didn't make it," Naia said flatly, as if to deliver the sad news as quickly as possible and be done with it. Maybe it was for the best. Kylan had no idea what to say to her about it, and he imagined Rian would feel even more at a loss if they dwelled on it too long. "This is Kylan, a song teller of the Spriton clan. We're here to..."

No one wanted to say what needed to be said next, though it was the reason they were meeting here so secretly. The reason neither Gurjin nor the Vapran princess who had also helped them was here with them. Kylan chewed on his lip, pushing back the feelings of remorse over their friends who hadn't escaped.

"We're here to figure out what to do about the Skeksis!"

The bright voice came from above. Mythra finished dressing the horner's wound and climbed down. She pushed Rian and Naia together, close enough that they could clasp hands.

"You two should dreamfast. Then we can make a plan."

Rian's ears flattened a little, though he wiped his palm off on his tunic in preparation. He held it out in offer, neither eager nor reluctant.

"She's right. It is the fastest way."

Kylan watched Naia, feeling a pinch of protectiveness. If she had not felt well enough to dreamfast with the horner, was she really in a safe place to open her heart to another Gelfling, to share what had broken it? They had heard Rian's name many times, and sought him for days, but he was still a stranger. An ally, but not a friend.

When Naia glanced at Kylan in hesitation, that was all he needed to know. He stepped forward and offered his own hand.

"Naia's heart is broken now," he said. "But I was there, and she told me what she saw. I can't give you her memories, but I can give you mine and my memory of her tale."

"Very well," Rian said.

He didn't seem to care either way, all action and little emotion. Kylan reminded himself that Rian had gone through his own trials since his escape from the Skeksis—trials Kylan was likely about to be witness to himself.

He braced himself. They grasped hands, and the dreamfast began.

CHAPTER 2

Dreamfasting was like diving into a pool of water without knowing its depth or what might wait below. Kylan remained at the surface at first, sensing Rian's memories and knowing at the same time Rian could peek into his. It was often disorienting in the beginning, to dreamfast with someone for the first time. Even when they had agreed to dreamfast, there were still so many thoughts and visions, protective barriers and waves of wariness.

After a moment the waves calmed, and Rian began. His mental voice sounded far away and inside Kylan's mind all at once.

I was a soldier, like my father . . .

The vivid image that came first was of the Castle of the Crystal, obsidian and magnificent, towering over the Dark Wood like a claw and crown. Rian's memory of the castle was powerful and detailed. He knew every spacious hall and stately room, had traveled and patrolled every spiraling passageway. The only chamber he had not seen was the center pavilion, forbidden to the Gelfling guards and servants. Only the Skeksis Lords, the raptorial velvet-cloaked keepers of the castle, were allowed to enter that place. There, they and they alone communed with the Heart of Thra—the heart of the world. After they heard Thra's song,

they entered its words in tomes and sent out orders to the *maudra* of each of the Gelfling clans. So the will of Thra was passed on.

Or so it seemed. Kylan already knew the terrible secret the Skeksis kept. He had seen its evidence himself and in dreamfast with Naia after the nightmare they had survived. Now he waited to see it as Rian had.

Our friends went missing, one by one. When we asked the Skeksis, they paid no heed. Then they called for Mira . . .

Kylan saw a flash of a Gelfling girl, all winks and tall tales. Rian walked with her, back to the castle after an evening patrolling the wood that bordered the grounds. In Rian's hand, hidden in his uniform cloak, was a glowing bellflower. He would give it to Mira when they said good night. He would tell her that even though they had been on duty, he had enjoyed their time together, and perhaps they could enjoy time together some other evening . . .

Two Skeksis were waiting at the castle, the decorated Chamberlain and the Scientist, Lord skekTek, a shrewd, tendony beast with a metal-and-glass eye. They crowded around Mira, the Chamberlain beckoning her for official business.

"Vapra, are you? Oh yes, lovely Silverling . . . come for orders . . ."

The Skeksis with the mechanical eye jabbed a talon-like finger at Rian.

"Retire for the evening, guard."

Kylan felt Rian's memory more than he saw it: anger, fear, anxiety. He knew he should trust the lords, or at least obey them, but his gut was telling him that something was wrong. Then impulsiveness as Rian followed, knowing if he were caught, he might be discharged, but if his instinct was right, Mira could be in danger.

She was. The memory was a rush of disorganized fragments of sounds and images: Rian's path through the castle, the jarring echoes of the Skeksis' harsh laughter. Mira's questions that started calm but escalated into alarm. Over it all, Kylan heard the memory of a grating crank, as if an enormous piece of architecture was in motion on a hundred gears and cogs.

Here the vision was sharp and painful. Rian found his way to where the Skeksis had taken Mira. The Skeksis Scientist's lab, deep in the gut of the castle. The door was open a hair, just a sliver of fiery red in the dark hall. Mira's voice was quiet now, just whimpers, and Rian peered through the crack in the door. He saw her bound to a chair, facing a panel in the stone wall. skekTek, the Scientist, stood near the panel with his claws on a lever. The cranking and shuddering of machinery intensified, and then the panel opened and flooded the room with brilliant red.

"*Look into the light, yes, Gelfling,*" skekTek said. He reached to another lever and maneuvered it, bringing a second piece of the contraption into view—a reflector, suspended in the cavern of fire beyond the wall. Mira began to cry out for help, struggling against the bonds. Rian almost burst in then, but skekTek rotated the reflector, placing a blinding dagger of light on Mira's face. The instant she looked into the light, she went still.

Kylan felt the memory weaken as Rian's focus lapsed.

It's all right, he said. *You don't need to show any more. I understand . . .*

No, Rian replied. *No, it's important. You should see it. You should see just how terrible the Skeksis really are.*

Kylan watched through Rian's eyes as Mira's limbs went limp. Her skin paled and dried, her hair turning withered and brittle, as if her life force was being drained from her body. As she slowly died, her eyes turning milky and unseeing, another machine went into motion. A series of tubes shuddered to life, slowly filling with a glowing liquid. The substance was pristine, blue tinted, almost like liquid crystal, and it passed slowly through the conduits until it finally filled a glass vial, drop by drop.

The worst came next. The Skeksis Scientist plucked the vial once it was full. He sniffed it and gave a pleased sigh, and then, to Kylan's horror, tipped the vial into his mouth for a tiny, sickening sip. As the drops touched his tongue, light flashed in his eyes, clearing them of their aging haze. The wrinkles and distortions in his withered face and beak smoothed, the hairs on his scalp growing thicker and filling with a glimmer of shine. Mira's life force was now his, her youth flowing into his old and deteriorating veins.

Her vliya, Rian said. *As if it's wine.*

Kylan shuddered. Naia had told him as much, but seeing it so clearly in Rian's memory was horribly different. He was relieved when the vision dissipated.

I'm sorry about Mira, he said.

Me too, Rian replied. Yet the grief had given birth to courage and purpose, it seemed, *Now tell me the tale you and Naia share. Tell me how you came to join me in the fight against the Skeksis, who've sent the rest of our people after me as a traitor and a liar.*

Kylan took hold of the dreamfast, remembering what he knew of Naia's journey. He had to speak for her as well as himself. Although they had dreamfasted together during their travels, and she had shared with him the story of how she'd left her home and traveled north, it was impossible to dreamfast another's dreamfasted memories. Instead, he had to speak it, so he kept it short and to the point.

Tavra, one of the All-Maudra's daughters, came to Naia's village searching for you and Gurjin. When Tavra didn't find Gurjin there, Naia left for Ha'rar to defend Gurjin's honor. I met her north of Sog, when she passed through the Spriton plains.

Kylan remembered the day Naia had come to his village, knowing that as he called up the memory, Rian would see it, too. He remembered Naia's aloof appeal, and how reluctant she had been to make friends, but Kylan had liked that about her. He had seen his own outsiderness reflected in her. It might not have meant much to her, but for Kylan, it had been the beginning of the journey that had eventually brought him here, to share in this dreamfast with Rian, and to fight against the Skeksis.

The lands were filling with darkness, he told Rian. *We saw the darkened creatures, mad with a sickness from looking into the earth. Even the trees in the Dark Wood were ill.*

He showed Rian the night they had been lost in the woods. Kylan stood watch while Naia dreamfasted with the Cradle-Tree, trying to calm its madness. She had healed the tree, but it hadn't soothed the darkness. Those shadows had been born somewhere else.

In the end, we went to the castle . . .

That was where he'd learned that the Skeksis Lords had betrayed them. That they had captured Tavra, the All-Maudra's noble daughter, and put her in front of the reflector in the Scientist's laboratory. That the Crystal itself was the source of the darkness, and the Skeksis were responsible.

And Gurjin? Rian asked.

The solemn question brought only one memory to mind: the terrifying Lord skekMal hunting them in the wood, chasing them like a shadow storm with glowing, fiery eyes. That was all Kylan had seen, and so that was where the dreamfast ended.

Kylan folded his arms around himself. His senses returned to reality, but it wasn't immediate, just as one couldn't be instantly dry after emerging from a swim. Naia sat on a patch of moss, waiting attentively beside the sleeping horner, while Mythra ate a fat peach-berry plucked from her traveling pouch.

"He sacrificed himself so that we could meet you and warn the rest of our people," Kylan said. "As did Tavra."

Kylan watched Rian's face, trying to guess what was going through the soldier's mind. Seeing Rian's memory had been difficult, and he couldn't imagine what it was like to relive it. Rian shook his head, thick brows eternally furrowed.

"Gurjin died proud as ever," Rian said. "We won't waste his effort. Nor Tavra's, nor Mira's. The Skeksis will pay for what they've done. I'll see to it single-handedly if I have to."

"You won't. Gurjin is—was—*my* brother," Naia said. "If anyone will teach the Skeksis what Gurjin's sacrifice meant, it will be me."

"You? Who haven't seen a day of duty in the castle?"

"I've seen plenty of days in other places."

"The Skeksis would crush you a second time! I will do it alone."

"Stop it!" Mythra scolded, so forcefully that a bit of fruit flew out of her mouth. "Rian always tries to go it alone. Look how that's worked out for you so far, big brother!"

Rian scoffed, blowing his shaggy bangs away from his face.

"I do it for you. And for Timtri, and Mother. I always have, and I'll continue to do things on my own if it saves the Gelfling people. I don't need anyone else's help."

Naia rolled her eyes so hard, her whole head moved. Kylan couldn't decide what to think of the Stonewood soldier. He was certainly brave and willing to act, but he had a streak of nerve that had nearly been the end of him at least once. Following the Skeksis scientist into the depths of the castle could have been the last thing he had ever done, but instead he had escaped and lived to tell the tale. Either his courage was being rewarded or he was just plain lucky.

Mythra finished the peach-berry and threw the pit at her brother, who deftly avoided it.

"Speaking of Mother. She wants to invite you all to supper—like we used to do, before Rian left to serve at the castle."

"I should stay here in the wood," Rian said. "I'm a traitor, remember?"

"Mother says it's important for you to come home. She left early this morning to go digging for your favorite merkeeps. She wants to thank Naia and Kylan for believing in you. Joining us is the least you could do to show some gratitude, since you don't seem very interested in thanking them yourself."

Rian flinched.

"I'm not ungrateful. I just don't want anyone else to get hurt. After what you've done and seen, you might want to consider keeping out of sight, too."

The warning was all too practical. It didn't matter if they were innocent. The Skeksis' accusations were more important than the truth.

Mythra snorted. She hopped down from her perch and headed up the path, back toward Stone-in-the-Wood.

"Just be home in time for supper."

CHAPTER 3

After Mythra left the three of them alone, the glade was silent save for the sounds of birds chirping beyond the tree line.

Kylan didn't know what to do or say next. The problem at hand was immense, almost too big to think about. How could they take on the Skeksis, those who were lords among the Gelfling and held the Castle of the Crystal? The Gelfling were peaceful and spread in seven clans across a great land. Some clans were so far afield, Kylan had only heard of them in song.

On the other hand, the Skeksis were few and focused. They controlled the Heart of Thra, and because of that, their word was law.

Kylan hoped that Naia or Rian might initiate the conversation that needed to be had, but both were too stubborn and lost in their own thoughts. It fell to Kylan, then, so he broached the topic as gently as possible.

"What do you think we should do?"

"We need to tell the All-Maudra," Rian replied immediately, as if the answer were so obvious, the question had been unnecessary. "I'm leaving for Ha'rar soon. I have a vial of the horrible essence. If I can just get to Ha'rar and show the All-Maudra and her court, they'll know that I'm telling the truth."

"Have you tried telling your own *maudra* first?" Kylan asked. "The journey to Ha'rar is long, and you don't know that the All-Maudra will believe you. But it's your *maudra*'s duty to care for her clan. Maybe she would surprise you..."

The soldier shook his head and lowered his voice, almost talking to himself.

"I used to think telling everyone, as many as I could, was the answer. I tried it after I left the castle. To reach people I knew before... but the Skeksis have turned everyone against me. They even sent my own father after me. If I tell Maudra Fara and she sides with the Skeksis, my family will be at risk. At least if the All-Maudra fails me, I'll know I did all that I could."

Naia struck the earth beside her with a fist.

"Not everyone is against you! We're here. And we're going with you. No matter how much you want to go alone. I've seen the darkened Heart of Thra, and what happened to Tavra after they put her in front of the crystal mirror."

"Naia's right," Kylan agreed. "We're in this together."

Kylan could see that Rian was calculating the benefit they would bring if he took them along. Perhaps Rian would have preferred Gurjin as his travel-mate, but that was no longer an option. Three Gelfling who sang the same song was better than one who sang alone. Rian tossed his hair and huffed.

"You'll only slow me down. I'm leaving in two days—"

"Are you going to see your mother tonight?" Naia interrupted.

Rian's cheeks turned pink. He crossed his arms and muttered, "Of course I'm going to see her. That's the only reason I'm here."

"Then you can tell us the details of our departure tonight. In the meantime, we'll leave you alone with your glorious troubles right now."

Naia sheathed her dagger to punctuate the sentiment and left the way Mythra had gone. She was not one to soften her feelings with words, and Rian was not being particularly inviting. Kylan waved an awkward goodbye to Rian and trotted after his friend.

"He's quite a charm, isn't he?" Naia said when he caught up.

"I'm sure he's been changed by the things he's seen."

"So have we." She sighed. "At least we'll have someone who knows the way to Ha'rar with us when we go. Tavra showed me in dreamfast, long ago, but it was a direct route. I don't think she expected any of this to happen. Now we've got to get there without the Skeksis finding us."

Kylan agreed, though he envied that Naia had the gift of the dreamfasted memory. All he had were ancient songs telling the path to the fabled Gelfling capital.

Stone-in-the-Wood emerged from the lush wood ahead of them, a crescent-shaped rise of rocks and boulders of every proportion. It looked as if a giant had stacked pieces of mountaintops there and left them to grow together over time. Nestled within the rocks and trees were dozens, if not hundreds, of Gelfling huts, all connected by narrow pathways and steps. Some of the huts were stone, others built of wood in the arms and trunks of the huge trees that grew in the spaces between the rocks.

At the bottom of the hilly formation was a clear lake, whose calm surface reflected the stone obelisk that stood watch from the very top of the rise. It was that impressive centerpiece that gave the village its name.

They paused to rest, even though the climb had not been particularly difficult. They'd had plenty of difficult days in the past, so any chance to enjoy the breeze was a gift, no matter how brief. Kylan took a seat on the rock beside his friend and looked down on the village. It looked so peaceful—so unaware. These people had no idea what was going on outside their corner of the Dark Wood. The inevitable truth-telling would be difficult. Wind blew through the forest, and the sound of the leaves rustling was like a thousand voices singing.

Naia rested her chin on her fists.

"Thank you, by the way. For dreamfasting with Rian in my place. I would have done it if I'd had to, but . . ."

She didn't finish, and Kylan shivered, though the wind wasn't chill at all. Rian's dream was enough to make him cold. No wonder the soldier was so standoffish, after all he'd been through. Kylan considered telling Naia the story Rian had shared, but he decided against it for now. She had enough to worry about, and they would have time to go over everything on their coming journey. For now, he wanted her to rest.

"Of course," he said. "That's what friends are for."

"You know, Kylan . . . you offered to go on without me so I could go back to Sog to see my family. What kind of friend would I be if I didn't offer you the same? You could stay in Stone-in-the-Wood. In the legendary home of Jarra-Jen. Isn't that what you left Sami Thicket to do?"

It was, but it seemed silly now. Kylan had failed at every part of being a Spriton, except for his studies in dream-etching under Maudra Mera. He had thought when he'd run away that he might find purpose in Stone-in-the-Wood... but now that he was here, he didn't feel like anything had changed. Jarra-Jen had lived hundreds of trine ago, maybe even before the Skeksis had assumed control of the Heart of Thra. Had Jarra-Jen discovered what the Skeksis had done to the land of Thra and his fellow Gelflings, Kylan wondered whether even he would have known what to do.

"When I met you, back home, I didn't have anything but those stories to tell," Kylan said, standing. "Their wisdom might help us once in a while, but now we have our own villains to defeat. The Hunter... skekMal. He's still out there, and he knows our faces. They all do, and they'll be coming for both of us. It would be irresponsible to hide in tales now, and I certainly won't leave you to fight them alone."

"I wouldn't be alone," Naia chirped. "I'd be with Rian!"

Kylan glanced at his friend and saw the grin, and they both laughed quietly at the thought. Naia followed his gaze toward the center-top of the village rise and elbowed him gently.

"Do you want to go look?"

Kylan did, more than almost anything, but it felt like a luxury he couldn't afford. The rock on the rise was where the stories of Jarra-Jen—and countless other tales—were inscribed.

"I don't know... We have more important things to worry about. Once we figure out this business with the Skeksis, and once the All-Maudra takes over, then I'll come back and do all the exploring and reading I like."

"Come on, let's go take a look. We have all the rest of the day."

Naia swung to her feet and stretched, nearly dislodging Neech, and pulled her traveling pack over one shoulder. The sack had been her father's, worn on one's back, but since her wings had blossomed, she'd taken to carrying it over one shoulder. It was a man's pack and would soon need to be traded for something that accommodated her new wings, especially if they meant to travel any farther than Stone-in-the-Wood.

"Just because we're hunted by the Skeksis and the world is falling apart, it doesn't mean you can't treat yourself a little."

It was a wry comment, but she smiled, and Kylan knew she meant well. The rock on the rise beckoned him from above, and when he gazed at it, he could almost hear the whispers of the songs that were etched into it. So, albeit with caution, he found an ascending path through the wood and followed it, Naia at his back.

CHAPTER 4

The rise turned out to be loftier than it looked, and it took them some time to hike all the way to the top. The boulders that composed the large mound grew more jagged and more ancient as they climbed. When they finally reached the flat slab at the top and looked down, Stone-in-the-Wood was minuscule and shrouded in the woods below.

The center obelisk was actually only one of many pillars like it, though it was the only one large enough to be seen from below. Half a dozen wide moss-covered stones were arranged around it, all etched with Gelfling writing and some with pictographs and swirling geometric diagrams. Kylan approached the big stone in the center and touched it, feeling the damp moss where it grew in the deep marks of the words.

"Can you read it?" Naia asked. She, like most other Gelfling, did not read or write. The combination of the two was one of Kylan's only talents, taught to him by Maudra Mera in the hopes that he might one day amount to something.

"It's the birth-song of Stone-in-the-Wood," he said in awe, tracing the words. *"In the summer ninet and the Age of Innocence, here stood Maudra Ynid the Tree Singer, called by the weeping-trees, at the heart of the Dark Wood where the Black River flows. She drew the shape of the suns in the ground. With the blessing of the Cradle-Tree, stones multiplied from the earth, and there was born Stone-in-the-Wood, and the Gelfling flowered."*

Naia's ears perked up.

"Maudra Ynid! I've heard that name . . . She was the sister of Maudra Mesabi-Nara, who brought the Gelfling race to the Swamp of Sog. Who planted Great Smerth, the tree where my clan lives. Written within Smerth's heartwood is a similar story."

"We have something like it in Sami Thicket, too," Kylan said. "The Six Sisters who left the northern shore and started the Gelfling clans . . . Look! This stone has a tale of Jarra-Jen!"

Kylan went from stone to stone, reading the songs and telling them to Naia, who trailed behind him. He wasn't sure if the songs interested her, but she listened anyway. One was a song from the Age of Harmony, of a song teller named Gyr, who traveled the world in search of the true song of Thra. Another stone told how Mother Aughra had come down from the High Hill and brought wisdom to the Gelfling of Stone-in-the-Wood—wisdom of the seasons and the stars—and taught them the shape of Thra's three suns. Knowing the shape of the Brothers and the path of the heavens taught the Gelfling to understand the ninets, the greater seasons. In turn, the understanding of the seasons led to understanding of the land, and crops, and the cycle of life in the grander sense.

It wasn't until the sky was too dark to read any longer that Kylan realized he had spent the entire day with the stones on the rise. Naia had fallen asleep against one of the tablets, snoring gently, while Neech darted in and out of the shadows, snapping up fluttering unamoths and other insects for his supper.

Kylan shook Naia's shoulder.

"Sorry," he said. "I didn't mean for this to take all day."

She yawned and stretched.

"You needed to read. I needed to nap."

"Well, now we need to get moving or we'll miss supper."

They watched the sky turn from orange to a deep blue as they hurried down the rise. The village torches flickered on, one by one, and as they walked down, it looked as though they were coming back to a sea of fireflies. Somewhere, a musician played on a lute, and the village hearth crackled with flames within and Gelfling laughter without.

As dismal as Rian's suggestion to keep their distance had been, Kylan and Naia avoided the hearth. A meal among others sounded nice, but every time Kylan looked at the peaceful faces of the Stonewood, all he could think about was how those faces would change if they knew what he knew. Yet he knew they would have to know, and soon—or what they didn't know could quite possibly kill them.

"I feel guilty, almost," Naia said quietly, undoubtedly thinking the same things. "As if it's my fault that the Skeksis have betrayed us. That it's our fault, somehow, that things are the way they are. I don't want to tell them. I don't want them to be afraid."

"Naia! Kylan!"

The chipper voice came from below. Mythra was hopping up the steep steps, waving a hand.

"There you are! Guess what? It's time for supper. My mother sent me to get you. Are you hungry? I hope you are, because she's made a lot of food. Come on!"

As quickly as she had arrived, she was off, bouncing from stone to stone toward the stone hut where Kylan and Naia had stayed the previous night. Smoke came from the chimney, and the windows were warm with hearthlight. His stomach rumbled in anticipation, and they hurried after the young Stonewood girl.

CHAPTER 5

Inside the hut, the small fireplace was lit, and some fire jars had been set out on the windowsills. The room radiated warmth with a gold light. Rian sat on the floor by the hearth, toying with something small and blue. When they entered, he pocketed it and raised an eyebrow in acknowledgment.

Mythra greeted them in a more forthcoming manner. She led Kylan and Naia into the cooking room, where her mother was chopping merkeep tubers and humming softly to herself. Like most Stonewood Gelfling, she had long dark hair, and her soft wings were brown and red, with two large black eyespots accented by other dapples of orange, gold, and tan. A youngling sat on the floor by her feet, chewing on his fist.

"This is my mother, Shoni," Mythra said. "And my little brother, Timtri."

Though Kylan and Naia had spent the night in the hut, Rian's mother and younger brother had been asleep when they had arrived and away early in the morning before they had awoken. Shoni set down her chopping knife and rounded the table to cup Naia's face and then Kylan's. Her hands smelled of spices and carrots. It was a warm gesture Kylan had seen many mothers do, although he couldn't remember much about his own mother, and certainly Maudra Mera would never have done something so kind to him.

"Hello, my sweets. I'm glad to finally meet you. Please, sit down. Ignore Rian if he's cold to you. Rian! Fetch our guests something to drink, would you?"

"I can do it, Mother," Mythra suggested, but Shoni waved her away.

"I want him to do it. It will be good for him."

Rian didn't protest, though he showed the bare minimum in care as he splashed water from a gourd into two clay cups. He held out a cup each to Kylan and to Naia. Once they'd taken the offering, he went back to his place by the hearth.

Kylan took a polite sip of his water, elbowing for Naia to do the same when she stood and stared after Rian in mild disapproval. The water was earthy, likely from a well. Though he had grown to enjoy the flavor of river water, the well water reminded him of home, and he drank slowly to savor the taste as long as he could.

"Can we help at all?" he asked. He wasn't very skilled with proper cooking, though he had learned to roast just about anything over a campfire.

"No, no. We're almost done. Please, sit."

She waved them toward the table, a large flat stone that grew straight from the floor near one wall of the hut. Kylan wondered which had come first, the stone or the hut. Shoni set the table with three serving bowls of nuts, spiced peach-berries, and diced root. Rian was the last to join them, sitting next to Mythra and focusing on slowly eating a modest portion.

"So. Swamp of Sog, and Sami Thicket," Shoni said. She pushed more food onto Naia's and Kylan's plates. Mythra needed no help, though she clearly favored the spiced peach-berry, taking twice as many of the fruit than nuts or roots. "That's quite a long journey. I've never traveled farther south than the Dark Wood reaches. Did it take long?"

Naia licked her fingers before replying.

"Not too long. I traveled only a few days before I reached the plains, though we were carried by Landstrider to Stone-in-the-Wood. I guess it would have taken much longer if we were on foot."

"I can believe it! Was it your Landstrider, Kylan?"

Shoni asked because the Landstrider was the sigil creature of the Spriton. Although it was an unsurprising assumption, Kylan couldn't help but feel mildly ashamed when he shook his head.

"No. It belonged to a friend of ours."

"Are Spriton Landstriders as tall and fast as those we have in the Dark Wood?" Mythra asked. "I've only ridden once, on a fawn—and it was not on top of its legs yet. Is it as fun as it sounds? Galloping across the plains!"

Kylan shook his head again. He didn't want to tell them about his brief foray into riding, the majority of which involved falling off, spooking the beasts, or a combination of the two. Galloping across the plains was one of the many Spriton traditions Kylan had seen much and done little of. There was that, and spear mastering, and *bola* throwing . . .

"I don't do much riding," he said.

"Enough that you could guide ours," Naia reminded him. "I'm thankful."

Rian had already finished his meal, though the rest of them had hardly begun.

"You should be," Rian said. "If you hadn't had a Landstrider, you would certainly have been caught by the Skeksis."

"Rian!" Shoni scolded. "Now's not the time. Can't we enjoy one meal as a family without mentioning . . . that?"

"I don't know, Mother. Can we even call ourselves a family when Father—"

"Enough."

Kylan hurriedly put a piece of fruit in his mouth, giving himself something to focus on as the air between mother and son grew hot. Rian didn't press the matter, though. Shoni flicked her wings once, shrugging off the little argument, and turned her attention back to her guests.

"What about you, Naia?" she asked. "What kinds of sport do the Drenchen do for fun?"

Naia perked up at the opportunity to share.

"Oh! We do *bola* tourneys, and during festivals, sometimes compete with feather-darts. When I was younger and argued with my sisters, my mother used to throw gems into the deepest parts of the swamp and make us find them before they sank into the mud. If we couldn't find a gem, we had to do chores under Great Smerth, cleaning mites from the roots and such. Oh, and during fall, when the apeknots droop, we do pole-vaulting dashes! Even the children play with us for that one."

Kylan thought it bordered on bragging, in an endearing way, and he welcomed the change of subject. The farther away from him, the better. He picked at his food and listened to Naia explain pole-vaulting dashes to Mythra, who got just as excited about it. Even Rian twisted an ear toward them.

"Gurjin told me about the *bola* tourneys," he said, his voice a sudden, but not unwelcome, surprise. "He showed me his Drenchen *bola*. With shorter rope, so it has more force, but less to tangle in the swamp."

Naia agreed readily.

"Yes! They're heavier, and take more to swing, but they're so much better in Sog. Or the forest, I suppose . . . Though in the field, I think the Spriton have it right, with longer rope and smaller stones. Isn't that right, Kylan?"

Kylan shrank a little into his shoulders. He appreciated her attempt to include him, but the truth was, he didn't know how shorter or longer rope changed a *bola*, or whether smaller or larger stones would be better in the field or forest. He didn't know, and a part of him didn't even care. He shrugged.

"I guess," he said.

His contribution was so small and green, it almost killed the tiny flame of conversation entirely. Naia was ready with kindling words.

"Kylan is a song teller, and a dream etcher. A very good one! And even so, he can still throw a *bola*. He struck skekMal the Hunter square in the face."

Again, Naia was only trying to help, but to Kylan, it sounded less like an endorsement and more as if she were trying to excuse him. As if being a song teller explained his athletic ineptitude, and his single victory in combat redeemed him.

Rian said, "Hm!" almost in approval. Then added, "I would love to knock skekMal one or two in the face. I will, someday."

A tap on the door brought Mythra to her feet. Rian stood, too, not in fear but in duty, moving to the back of the hut so he was out of view of the doorway. Once he had moved out of sight, Shoni waved for Mythra to open the door.

An older Gelfling stood outside, dressed in indigos and greens, her dark burgundy-and-gold wings folded along the length of her back like a cloak. From the beads and ornaments woven into her dark hair, Kylan realized who she must be.

"Maudra Fara!" Shoni said. "Good evening . . . come in."

"Good evening, Shoni. Little Mythra."

Kylan pretended he didn't hear Rian move to the back of the hut, softly closing the curtain to one of the rear rooms. Maudra Fara came in, ruffling Mythra's hair. It was not the youngling or her mother who had brought the *maudra* to the hut, though. She looked over Naia and Kylan, and reached into her sleeve.

"So there is a Spriton here. I *thought* I saw you on the rise this afternoon. Are you called Kylan?"

He stood when he was addressed by the Stonewood *maudra*. She withdrew a note from her sleeve.

"Yes, Maudra."

"This just came from Sami Thicket. Before you wonder—it is bad news."

Kylan's heart raced. No one spoke, though Naia put her hand on Kylan's shoulder as he unrolled the note and read it.

To my maudra sisters:

> *Take note. Lords skekLach and skekMal arrived early this morning. They sought one of mine, a runaway named Kylan. They say he is a traitor. When they did not find him, they took three others as collateral. If you know of Kylan's whereabouts, send him to me, and I will take responsibility for him.*

In Thra's song,

> *Dream Stitcher Mera*

"They went to my home," Kylan said, cheeks cold with fear. "They took people from my village..."

"It's not your fault," Naia said sternly, before he could go that far. "They're not even hiding it, then! They didn't find Kylan in the Spriton village, so they just scooped up a few others? For what, a traveling snack?"

"You should not say such things." Maudra Fara's warning was quick, though from the urgency, Kylan felt it was born more of fear of the Skeksis than of loyalty to them. She grimaced, her face a knot of responsibility and regret. Naia didn't quit.

"You can't believe he's a traitor," Naia said. "He's not the first to say it."

Maudra Fara looked Naia straight in the eye, then turned away as if nothing had been said.

"If Shoni has welcomed you to her home, I won't betray her hospitality tonight. But the Skeksis are looking for you, and my duty is to my clan. By the time the suns rise, you must be gone from here. Go to your *maudra* or do not. Go anywhere but here. I've got enough on my hands with Rian missing in the wood we share with the Skeksis. I can't risk the safety of my people any more. Please understand."

Kylan understood the words, but they left a hole in his heart. He tried to remind himself that this was the *maudra* of the Stonewood clan, the same *maudra* Rian did not trust to protect him when he had been labeled a traitor by the Skeksis. Now Kylan stood with the note in his hand and the same sentence. She was not his *maudra*, and this was not his home. In a way, he was not surprised. Had the Skeksis come for Naia while she had been in Sami Thicket, he guessed Maudra Mera would have done the same to her.

"It's all right," Naia said quietly. She squeezed his shoulder. "We'll go."

Maudra Fara touched Kylan's cheek.

"I am sorry about your people. But this is for the greater good."

The *maudra* left without another word, but Kylan wasn't sure what else she might say. It was the *maudra*'s burden to do what was right for her clan. That much was the same for all the Gelfling. Yet to be kicked out so suddenly, and with so little compassion . . . Kylan threw the note from Maudra Mera into the fire, watching as it wilted. It was enchanted to resist dream-etching heat, so it would take time to burn, but soon it would be gone.

Once Maudra Fara had gone, Rian came back, knuckles whitening in his fists. Shoni waved Mythra toward the table to clean up, giving the rest time alone. Kylan sat heavily near the hearth. Naia stood beside him, and Rian joined them, keeping his voice low.

"This is bad," Kylan said. Naia was more offended than worried.

"I just can't believe your *maudra* would kick us out like that!"

"I can," Rian said. "She would have sent me away, too, if she'd known I was here. I can't fault her for it. It's her duty to do what's best for the entire clan, not just one or two, or even three of us... The Skeksis will eventually come here, and they will do what it takes to scare the others into giving us up. The only thing that may save us is if no one knows our whereabouts and if we reach the All-Maudra as soon as possible. We should do as Maudra Fara says and leave. Tonight."

Kylan cupped his hands together to keep them from shaking. He couldn't stop thinking about Maudra Mera's message. Whom had the Skeksis taken? Phaedra, the village sandal-stitcher? Little Remi, the one who rang the hour bell? Were they being taken back to the Castle of the Crystal to be drained like all the others, or had skekMal killed them right away, as he had Kylan's parents? Should they try to find the two lords and rescue the Spriton captives—or was that a waste of time? Kylan and Naia had barely been able to escape one Skeksis alive, let alone two.

"It's not good enough for us to leave," Kylan said. "That might keep the Skeksis from Stone-in-the-Wood, but what about the other villages? The other clans? The Skeksis won't stop coming after us now that we know the truth. The All-Maudra needs to know, but so do the rest of our people. If Maudra Mera or my friends in Sami Thicket had known the truth, maybe they could have been prepared when skekMal came. Even now, they don't understand what's happened. Wasn't that what you were fighting for all along, Rian? A way to tell the truth?"

"Yes. And the fastest way is to tell the All-Maudra."

Kylan didn't want to say what he thought. Maudra Fara hadn't even asked whether he had a response to being called a traitor. She hadn't even cared. He and Naia were a risk to her, just like Rian, whether or not they were what the Skeksis said they were. It only proved what Rian had said in the forest: People were unwilling to listen to the truth, especially when it was dangerous.

"We will tell the All-Maudra," Naia announced. "But Kylan's right. The rest of the Gelfling need to know, too. If we focus all of our efforts on reaching the All-Maudra and waiting for her decision, many of our people could be taken by the Skeksis in the meantime. We have to find a way to spread the message faster, and sooner. Like dreamfasting."

Kylan held on to his elbows and hugged himself.

"Even with your powers, Naia . . . we'd have to touch hands with every Gelfling alive. We simply don't have time for that."

He hated being the one to bury the idea, but it was true. The three fell quiet. Kylan hoped Naia or Rian could come up with another plan, because when he tried to put his mind to work, all he could think of was Maudra Mera's message.

"There is always the path to the High Hill."

The voice was Shoni's, who had joined them after they had said nothing for a long time. Rian groaned, shaking his head.

"No, Mother. Aughra will be no help."

The name was like a beacon in the dark. Kylan struggled to respond, not sure if he had heard correctly.

"Aughra? As in . . . The three-eyed? The Helix-Horned? Mother Aughra?"

Shoni nodded.

"Her home is near our wood, though few make the trek to see her. Even those who arrive often do not find the answers they are looking for . . . Some find nothing at all. But I think, given how empty our table is, even a crumb would look like hope."

Kylan couldn't believe how casual Shoni sounded; she was speaking of a figure Kylan had only heard of in songs—songs that were as old as the three suns that crossed the sky each day. Mother Aughra—the mother of three, some called her, or the *maudra Thra*. She had been there at the first conjunction, and the second. She had known the world before the Gelfling had even come to be, or so the songs said. Yet Shoni spoke of a journey to her home as if it were a spring trip to the mountains.

"She's nothing but a mad witch spouting nonsense and riddles," Rian grumbled.

"You've met her?" Naia asked, as surprised as Kylan but more practical about how the news could serve them. "So you know the way! We can ask her if she knows how we can send our warning."

"She won't help!" Rian snapped, his voice escalating suddenly.

When Kylan and the others fell quiet, he tried to settle down. Still, his fingers twitched and his thick brows drew tight. "She's existed since the beginning of time, and the years have eroded her mind. She's not interested in us. In the Gelfling. She won't help, and I'm not about to waste my time on her."

His irreverence was astounding. He had *met Aughra*, yet described her as a senile nana, all raving and superstition. Kylan would have given anything to merely step foot in her presence, to hear any word at all that she might have to bestow on him. If anyone would know what to do about the Skeksis, it was Aughra!

"Listen. Look."

Rian removed the object he'd pocketed earlier and held it out for them to see. It was a glass vial, plugged tight with a cork stopper. Inside was a sparkling blue liquid. The same Kylan had seen in Rian's dreamfast. It was *vliya*: bottled Gelfling life essence. It was beautiful and grotesque all at once, and Rian put it back in his pocket before they all grew sick from the sight of it.

"*This* is the fastest way to fight the Skeksis," he said. "Our time is best spent getting it to the All-Maudra before the Skeksis find us. Aughra's riddles will only waste our time. I choose to put my faith in Ha'rar and the All-Maudra."

Naia sighed. "There are so many things that could go wrong between here and Ha'rar! I don't like putting all our reeds in one satchel."

"Great. I already said I wanted to go alone," Rian replied.

"And I already said we'd go together!"

"We should split up." Naia, Rian, and Shoni looked at Kylan

when he finally spoke. "You're fighting over it, but you're saying the same thing. If we all stay together, it will be easier for the Skeksis to find us and capture us all at once. Rian's right that the All-Maudra needs to know, and Naia is right that we shouldn't put all our effort into something that may not work. If we can ask Aughra for help—for a way to send a message to all of the Gelfling—then maybe we could save others. We need to work together, apart."

Kylan shrugged, in case they didn't like the idea. They were both leaders, and he was a follower, but they weren't looking at the big picture. To his surprise, though, the suggestion brought a calm to the room. Naia nodded at Kylan, a flash of respect in her eyes.

"Just so," she said. "That settles it. Rian will go to Ha'rar and see the All-Maudra. Kylan and I will find Mother Aughra and get her help. There has to be a way to tell all the Gelfling about the Skeksis, and we'll find out what it is. Maybe she knows more about the Skeksis, too. We'll put an end to their fearmongering, and make sure what happened in Sami Thicket never happens again."

"Fine," Rian said, but his steam had run out. He waved his hand in peace. "As you like. It won't matter, anyway. Once the All-Maudra sees the vial, she'll know what to do."

"You'll tell us the way to the High Hill, then?" Naia asked, raising a brow.

"I'll even walk you partway there if it'll keep you out of my way."

Naia accepted the offer despite the cheeky remark. She glanced at Kylan, and her confidence was like a wash of cool water from the wood creek.

"When should we go?" she asked.

Though he wasn't eager to forsake the warmth of the stone hut for the cold wilderness of the wood, he felt it was the right thing to do. He had wanted to rest, but it seemed rest was a luxury for which they would find less and less opportunity. Knowing that Maudra Fara thought they were endangering all the Gelfling of Stone-in-the-Wood—and that they were under orders to leave—robbed the warm hut of much of its comfort.

"It is safer for us and the Stonewoods," he said. "I say we leave right now."

CHAPTER 6

In the dark of the night, they walked with Rian and Mythra to the edge of Stone-in-the-Wood. The gentle glow of the village was barely visible through the trees, and only a sliver of the rock on the rise could be seen, illuminated in the moonlight.

"Best wishes!" Mythra said. "When I'm big, I'll come and join you. I fear no lying Skeksis!"

Rian gave his sister a friendly shove, sending her toppling onto her rear in the moss. He came prepared for a journey, with his pack strapped on his back and his walking spear in hand.

"Once you're big enough to not be eaten in one gulp. Then I'll welcome you."

It was the first playful thing Kylan had heard the soldier say, and it was endearing. Mythra jumped to her feet and gave her brother a tight hug and a kiss on the cheek.

"Please don't die," she said. "Any of you!"

"We'll do our best," Rian replied. Then the three of them turned away from her and the village, and went into the wood without a glance back.

For the first part of the journey north, they said little. Rian's steps were solid, never wavering, and Kylan followed with Naia behind. They had taken the formation instinctively, with the soldier guiding at the front and the warrior at the rear. Kylan was the song teller in the middle, telling himself he did bring value to their party in some way, even if he didn't know what that was yet.

After they had traveled for some time, Kylan felt the initial wariness of the unknown fade away. Their footsteps crunched against the underbrush, and he lost track of their direction, trusting Rian to know the way.

"The Skeksis have been doing this for a long time, I think," Kylan murmured, more to Naia than to Rian, who turned his ears back to listen. "Do you remember the night you came to Sami Thicket? It was the night of the census, and Lords skekLach and skekOk were there. They came twice a trine and recorded the numbers of all our people."

"They do the same in Stone-in-the-Wood," Rian said. "And in Ha'rar, I hear. Probably along the Sifan coasts as well. Do they not in the Swamp of Sog?"

"No. I'd never seen a Skeksis before I left Sog."

"Do you suppose they take the census as part of their . . ." Kylan swallowed, unsure of what to call the Skeksis' apparent plan.

"Harvest?" Rian asked bluntly. The word sounded awful, but Kylan couldn't think of a better one. He tried not to think of Maudra Mera's message, and his clanfolk who had been taken.

Taken, he told himself. *Not harvested . . . but is "taken" really any better?*

Rian whacked an errant shrub with his walking spear.

"We count the peach-berry trees every spring, and pluck half the blossoms so they bloom in the summer. That way we know they will all bear fruit, and how many. Mother Aughra taught the Gelfling these things long ago, and we've performed the counting and plucking every year since the Age of Innocence... and yet we couldn't see that the Skeksis were doing the same to our people, in front of our very eyes."

Naia said, "You've given this a lot of thought."

"I've had a lot of time to consider."

"What about the other clans?" Kylan asked aloud, to no one in particular. "The Dousan and the Grottan? Do you suppose the Skeksis send skekLach the Census Taker to them as well?"

"We had only one Dousan guard at the castle, and none from the Caves of Grot. Who knows if any Grottan even exist. Perhaps the Skeksis finished them off long ago and no one even noticed."

It was hard to tell how much of Rian's depressing attitude was because of the nightmare he had endured. In their dreamfast, Kylan had seen a Rian different from the serious, angry soldier who walked ahead of him. Someone who had taken pride in his work as a guard, but also someone who had been sentimental. In love, in fact, and vulnerable enough to be terribly wounded from what had happened in the Castle of the Crystal.

He knew that he could do nothing about Mira. Nothing except know that it had happened and understand why Rian might behave the way he did. It was tragic, but in it Kylan saw beauty. Like a song-for-tears, crafted to sing to the heart in sadness.

Maybe there was something to that. There was kindness hidden in Rian; Kylan had seen hints of it around Shoni and

Mythra. He had seen it in the dreamfast. Rian had hardened himself against other Gelfling, but maybe there was another way to ease his troubles. Maybe there *was* something Kylan could do.

"Uh . . . I was thinking. Well, there was a song I read on the stones on the rise, about Jarra-Jen. I could tell it to you both, if you'd like?"

Rian didn't respond, but Naia said, "Yes, do. I could use a break from the stories of our real life."

He could do this. Or if he couldn't, he might as well try. Reassuring himself, Kylan put his thoughts in order, cleared his throat, and sang:

> Many songs of our lightning-born hero are known
> From courage and cleverness are these stories grown
> But no song is filled with such heartache and yen
> As this one of the Dew-Tree and brave Jarra-Jen
>
> Jarra-Jen was known well through all of the land
> As a brave hero: kind of heart, quick of hand
> But little is told of Jarra-Jen's first love true:
> Amiris of Darkwood, the Singer of Dew
>
> Brown of skin, green of hair, with the bluest of eyes
> Amiris sang Sister Moons sweet lullabies
> And then every morning to break nighttime's fast
> She laid one loving raindrop on each blade of grass

Jarra-Jen loved Amiris, as a singer loves song
So often he'd visit her Garden of Dawn
Together they'd dance till the morning light glowed
And away to her dew-singing Amiris would go

Now, the Garden of Dawn was the life of the land
And its melody charmed Kaul, the Dark King of Sand
His thirst for its power could not fast be quelled
So he kidnapped Amiris to the dunes where he dwelled

On the next evening when Jarra-Jen came to call
The Garden of Dawn was barely living at all
Without the Dew Singer, all green turned to brown
The tree-branches withered with the roots in the ground

In Kaul-Dunes, the Dark King bade Amiris kneel down
And call forth green life from the parched golden ground
She tried, but no seed could grow root in the sands
Not even when bidden by a Dew Singer's hands

So the King, at her failure, grew wrathful in spite
He took her out in the desert, upon sands hot and white
There he punished her, holding her face to the suns
"If I can't have the Garden, then neither will no-one."

There he left her, the sands draining life from her eyes
Amiris sank to her knees, sang a song of goodbye
For three nights and three days she prayed, and then
On the fourth morning dawn, from the dunes came her Jen

He ran to her, held her—she wanted to cry
But even joy-tears had long since been burned from her eyes
Though he'd found her, she knew she was headed to rest
So she blossomed blue fire, drew a seed from her breast

Jarra-Jen pleaded and begged, cried for her not to go
She put the seed in his hand, bade him help it to grow
Then she melted to stardust. The wind took her away
Jarra-Jen left with the seedling on his loneliest day

Sad one in the desert, the seed cracked in his palm
Jarra-Jen had to act soon. He didn't have long
So in the sand did he plant it, though futile it seemed
As the desert had nothing to water the seed

He called to the earth. He called to the sky
But nobody answered. The dew-seed would die
With no other hope, Jarra-Jen fell to his knees
And wept . . .

> Bursting forth from the sands came an enormous tree
> Brown of skin, strong of branch, and emerald of leaf
> Its roots rippled the earth, its crown brushed the sky
> And Jarra-Jen poured forth every last tear he could cry

> Kaul-Dunes and its Dark King were lost in the storm
> In the desert, a new Garden of Dawn became born
> The Dew-Tree split open the sands of the dunes
> Strong, graceful, at peace, and with silver-drop blooms

> And from that day forward, and for all the trine after
> When the Sisters grow tired of twinkling star laughter
> In the Garden of Dawn, the Dew-Blossoms appear
> Left on each blade of grass
> Nectar shaped like a tear

It seemed as though the entire wood had been listening, hushed in anticipation, and when Kylan finished telling the song, it was quiet for a moment longer in reflection. Naia gave a hum of approval from behind.

"I liked it," she said. "I think it's a good lesson . . . We will always face hard times, but it's important to remember that our sadness can often be what becomes our strength. There's no weakness in sorrow or grief."

Rian said nothing from ahead, treading on with the same steady cadence as before. Just as Kylan thought the soldier had been unaffected—or maybe not even listening—he sniffed once and raised his hand to wipe his cheeks. He cleared his throat and said, "We're here. This is where we part ways."

In the dark and so focused on Rian's reaction, Kylan hadn't realized they'd come abreast of the Black River. It gurgled, inky and wide, on the other side of a line of straight trees and reeds. The path they'd taken ended in a short wooden dock where two small boats were tied. The river flowed north, where it would eventually empty into the Silver Sea at Ha'rar, the Gelfling capital.

Rian pointed upward, almost to the Sisters themselves.

"Head northeast, toward the cliffs, a day. Moss in these woods grows on the north side. Follow the incline through the night. On the second morning, you'll see the High Hill. You can't miss it. That's where you'll find Aughra. The river will take me all the way to Ha'rar. If I'm lucky, I may finally fall asleep and wake up in the All-Maudra's keep."

Farewells were in order, but no one was eager to be the first to say goodbye. Circumstances were dire now, and it was all too possible that they might never see Rian again. Naia clasped wrists with Rian, and when Kylan's turn came, he held on to the other boy's arm a moment longer.

"You're not alone, Rian," he said firmly. "We may be strangers by blood, but we're family in arms. Please trust us as you trusted Gurjin."

Naia saluted. "Yes. If you should need us, we'll find a way."

It took a moment, but Rian's callous features softened, and he let out a sigh. For a moment, Kylan knew he was seeing the real Rian, from before the nightmare at the castle.

"I miss Gurjin and the others very much," Rian confessed. "I don't want to put anyone else in danger. Every night I dream of the Skeksis hunting me, killing anyone nearby. Gurjin, Mira. Mythra, Timtri, my mother . . . The only way I can rest is if I'm alone. Once the All-Maudra has been told, maybe I will stop looking over my shoulder, but until then . . . I couldn't see you in danger when Gurjin died to protect us."

They helped him untie one of the boats and steadied it as he climbed in. Kylan regretted meeting this Rian so late, now that they were parting ways. As if feeling the same, the soldier let slip a small, sad smile.

"I do trust you both, though. As I trusted Gurjin. I only fear that my sorrow will not be enough to grow anything."

"Only if it's salted with remorse," Kylan said. "Good journey to you, Rian. We'll meet again in Ha'rar, with help from Mother Aughra and stories of our adventures on the High Hill."

They pushed him away from the dock, and Rian pulled the oar out from beneath his feet, handily maneuvering the little boat so it was pointed downstream.

"Till Ha'rar, then!" he called. "Be safe . . . Oh! I forgot to mention one other thing about the High Hill!"

"What's that?" Naia called.

The Black River had caught hold of him, carrying him away at a surprising speed. The soldier's voice seemed disembodied in the dark of the night as he drifted farther and farther away.

"Stay away from the finger-vines!"

Then the boat with Rian disappeared into the shadows.

"That song of Jarra-Jen was really something," Naia said as they untied the second boat. They would need it to cross the river, as it was far too wide to ford. "I think it really moved him. I wouldn't mind meeting the song teller who wrote it. The song that soothed the soul of the boy who first saw the Skeksis betrayal!"

They climbed in the boat, and Naia used the oar to push them away from the dock. Kylan let her do the rowing, since she knew her way around the water much better than he.

"You don't have to wait to meet that song teller," he said. "You already did, in Sami Thicket, when he was running away from home."

"When he was . . ." Naia coughed in surprise as she put one and one together. Then she crowed with laughter. "You devil! You made it up just for Rian?"

"I thought if he knew I'd done it for him, he wouldn't listen!"

Naia rowed them across the river, beaming with pride in the moonlight. Kylan absorbed as much of the feeling as he could. He'd done something right. Naia hummed a little as she worked.

"I don't regret it one bit, Song Teller," Naia said, as the opposite bank came into view in the dark. "Taking you along. I would have been a fool not to. I hope you know this as I know it."

It was possibly the sweetest thing she'd ever said to him, and Kylan finally let out the smile he'd been holding back.

CHAPTER 7

The jungle on the other side of the Black River might as well have been a different world from the wood they'd just left. The trees were lush and plump, with succulent fronds, and undulating with tentacled creepers. A scent lingered in the air that Kylan couldn't place, tart and strong, as if a grove of fruit-bearing plants were just beyond the reef.

Naia tied the boat to a root on the bank, and Kylan squinted into the deepening dark. Only one of the moons had a full face on, and the tree cover was dense. The other side of the river was barely visible, Stone-in-the-Wood long enshrouded by the wood and the night.

"I can take the pack back now," Naia said, holding out a hand.

In response, Kylan slung it over his shoulders. It was heavy, but manageable.

"Let's get going!" he said.

Naia opened her mouth to protest, but instead only shrugged. Even in the dim light, Kylan could see her wings at her back, still gaining volume since sprouting so recently. They would never grow out properly if she kept wearing the pack, and he was ready to share their burden. Before she could change her mind, he sighted the nearest tree and inspected its woolly trunk.

"Just like Rian told us," Kylan said. He pointed at the moss, thick as fur, growing green and hairy on one side of the tree. Together they hiked into the forest.

"Do you smell that sweet scent in the air?" Naia asked, more rhetorically than anything. The aroma was so strong that anyone with a sense of smell would have caught wind of it. "Do you know what it is?"

"I've never smelled anything like it before. It does smell delicious, though. Perhaps some kind of fruit that grows on the higher grounds?"

Naia patted her stomach. "Maybe we can make a snack of it."

Neech found no short supply of food in the insects and other critters that flitted, buzzed, and swooped through the air. Kylan touched stones every once in a while as they walked, leaving a small dream-etching the size of his fingerprint in case they should need to find their way back to the boat. The small shapes glowed with heat and blue *vliyaya*—Gelfling magic—after he made them, though by morning they would cool. They trod through brush and crossed creeks of slow-moving water, letting their fingers brush against the mossy trunks of trees here and there to fix their direction. Things moved in the wood beyond their path, but the forest went about its business, ignoring the two Gelfling travelers.

"Whatever smells so good must be close by," Naia remarked after a while. "It's like . . . perfectly ripe fruit, sweet nectar. I've got to know what it is!"

Kylan started to protest that they shouldn't leave the path, but when he looked around and saw only bushes, trees, moss, and plants, he kept his mouth shut. They were hardly on a path anyway, and the mystery fruit *was* piquing his appetite. Together, they waded into the forest in the direction of the lovely scent.

"Do you ever hear songs about those fish that dangle tasty-looking snacks in front of other fish, and when the smaller fish swims close enough, the bigger fish . . ." Kylan made a double-handed gesture, mimicking the jaws of a large creature consuming the body of a smaller one. Naia looked over her shoulder.

"Are you saying you think this is some kind of trap?"

"I'm just saying let's be careful."

"What happened to *always trust a Drenchen's gut?*"

Naia pushed back a heavy bough of leaves, revealing a glade lit by moon and starlight. At the center was a large plant with a fat, smooth trunk bulging like a sack of rocks. The plant's roots were exposed, splayed out beneath its bloated body like feet. Its branches were long and slender, protruding from the top and curving back toward the earth, weighted down at the ends with clusters of glistening blue fruits large enough to hold in two hands. They looked juicy and sweet, and each fruit had a six-petaled white flower blooming from the bottom, dripping with nectar.

Despite her earlier eagerness, Naia stood at the edge of the glade, and Kylan waited with her.

"Something about it doesn't seem right, does it?" she asked.

Kylan glanced at his companion, then back at the strange plant. It was big enough to be considered a tree, though it had no bark and something about it did not seem treelike. Trees were mostly stationary—and something about the plant at the center of the glade did not feel rooted.

"Is that your gut talking, or . . . ?"

"Look at how there are no other plants near it. Listen to how quiet the wood is here. Let's just leave it alone."

Kylan's stomach grumbled, but he agreed. Despite the wonderful-seeming fruit, there was something unsettling about the plant. As they stood there, watching it, the wind blew and the plant leaned, drooping one of its fruit-laden branches closer to them.

"Yeah," he said, inching away. "Let's go."

Together, they backed away and then turned from the glade. As soon as they did, Kylan heard a low *creeeakkk* from behind them. He reached out and grabbed Naia's wrist, pointing. They looked up in silence as two branches descended from above. Blue nectar dripped off the petals of one flower and landed on Kylan's nose. Without thinking, he licked at it—it was the stickiest, sweetest thing he had ever tasted.

He made the mistake of looking back. The plant was leaning toward them with all its weight, and one by one its tentacle-like boughs swept through the air toward them.

"I think we should run," he whispered.

"Agreed," said Naia. "On three. One . . . two . . ."

Kylan leaped forward with his friend, but the boughs with the fruits crashed down upon them, coating their hands and clothes in sticky nectar and fruit pulp. Kylan yelped as he fell, his limbs stuck to the traveling pack and the branches. Naia had avoided some of the nectar, but not enough to escape. Tendrils shot out from the top of the plant and tangled around their legs. Kylan and

Naia grasped at the earth, tree roots—anything!—as the tendrils dragged them back toward the plant. Naia pulled out Gurjin's dagger and plunged it into the ground, holding on to the hilt with one hand and grabbing Kylan with the other.

"I thought Rian said to watch out for finger-vines!" Kylan cried. "This isn't a finger-vine! Why didn't he warn us about this thing?"

Naia's dagger gouged the earth. Kylan scrambled to grab its hilt and looked back.

He wished he hadn't. The plant's body bent toward them, revealing a toothed maw at the top of its trunk and six black eyes that focused ravenously on its prey. Inside its horrific mouth, Kylan could see the remains of other creatures, and it let out a loud nauseating belch that smelled of everything dead inside it.

Dozens of tendrils snaked out of the plant, lunging toward them and tangling in thick knots around their ankles. No matter how hard he kicked at them and struggled, more came. One tendril, fatter than the rest, struck from below and lifted Naia up and away, ripping her from Kylan's grasp as it hoisted her into the air.

"Naia! *Naia!*"

Something silver and flame-red flashed, and the plant—was it a plant?—shrieked. Flayed tendrils exploded in the air, and Naia fell. The plant screamed again and uprooted itself, pulling six woody appendages from the dry earth. It lurched back from the torch- and sword-wielding cloaked figure that now stood before it. Kylan kicked the severed tendrils from his legs and scrambled to

Naia, helping her up. She leaned on him, favoring a leg that had been slashed from the thorns on the plant's tendrils.

"Back! Out of here, you big weed! Back, I say!"

The rescuer's feminine voice was refined and familiar. She strode forward and waved the torch, spraying embers. Kylan grabbed a stick from the ground, quickly lighting it from the silver-haired Gelfling's torch, and together they beat the carnivorous plant back from the glade. When it reached the edge of the clearing, it turned and clambered into the wood, its screams of defeat fading into the night.

Kylan caught his breath, and Naia joined him, walking off her limp and giving him a pat on the shoulder. Together they watched the back of their rescuer, whose sheer, prismatic wings were half-hidden in the silver folds of her cloak. She pulled back her hood and turned, and Naia let out a cry of surprise.

"Tavra!"

The soldier returned the hug when Naia gave it. Kylan had not spent much time with the All-Maudra's daughter, but in the torchlight, her pale Vapran features were unmistakable. Though she looked tired, with deep circles under her eyes, it was definitely her.

"You're alive," Naia said. "Even after the Skeksis made you look into the Crystal—I thought you were dead!"

"Aren't you glad I'm not?" Tavra asked. "I've been looking for you two. Glad I found you when I did."

Naia brushed dirt and vines off her front and then went to retrieve Gurjin's dagger from where it was still upright in the earth. Tavra skewered one of the blue fruits on her sword, taking a bite out of it.

"You can come out now," she called into the wood. "We've found her."

Kylan's heart was just calming from the confrontation with the blue mouth when he saw a lean figure step out of the shadows, leaning against a tree for support. Naia gasped when she saw him, eyes tearing at the sight of his clay-green skin, thick dark locs, and round face that mirrored hers.

CHAPTER 8

Gurjin nearly toppled over when Naia tackled him. Though he held on to his sister, he shook with weakness, and she helped him stand. Tears flowed freely on Naia's cheeks, and she held her brother.

"How?" she whispered. Then she raised her voice: "*How?*"

Gurjin shook his head. He looked even wearier than Tavra.

"I don't remember much. skekMal threw me against that tree, and I fell unconscious. The next thing I remember is being out here in the woods with Tavra. She's been trying to find you two."

Kylan made his way toward them as Tavra approached. Kylan couldn't help but notice how impressive the Vapra appeared in the moonlight, all in white and silver. He had not traveled with her long, and learned most of what he knew of her from Naia. She looked as he expected a daughter of the All-Maudra should: strong and beautiful, worldly and noble. He clasped the Vapra's wrist when she offered it.

"Kylan. Naia."

"It's good to see you again," he said. "And you, Gurjin . . . we thought . . ."

"I did, too."

Tavra did not sheath her sword, as if they could be attacked at any time.

"After you fled the castle," she began, "the Skeksis were in such an uproar that I was able to escape. I stumbled out of the castle through a turret window and flew down, but I was too late to stop skekMal from his hunt. I watched you escape and waited until skekMal returned to his brothers at the castle before finding Gurjin. I expected to have to send him to his final resting place, but he was still alive. You Drenchen are all clay, aren't you?"

She gestured, and they fell in line beside her, hiking up a path that cut through the steep hills. Kylan didn't know where she was taking them, but her footsteps were so confident that he didn't think to worry about it. Eventually they came across a landing in the trail, wide enough to make a fire.

"We'll camp here tonight," Tavra declared.

And so they did. Kylan started the fire while Naia helped Gurjin find a place to settle in. Neech came out of hiding in Naia's cloak and erupted with chirps and purrs, stopping only for chin scritches before launching into happy circles in the air.

"Oh, you should know," Naia said, "we met Rian, in Stone-in-the-Wood. He's left to go to Ha'rar to tell the All-Maudra everything that's happened."

"Rian's alive?" Gurjin exclaimed. "Thank the suns!"

"When did he leave?" Tavra asked. She looked almost as if she might snatch up her sword and leave that instant.

"This night. We saw him safely on the Black River just before we ran into trouble."

Tavra looked out into the wood in what Kylan could only assume was the direction of Ha'rar. While she was still, Neech hovered close to her, sniffing her hair and neck. He let out a chirp, but she batted him away. Sulking, he glided back to Gurjin, and Tavra returned her gaze to the fire.

"Is everything all right?" Naia asked. She sat next to her brother, hand on his back, protective and loyal. "How are you feeling, after what the Skeksis . . . did . . . to you?"

Tavra's eyes were hollow and hazy when she looked up, but the empty expression came and went like clouds in high wind. She flicked her ears and shook her head, brow stern and jaw set.

"I'm fine. And no, everything is not all right. The Skeksis are looking for us. The two of you nearly became dinner to an oversize flower. Gurjin can barely walk. And now you say Rian was here and you parted ways—things could not be *less* all right."

Kylan stiffened.

"We decided it was better if we split up. We're going to see Aughra. We're hoping she can help us find a way to send a message to all the Gelfling at once."

The Silverling soldier barked a laugh of disbelief.

"At this rate, you won't arrive in one piece! Maybe if Gurjin were strong enough to make the journey, but not now. He needs to rest, or you'll lose him again before long. Whether to blue mouths or finger-vines or sheer exhaustion. We'd be better off taking a boat to Ha'rar to catch up with Rian."

"We promised we'd find a way to warn the Gelfling," Naia protested.

"If you want to be well, then you will have to break that promise. You can't truly be thinking about choosing Aughra over his well-being. I will not have us traipsing about in the high hills with him in such a state!"

Kylan didn't want to admit it, but Tavra had a point. Gurjin needed rest. Would they have to split up again, just as soon as they had been reunited? It would be better if they could find a way to help Gurjin and convince Tavra to come with them. Naia had told him about Tavra's prowess in conflict and wisdom in travel, and Gurjin was an ex-soldier of the castle, like Rian. Their help could be invaluable in the journey to Aughra and beyond.

Naia stood and shrugged out of her cloak.

"Then I'll heal Gurjin."

"Wait, Naia..."

Kylan wanted an option, but the one his friend suggested was dangerous. Drenchen healing *vliyaya* was powerful, but only to a point. It could only mend surface wounds, like cuts and bruises. Gurjin's state was the result of starvation, dehydration, and lack of light and air. He had been a prisoner in the Castle of the Crystal. Normal healing *vliyaya* could not replenish the life force he had lost from his time in the castle. That was something that would have to come from within Gurjin over time, and Kylan said so.

"Even if you could normally heal a bite or scratch, Naia—even a broken bone—"

"He was locked in the castle because they were waiting for me," Naia replied. The fire reflected off her eyes and the beads in her locs. "Because we're twins. Because our life essence could heal the Emperor. Gurjin heard them say so himself. If our life energy can be shared, then we should be able to use it ourselves—for good. I will share my own life force with you, to use until you can rest and grow it on your own."

Even Gurjin looked wary, and he had the most to gain. "I don't know, Naia. It could be dangerous. It could certainly leave you weak. And that's only *if* you can do it."

Naia snorted and sat back down beside her brother.

"If the Skeksis can do it, then so can I. Now, hold still."

Naia settled and closed her eyes, holding her hands out so her palms touched Gurjin's chest. Gurjin hesitated, but knew his sister's stubbornness as much as any of them. He turned toward her and closed his eyes, too.

"You're not going to stop her?" Kylan asked Tavra. In the firelight, he noticed a sparkle at Tavra's neck—a purple jewel dangling from her ear on a shimmering thread. It accented her regal, if dour, complexion as she watched with aloof interest.

"No. If she can do it, I want to see it."

Naia's palms glowed blue. The calm, healing light crept up each of her three fingers and thumb until both hands were enveloped in it. Although it was yet unheard of for a healer to share her life essence with another, Kylan had no doubt in his mind that Naia could do it. The sturdy girl was special, in more ways than one. She could dreamfast with trees and non-Gelfling creatures. Her bond with Thra was different, and her bond with Gurjin was special. It was no wonder the Skeksis sought the two of them.

The light in Naia's hands intensified, then seeped into Gurjin's chest, over his heart. A soft blue glow surfaced where Naia's heart was, as well. The healing process had begun, and it was working.

"If Naia can do this, then it means the Skeksis might be able to do what *they* want, doesn't it?" Kylan whispered to Tavra as he watched Naia work. "The Skeksis can't find out about this. If they do, they'll work even harder to capture them both."

"Don't get so caught up in *ifs*, Song Teller," Tavra advised. She watched the healing miracle with a closer and closer eye.

The blue light enveloped the two Drenchen for some time. Although Gurjin's arms remained thin and his cheeks wan, his posture straightened, and his breathing became steadier. When Naia was done, she let out a big sigh and lowered herself to the ground so she could rest.

Kylan knelt beside her and assessed Gurjin. By no means was he ready to wade into battle, but his constitution had wholly changed. Energy had returned to his face, lighting his eyes with alertness. Kylan imagined the Gurjin he saw now was leagues closer to the Gurjin that had left the Swamp of Sog to join the guard of the Castle of the Crystal. Once he regained his lost weight and spent some time recovering his warrior's build, he would be formidable.

"It seems like it worked," Kylan said. "For better or for worse. Are you sure you're all right?"

"We had a long day. I'm tired. But you're right. It did work, and I will be just fine."

Kylan took it for what it was and moved to the next step: appealing to Tavra.

"In the morning, all four of us will head on to see Aughra."

Tavra grimaced and said nothing.

CHAPTER 9

Kylan was the second to wake, though the only evidence that he was not the first was that Tavra was nowhere to be found. Coals smoldered in the fire, but the morning was still cold and a bit damp. Kylan pulled his cloak tight and took his tablet and scroll from the traveling pack he shared with Naia. His friend and her brother shared a deep sleep nearby as Neech finished his morning preening on Naia's shoulder. Neither Drenchen stirred as Kylan sat up and propped his tablet on his knees, spreading the scroll across it and taking time in the quiet morning to record his journey thus far.

It had been several days since the last time he chronicled their journey. Dream-etching the words that described all that had happened since first arriving at the Castle of the Crystal took time. As the second Brother rose and the air began to warm, he heard footsteps coming from the forest. Kylan looked up from his tablet to see Tavra emerge from the brush, bearing a weighty bundle wrapped in her cloak.

"You're almost at the end of that scroll," she remarked as she lowered the bundle of breakfast to the ground. She let the corners fall, revealing a collection of fruit, fragrant flowers, tubers, and nuts.

"I've got more," Kylan said. He rolled the paper and stowed it once more in the traveling pack. "But I suppose this story is far from over . . . Do you think that there are scrolls for trade in Ha'rar?"

"Daughters of the All-Maudra do not trade. They are given whatever they desire."

The boast seemed strange coming from a Gelfling who had kept her lineage a secret for so long. Tavra sat cross-legged and plucked a red-and-white blossom from the collection, picking a petal off and munching quietly on it. It was hard to believe the serious Silverling was truly one of the All-Maudra's daughters. Kylan wondered what it was like to have siblings—he thought back on Mythra, and her tireless attempts to cheer her brother. Even Naia had Gurjin, and her sisters back in Sog.

Kylan realized he was staring when Tavra met his eyes. Hers were lavender, though somewhat sunken in her weary face. The draining had certainly taken its toll on her, but despite the worn, almost deathly exhaustion, the soldier still had an ethereal, ghostly beauty. He looked away and felt his cheeks warm.

"I climbed a tree and saw the High Hill this morning," she went on. "The directions Rian gave you are good. As expected of a Stonewood. Assuming the twins wake up and are able to travel, we're in good standing to make it there without much time lost. We can exchange our words with Aughra and get moving to Ha'rar."

"Have you spoken with Aughra before?"

Tavra shook her head. "She rarely leaves the High Hill, and

few bother to venture to her orrery, so we rarely hear from her. She keeps to herself."

"You sound as if you don't believe she'll help us."

"Why should she? She's the voice of Thra—she hears the songs of the world that many do not. She must have known what the Skeksis were doing, and yet she said nothing. If she said nothing then, and all this time, why would she say anything now? She has no interest in politics."

"This isn't politics, is it? The Skeksis are supposed to be the protectors of the Heart of Thra. The Crystal. We, and all creatures of Thra, entrusted the castle to them."

"Perhaps some creatures believe we still should."

It was an abrupt and peculiar thing to say, and Kylan didn't know how to react, so he said nothing. Tavra finished the flower and tossed her hair.

"Wake the twins. We need to get moving if we're going to catch up to Rian."

Naia and Gurjin joined the others around the dying fire for a breakfast of petals and pulpy fruit. They left the fruit pits and seeds in the cool ashes of the fire to sprout, packed up, and continued northeast. Tavra took the lead, always plowing ahead without looking back, left hand on the hilt of her sword while the right held a stick that she used to push brush aside as they passed. There was a path, albeit a not-well-traveled one, and up the trail they went.

Kylan walked with Naia, who took the rear and watched Gurjin from behind. The ailing Drenchen guard was not spritely, but he had energy to his step, and the color was returning to his skin, deepening in its dappled gray-green hues. Naia, on the other hand, had paled slightly, though only enough to seem tired, which would have been understandable even if she hadn't shared her *vliya* with her brother.

"How are you feeling?" Kylan asked her.

"Could have slept better, but not bad. It feels good to be moving. It feels good to have Gurjin and Tavra both here."

Kylan adjusted the pack on his shoulders. He was already sore, but he knew there was no other way to grow into it. Naia reached over her own shoulder and massaged where her wings joined her back. It seemed she was in the same situation.

"The past couple of days have been quite an adventure," he agreed. "Tavra offered all the scrolls I could need to write it down, so at least it'll be quite a tale for others someday. They won't have to worry about all the unglamorous aspects."

"You'll change the bit where we were almost eaten by a plant?"

"Absolutely."

She laughed, and Kylan laughed with her. It felt good. He had been worried about her, especially after her resolve to share her life with her brother. Instead, though her body was weakened, her heart seemed rejuvenated. That would go a long way.

The highland was less dense here than below. From their vantage as they climbed, Kylan realized that they had been on a consistent ascent since they'd left the Spriton Plains so many days ago. The Dark Wood, and the Castle of the Crystal, nestled in the arms of the highlands, were lush and bountiful from the Black

River that flowed down and within it. The landscape reminded Kylan of a youngling basket, a cradle—from which Olyeka-Staba, the Cradle-Tree, was named, he guessed.

They had not gone far when Tavra signaled for them to stop. She proceeded slowly and the others followed, Naia putting her hand on the hilt of her dagger and picking up her pace to join the Silverling at the front. Kylan stayed back with Gurjin, who stooped to pick up a hand-size rock as a makeshift weapon.

"Slowly now," Tavra said over her shoulder. "There's a blockage up ahead. Spiders. If we're quiet and don't disturb them, they'll leave us alone. If we wake them, though, we're in for big trouble. These are death-sting spiders, and like other spiders, they care not for Gelfling one bit."

The path widened and curved to accommodate an outcrop of boulders, half a dozen big things that were probably the last remains of an ancient avalanche. Most remarkable about the structure, though, was the frothy white mass of cobwebs that covered it. Had Kylan not heard Tavra say *spiders*, he might have thought the rocks had grown fur or some kind of mold or fungus. No spiders were in sight, but the boulders had plenty of nooks and crannies for a dark sleeping space.

Kylan had never heard of death-sting spiders, but he could infer enough from the name to be careful. Just to be sure they understood, Tavra added quietly, "One sting will kill you. Don't do anything stupid."

Tavra stepped lightly, circumventing the rocks, and they followed. Kylan marveled at the webbing, despite what dangers it might hide. It shone in the early morning sun like spun silver, draped in thick tapestries inlaid with delicate patterns.

They had nearly passed the formation when Kylan saw something beneath the webs. At first he thought it was a trick of the eye, but he squinted and took a careful step closer.

"Kylan, don't," Naia said.

"I'm just looking . . . There's something there. I think it's dream-etching."

He edged forward, but the motion brought a chittering noise from deep inside the boulders. He dared not get closer at risk of waking the nest, but there was definitely something written on the rocks where the web was thickest. He could only make out one of the words:

HER.

"Leave it alone. You'll wake them," Tavra urged.

"You all go on ahead. If I'm quiet, and gentle, I think I can make it out. So few can dream-etch. If someone took the time to write something, it must be important."

Naia crossed her arms. Though she whispered, her voice was no less firm.

"I'm not leaving you with a swarm of death-stingers that are sure to be cranky if you wake them. If you stay, I stay."

Tavra would not have it. She said, "None of us are staying. We're leaving. *Now.*"

"Maybe Tavra's right," Gurjin said. "One or two spiders is no problem, but a whole nest . . . Who knows how deep it goes. These mountains are probably full of underground caves and tunnels.

There could be thousands of them."

While the others argued quietly, Kylan scooted closer yet, as quietly as possible. He could almost make out the other words. He was so close!

"You two go ahead," Naia said. "I'll stay here with Kylan. If he thinks this is important, then I do, too. If the spiders wake up, I might be able to dreamfast with them and explain we mean no harm. If worst comes, I'll throw Kylan over my shoulder and run if I have to."

"They will not—" Tavra began, but Naia wasn't asking.

"Go!" she said, loud enough that the clicking, chirping, skittering noise from within the nest intensified. Gurjin stepped back, and Tavra glared at the Drenchen girl.

"Fine," the Silverling said. "But I warned you."

Then she continued up the trail. Gurjin hesitated, but Naia shooed him.

"You're not in a state to outrun anything right now," she said. "We'll be fine. Kylan and I have been through worse. We can handle this. It won't take long."

"Be careful," Gurjin said, and hurried after Tavra.

Naia faced the rocks with Kylan.

"I hope this is worth picking a fight with a Silverling," she said. "Something must be bothering her. She's as touchy as a . . . well, as a sleeping spider nest. Ha!"

Kylan and Naia took slow steps closer to the rocks. No matter how quiet, each step stirred the shadows within the nest. Veiled by the gauzy web, the spiders inside were almost impossible to see, though as they neared, Kylan thought he could make out a rolling coat of shining black bodies. Web-wrapped lumps hung in the draped nest, some with the feet and tails of woodland creatures sticking out.

More words etched into the rock also became clear, written in Gelfling hand:

TRUST HER.

Kylan almost took it for what it was, whatever it meant, but he could see there was still more hidden beneath the web. To reveal the last part of the message, he would have to brush the web aside. He picked up a stick, glancing within the nest, where some of the spiders were emerging, tiny black things crawling along the strands of the webbing. He held the stick carefully, to show he was not a threat, and to indicate to Naia what he was about to do.

"You don't have to stay," Kylan whispered.

"I know," Naia replied.

He took the last step, close enough to reach the rock with the web. Naia stayed back, watching the nest as it slowly came to life. Kylan reached out with the stick and poked at the web near the writing. As soon as the stick touched the web, spiders emerged, in small numbers at first, and then more.

"Hurry," Naia said.

The web was sticky and thick, and he had to exert more effort than he expected to tear the netting to the side. The sounds of the nest grew louder as the larger spiders awoke, some the size of Kylan's hand.

"Hurry," Naia said again, more urgently.

Finally, the web came away. The remaining words that completed the etching were startling, and Kylan forgot about the spiders. Naia grabbed him by the pack and yanked him away, nearly picking up him and the pack in the process. Kylan took his eyes off the writing and willed his legs to move. They sprinted away from the outcrop and up the trail.

When they were in the clear, they stopped to catch their breath. Tavra's and Gurjin's footprints marked the trail, and Kylan could make out their forms in the wood ahead. He panted and wiped his forehead, sweating more from shock than the physical exertion.

"What did it say?" Naia asked, less winded but still weaker than usual. "You went pale as a cloud, and that's saying something for a Spriton!"

Kylan tried to tell her two times before finally getting the words out.

"*DO NOT TRUST HER,*" he panted. "The words said *DO NOT TRUST HER.*"

Naia's eyes went wide, then narrow, and she looked up the trail, where eventually they would reach High Hill and the ram-horned mother-creature that lived there. Kylan wondered whether the message had been about Aughra. Or someone else? Did it mean nothing, or could it make all the difference?

"Who do you think wrote it? Who is it about?" Kylan asked, though there was no reason Naia would know any better than he did. "Do you think it means . . . Aughra?"

"I don't know. For now, let's keep this between us. We don't need to give Tavra any more reasons to avoid Aughra."

Kylan didn't like keeping secrets, but Naia was right.

"She really is set on finding Rian," he said. "Was she always like this? All duty and no joy?"

"No . . . I don't know. I wonder now if I ever really got to know her in the first place. Looking into the Crystal must have changed her."

"I think that would change anyone. No one else has even survived it. Perhaps now that she's free of the castle, she'll come around."

"Let's hope so," Naia said, and they hurried up the trail to where the others waited.

CHAPTER 10

On the second morning, a crag appeared in the mountains above. It was shrouded in fog, a big protrusion from the highlands that peered over the wood like the head of a beast gazing into the heavens. Aughra's High Hill was not casually named. Within the mountainous forest, it was the highest point in all the land, near where the Black River originated, closest to the suns and moons and stars. Not *a* high hill, but *the* High Hill.

Tavra never asked about what they had found written on the rock, and when Gurjin asked his sister, she shrugged and told him only that Kylan hadn't been sure what it had meant, and that she'd share its meaning if they ever decided they fully understood it.

With their destination finally in view, the party quickened their pace. Even Gurjin's steps were full of energy. He chatted with his sister as they maintained the rear of the group, leaving Kylan to watch Tavra quietly, to take in the misty, arid surroundings, and to think. That was his role, it seemed: to think. If that was his job in all of this, then he would gladly take on the burden.

So he thought about the message on the stone, hidden beneath the spiderwebs. If only he could understand who it was for and who it was about. He had always thought of words as the best way to pass on meaning, but in this case, they fell far short. Without context, they meant nothing.

He wanted to talk about it, and ask all the questions that didn't have answers, but he couldn't with Gurjin and Tavra around. Naia was right: If they asked Tavra's opinion, the Silverling would undoubtedly use it as an excuse to abort their journey to the High Hill and pursue Rian instead. After they met with Aughra, then maybe they could bring it up.

He scratched his arm where he still felt the phantom tingling of spiders crawling. It reminded him of something Tavra had said. He trotted ahead to where she was forging their path.

"Tavra, may I ask you something?"

She didn't say no. She didn't say anything.

"What did you mean back there, about the spiders not caring for Gelfling?" he asked.

To his surprise, she replied.

"Spiders hate Gelfling . . . All Vapra know this."

"They hate us? *All* of them?"

"Oh yes. From the death-stingers to the crystal-singers."

This was news to Kylan, though on reflection he'd never had a conversation with any spider before. The idea that an entire race might loathe his own was discomfiting. He wasn't even sure what a crystal-singer spider *was*.

"Why?"

Tavra thrashed a fern with her stick so it wilted back from the path. She pulled away, ending the conversation with a final suggestion:

"Next time you see one, maybe you should ask."

The way became rockier before long. Hundreds of round rock spires lined the winding path, some shining with veins of clear crystal still untouched by the darkness spreading from the castle.

By midday they slowed their pace, weaving single file between the stone mounds, shoulder to shoulder with the mist that cascaded over the cliffs.

Kylan would have liked to rest, but Tavra tirelessly marched on, glancing over her shoulder occasionally to make sure the others hadn't fallen too far behind. The Silverling's face was as pale as ever, but she was even less winded by the climb than Naia, who was otherwise the most hardy of the group.

"We'll reach Aughra by the evening," Tavra said. "Have you prepared what you're going to say?"

Naia crinkled her brow at the question.

"I plan to tell her the situation and see if she has advice. Is there more to it than that?"

"You're about to speak to Mother Aughra, the Ram-Horned. The mouth of Thra. She was born of the world, both child and mother. She has seen Thra before the Gelfling were but sprouts in the garden of all creatures. You would speak to her so casually?"

"I'll speak to her like I'd speak to anyone else," Naia said. "With respect—if she deserves it."

Gurjin's voice was a continuation of his sister's, carrying the same cadence and reasoning.

"If she is as old as they say she is, then she will respect hard-talk. It's the language of the natural world, after all."

Tavra shook her head in disapproval, but didn't push the topic and marched on.

Kylan had nothing to add. Aughra was said to be wise, to know all things—but as Tavra had said, she might already know about the Skeksis. Worse, she might already know and yet have done nothing. The Gelfling were her favored children, as their lore sang time and time again, but those songs had been written by the Gelfling. Did Aughra think of the Gelfling as much as any other flower in her garden? Would she be equally content to see one creature devour another, if it, too, were part of the circle of life?

More importantly, no matter what Aughra had to say, if anything—could they trust her?

"You're very quiet, Kylan," Gurjin remarked, second from the back and nearest to Kylan. It was strange to be around the boy, whose presence felt like Naia's, but wasn't. It was not hard to believe that they could share *vliya*, if their auras were already so similar. Maybe they really did share the same life energy between two bodies.

"I don't have much to say," Kylan replied.

It was a small lie, but might as well have been the truth. Naia cleared her throat, reassuring him that she had overheard and had the same concerns. He wondered whether she had shared the message with her brother, perhaps silently in dreamfast during their trek. Gurjin's dismissive shrug indicated she hadn't.

"If you say so," he said. He chuckled at his own joke. "Oy. I never got a chance to thank you for keeping Naia company. We were raised to be stubborn and never let go of the things we had.

I think if it hadn't been for you, she might not have let go of me back in the wood. And we'd all be up a creek now, wouldn't we?"

Kylan nodded.

"I'm glad you're alive. I'm glad we all are."

Gurjin patted Kylan's shoulder warmly. Both of them stopped when Tavra turned back, pointing up the trail. Kylan couldn't see far past the Silverling, but he could tell that the path widened and ended. He realized the High Hill was nowhere in sight, and hadn't been for some time. It was out of view because they had arrived.

"Don't touch the vines."

Kylan and the two Drenchen followed Tavra to where the trail opened onto a shelf large enough for them all to stand. Thick orange vines covered the cliff wall in front of them, finger-shaped and tangled like rope that had been left too long to its own devices. No further pathways led deeper into the crag, but Kylan could feel a draft coming from behind the vines. There was a tunnel there, but they would have to pass through the overgrowth, and if one part of Rian's instructions had stayed with Kylan, it was to stay away from the finger-vines.

Tavra plucked a rock from the path and tossed it underhand into the vines. As soon as it hit, the vines shivered and tangled, grabbing the rock and constricting around it like tentacles. After a minute of tasting the rock and deeming it inedible, the vines loosened, and the rock fell to the ground. Kylan expected it would not be the same for them, should they become entrapped.

Tavra turned to Kylan and Naia, brow peaked with skepticism.

"Now what?"

Kylan didn't have an immediate answer. Before he had to come up with one, Naia shouldered past and approached the protected tunnel entrance, wary of the vines but defiant in the face of Tavra's challenge.

"Aughra?" she called, her voice lost in the tunnel beyond. "Mother Aughra? We've come to ask your advice. Are you there?"

They waited, but no response came but the echoes of Naia's voice and the distant whistling of wind. The vines slithered among themselves, anticipating an early supper. Naia called again and again, but nothing happened. Tavra was unimpressed and unsurprised, almost smug at the situation.

"Don't you want Aughra's help?" Kylan asked her. "Even if you think she won't help, isn't it worth your time to hope that she might?"

"It would be worth my time if it weren't a waste of time," the Vapra replied. Then she raised her voice to Naia. "How long will we wait before you agree?"

Naia shot a glare back and flicked her wings in annoyance. She was about to do something brash, Kylan realized, but before he could stop her, she stepped right up to the finger-vines and put her hands upon them. They rustled and moved to grab her—but stopped. They dangled, unmoving, as Naia touched them.

"What's she doing?" Tavra whispered. "Is that . . ."

Kylan held his breath. The vines, so ready to ensnare their prey, had become transfixed.

"Yes. Dreamfasting."

Kylan had learned the language of the Landstriders, as all

Spriton did. Tavra had certainly learned the tongue of other creatures as well, in her training to serve the All-Maudra. But those were languages spoken on the tongue, in sets of words and phrases. Naia's unique ability to dreamfast with creatures other than Gelfling let her speak in the universal song of the heart.

It worked. The vines calmed and drew back, opening like a curtain on either side of the tunnel. Naia turned back with a triumphant wave and gestured widely for Tavra to enter.

"After you."

The tunnel was windy and dark. Kylan kept a hand on the wall as he walked, feeling the pressure change as they ascended. He was sure the tunnel remained the same width the entire way, but the dark and confined space still felt as if it were closing in on him. He kept reminding himself that when they reached the exit at the top, they'd be on the High Hill. Where they would meet Mother Aughra, no less—that is, if she showed herself to them.

A bug chirped from somewhere in the tunnel. Their footsteps were the only other sound. Tavra stopped, and they all bumped into one another in the dark.

"There's a door. We're here."

With a great groan, the mouth at the end of the tunnel opened. Kylan squinted as light flooded upon them—light, and a sound that he couldn't place: the scraping and grinding of metal and wood, of air and space. When his eyes adjusted he gasped.

The four of them stood at the entrance to a round domed chamber. The ceiling was made of frosted crystal, letting in the light of the suns above. Tables and shelves were scattered about, cluttered with mysterious devices, and flasks and bottles filled with even more mysterious liquids.

But most impressive was the enormous moving contraption that occupied the center of the chamber. It filled the space of the room with dozens of huge spheres, mounted on poles and swooping arms. The machine rotated and gyrated like a living thing, spheres orbiting spheres, circling yet other spheres, all of it shining in bronze, copper, iron, and glistening stones. Clearly, the grating sounds emanated from the machine, and the movement of its pieces stirred the air so it felt as though there were a breeze, even inside the crystal dome.

"Amazing," Kylan breathed.

He recognized some of the symbols etched deep into the metals: the symbols that represented the Three Brothers, others that represented the elements of the earth and water, air and fire.

"It's the path of the stars," he said. "The suns, and . . ."

"Gelfling!"

The hoarse shout brought them out of their reverie. A stout figure, hidden among the towers of papers, books, and other artifacts, raised a dark gnarled head with leathery and heavily wrinkled skin, like the bark of an old tree, and a knob in the middle of her forehead. A deep scar took the place of what was once her right eye. She had a mane of black and gray hair, tangled and matted around a pair of whorled horns on either side of her wide-browed face.

"Gelfling!" she repeated, her voice flavored with a strange, ancient accent that made some words alien in Kylan's ear, though she spoke the Gelfling tongue. "What, you just gonna stare? Walk right into my home just to stare, did you? Maybe you should draw a picture, take it with you!"

Naia took the lead when Tavra said nothing; the All-Maudra's daughter held rank among them, but they were the ones who had resolved to come here.

"My name is Naia," she began. "I'm from the Swamp of Sog. We're here to ask for your help, Mother Aughra."

Aughra—for that was the only thing the disheveled old creature could be—stared at Naia with a focused glower. She let out a big grunt and stood, pushing a table out of her way and lumbering close enough that her whiskers brushed Naia's chin as she sized up the Drenchen girl. Naia stood firm, though Kylan saw a tiny tremble in her hands when Aughra gave her a good sniff and then a swat on the chest before she finally backed away.

"*Mother* Aughra, eh? Ask for my help, eh? Why is it you Gelfling only call Aughra *Mother* when you need help? That's what children do, I guess . . . I guess that's what they do."

Aughra put her fists on her bulging hips, releasing Naia from her appraisal and taking note of the other three who stood near.

"Hmph! A Spriton. A Vapra—maybe? Another Drenchen. Hmph. Three out of seven ain't bad. It's still soon. Where are the others?"

"What others?" Kylan asked.

Aughra scoffed, loudly and forcefully enough that spit flew out from her throat. She turned her back to them and stomped over to where she had been working when they had arrived, waving her

hand and muttering to herself.

"What others, he asks? What others? The other clans, of course! Gelfling gathering. What else is there to know?"

Aughra sat heavily on her table stool, as if hoping they might go away if she ignored them long enough. Kylan's head spun, trying to make sense of the words. Was this what Rian had warned them about? She was not the Mother of Thra who Kylan had expected—she was rude, ungainly, and undecipherable. They hadn't even asked their questions.

"Please, Mother," he said. "We need to know what to do about the—"

"Please, grassling!"

Kylan snapped his mouth shut and bristled. They were rewarded for the persistence, though. Aughra waved a knobby hand, this time beckoning them closer.

"Come on, then, Gelfling. Children. Aughra already knows what you want to know. Whether it's what you want to hear, though, hmph! Might not be."

CHAPTER 11

Aughra did not offer them *ta* or even a place to sit, so the four Gelfling stood under the metal spheres of the heavens. Tavra kept her distance, leaning against the wall with her arms crossed, while the rest of them approached Aughra's worktable, hesitant even though they had been invited to do so.

Kylan began to feel light-headed if he watched the machine's movements too long, so he watched Aughra grumbling and grunting, sorting through the artifacts—or was it junk? It was hard to say. When she couldn't find what she was looking for, she let out a growl of frustration and swiped, knocking a pile of cluttered objects to the ground.

"Eh!" she barked. "Eh! Where are they? Probably buried somewhere. No matter. Not the time yet, no point. No way to know which one it is yet, anyway. All right, Gelfling. What you want to know? Too much to tell if I tell you everything, so you'll have to ask it one question at a time."

Kylan stooped to collect the items that had fallen. It was mostly scraps of paper with writing in letters he didn't recognize, a few pieces of sculpted metal, and a leather-bound book tied shut with a braided black cord.

"The Skeksis have betrayed the Gelfling," Naia began. "I've

seen the Crystal where they've darkened it. We need to send a message to all the Gelfling, all at the same time, so everyone knows what the Skeksis have done."

Aughra stared at Naia with her single eye, flat face unreadable except for a general sense of disdain. Kylan worried suddenly that she would not have an answer—or if she did, that it would be impossible to interpret or understand.

"And what's the question?" she barked.

Kylan jumped in. "Is there a way to send a message like this? Something that will reach every Gelfling, but that the Skeksis won't be able to interpret?"

"Would be, if all Gelfling could read, eh!" Aughra interrupted herself with a gruff laugh, then went on. "Oh yes, sure there's a way. There's always a way. Could be this way. Could be that way over there."

"Well, what is it, then?" Naia asked.

"Who knows. That'll be something Gelfling will have to figure out, isn't it? If it's something only Gelfling can understand, how can you expect Aughra to understand it?"

"It would be all right if you could understand it . . . You're helping us."

"If Aughra can understand it, so can the Skeksis! Who do you think taught Aughra to read? Well, it wasn't the Skeksis, I suppose. Not exactly. They weren't the Skeksis *yet* . . ."

"What do you know about the Skeksis?" Gurjin asked, before they lost her down the trail of her own thoughts. It wasn't the reason they'd come, but if she had information about the Skeksis,

Kylan would take whatever she would give.

"I know they love a good crawly. What do *you* want to know?"

Naia bit at the end of the question, finishing Gurjin's thought. "Everything!"

Aughra was a creature of constant motion, but here she paused long enough to stare. Kylan thought maybe she was angry, with the way she fixed them with her single eye. When she answered, he still couldn't tell if she was irate or amused.

"Everything!" she exclaimed. "HA! Didn't you hear what I just said? Everything's too much! Small questions, Gelfling. Small questions with small answers for your small head!"

Kylan held Naia back before she said something she regretted. Aughra's way of conducting conversations was like expecting them to find their way through a maze every time she spoke, and they would get nowhere relying on Naia's Drenchen sensibilities. Kylan gathered his words and put them in order before he stepped in, hoping to make it as easy as possible for Aughra to answer the question in an understandable way.

"We met a wanderer in the Dark Wood. An archer named urVa. He had a scar on his hand. We saw the same scar on the hand of skekMal, the Skeksis hunter. As if they're the same—shared one life force, but in two bodies. At first I thought it might have been just skekMal and urVa, but . . . all the Skeksis are after Naia and Gurjin because they're the same. Twins. One life force, two bodies. It was important enough to them that they didn't place Gurjin before the Crystal, and tried to get Naia to come to them first. Can you tell us how they are connected?"

Again, there was a long pause. Aughra steepled her brown fingers, joining them at the tips so they looked like tree roots growing from one stumpy wrist to the other.

"Skeksis were born at the last Great Conjunction. That's when the Skeksis appeared, and the Mystics. Can't have one without the other."

Kylan remembered skekMal the Hunter's rabid screams when Naia had guessed as much—that skekMal and urVa were somehow connected, the same entity, in two vastly different forms. What affected one affected the other. They were, somehow, the same, though urVa was gentle, wise, strong, while skekMal was vicious, shrewd, and unforgiving.

"Mystics—is that what urVa is? Are you saying each Skeksis has another half—a Mystic?"

Aughra's yellow eye went back and forth between Naia and Gurjin. Kylan could hear it clicking in the socket, and it made him grow tenser by the moment.

"Eighteen Skeksis. Eighteen Mystics. That's one for one, isn't it? If the numbers are right." She grumbled, talking to herself more than to the Gelfling in her observatory. "Twins, eh? I can see what they're thinking, but they're wrong. Twins are two souls, two lives, two bodies. A close connect, yes! Same blood in your veins, same Gelfling essence! But you and you, you're two, eh? Skeksis and the Mystics are one, split. What happens to one happens to the other. And the other way around, too."

It still wasn't a straight answer, but Kylan had to take it. It seemed she was confirming what he was asking, and he wasn't likely to get more out of her. It explained what they had seen with skekMal and urVa. It also meant there were other Mystics, as Aughra called them. One for each Skeksis. Where were they, and could they help, as urVa had helped?

"Is that what we should do, then?" Gurjin asked, voice quick with hope. "Find the Mystics? Can the Mystics stop their other halves?"

"NO!" Her response boomed over the sound of the machine. "Skeksis can't destroy Mystics. Mystics can't destroy Skeksis. What's one is the other. *You* know! *You* saw it! Maybe a Mystic could keep a Skeksis in one place. Stop him from doing the really bad thing. Maybe the other way around, too. Skeksis stops a Mystic from doing the really *great* thing. But it's just a wall. Just an impasse, not a defeat, not destruction."

"Then what if *we* destroyed the Mystics?" Gurjin asked. "To get at the Skeksis?"

"No!"

This time it was Naia who protested, and Kylan agreed.

"You didn't know urVa," he said. "But he wasn't the same as skekMal. It wouldn't be right to use him to get to skekMal . . . or any Mystic, to defeat the Skeksis."

He didn't have a better argument. It just wasn't right. He could feel it in his heart.

"Aughra, if the Mystics can't help us defeat the Skeksis, and if you don't know how we should deliver the message to all the Gelfling . . . can't you tell us anything that could help? What do we do?"

"Don't know," Aughra said. She gave a big groan, clearing her throat, and spat, right on the floor. *"Don't know."*

It was a dead end. If Aughra had no suggestion for sending their urgent message, and no solution to stopping the Skeksis, then what other questions could they ask? Kylan chewed on his lip, worrying that Rian and Tavra had been right all along. Maybe it had been a waste to come here. Maybe the only one who could do anything was the All-Maudra.

Aughra went on.

"Skeksis, Mystics. Born at the Great Conjunction. Maybe they'll die at the next. Maybe they'll go back to wherever they came from. Maybe the whole world will end! No way to know but wait. Nothing to do but wait until the next one. The next Great Conjunction."

When her words got nothing but a heavy silence, she scoffed.

"See? Told you it might not be what you wanted to hear."

Kylan felt like a child for putting so much hope in Aughra, after all the songs celebrating her infinite knowledge. She didn't seem to care about what was happening, but maybe it was because she didn't understand. She spoke of the birth of the Skeksis and the Mystics at what seemed like the beginning of time, but said nothing of the things that had happened recently, when it mattered. When Gelfling had died. Understanding the Skeksis and Mystics would not prevent skekMal's next raid on Sami Thicket or Stone-in-the-Wood.

"Did you know they'd started consuming our people?" he asked. "Draining our essence?"

"Eh?"

Her brow peaked above one eye, her mild surprise—if that's what it was—a tiny victory. Kylan chased after it, hoping to unlock her wisdom if he could only form his words into the right key. Maybe Aughra had been so preoccupied with the heavens, she hadn't noticed the problems that had taken place down on Thra. He tried again to explain, in less artful terms, hoping she had just misunderstood. They needed her, after all. She had to know what to do. How would they fix things if she didn't?

"They steal Gelfling away and bind them to a chair in a chamber. The Skeksis scientist makes them stare into the Heart of Thra—the Crystal, that they've perverted with their experiments. We all entrusted the Crystal to them, and this is what they've done. Their influence has darkened the Crystal, and now that darkness is spreading everywhere. Like a sickness! This is happening right now. We can't wait for the next Great Conjunction. We don't even know when it will be! It could be hundreds of trine from now, and in that time the Skeksis may take every last one of our people."

Aughra had become distracted by the contents of her worktable, sorting through it, though her motions were slower now, as if burdened. Kylan had never wished sorrow upon anyone, but at that moment he hoped the old woman felt at least a little. It might mean she cared. He stepped forth, still gripping the book in his hands so he had something to hold on to when it felt like everything else was slipping out of his grasp.

"At least tell us if it's possible," he urged. "Is this a battle worth fighting? Are you really saying the Skeksis are unstoppable and we should just . . . give up?"

Aughra sighed.

"The future is immutable. A single moment in the movement of all things—the Great Conjunction. More powerful than the Skeksis. More powerful than the Mystics. I haven't seen far enough, yet. Not far enough to know whether there is hope. Be patient."

Kylan didn't know what he had expected coming here, but this was not it. It was no map to navigate their way out of the wood, no rope to pull them out of the swamp. Aughra was wise, but her wisdom couldn't help them now. She couldn't even tell them there was light at the end of the dark. They couldn't wait for her to save them.

"I've had enough of patience," Kylan said with a sigh that left him completely deflated. "And I've had enough of you."

He regretted the words as soon as they escaped. Even Tavra looked surprised. Aughra fixed him with her one eye, the last of the three she'd once had. For the first time, he saw real emotion in her face. She looked down from his face to the book he clutched tightly in his arms.

He thought she would reproach him for speaking to her in such a way, but all she said was, "Take that book. Aughra thinks it was meant for you."

Then she turned her back on them and shuffled away, making no further invitation to follow. He thought about apologizing, but the room had become so damp with sadness that he didn't want to provoke it further. Their time with Aughra was over, and Kylan had been the one to end it.

"Come on," Naia said. "Let's get out of here."

No one spoke a word as they left. They had no destination except away from the High Hill, Kylan so wanting to put it behind him that he almost considered asking Tavra to take them straight to the Black River as she'd wanted to from the beginning.

When they reached a wide, flat rock pocked with rain-filled holes, they stopped to rest. The water in the pools was clean and cool even as the suns shone down. Kylan tried to enjoy it and focus on the moment. He washed his face, hoping it might cleanse the memory of Aughra and her orrery from his mind.

Maybe it hadn't been all bad. He held out the book she had given him. It bore no markings save for a symbol Kylan didn't recognize written in black ink on the spine. The worn, dark blue-gray leather that bound it had long ago lost a corner but was otherwise in good shape.

He flipped through the book and found most of the pages filled. The writing within was in ink—not dream-etched like Gelfling writing. Some of the words were illegible, and the hand in which it had all been writ did not match the many other scrolls and parchments in Aughra's orrery. Splatters of black dotted the paper around scrawled sketches, diagrams, and sometimes completely unintelligible shapes that did not fit into any category. Given it was done in ink and not dream-etching, he guessed the author was not Gelfling. Yet in many places, the writing was in Gelfling letters and very fluent for a non-Gelfling. The subjects of the text were unfocused, sometimes geographical, sometimes astronomical. Sometimes they even seemed to be a record or diary, longhand for a few pages. These entries were almost always in a writing Kylan could not read, but they were dense, often accompanied by messy ink splatters and sometimes the remains of torn-out pages.

"The message on the spiderweb rock was right, I think," Naia said when they stood to continue their journey. Kylan would have loved to rest longer, but he knew better. Perhaps if they made it to the Black River and made a boat, he could read the entire way there.

"Oh?" Gurjin asked with a raised brow. "You decided what it meant?"

Kylan let Naia share the expired secret, glad to have it out in the open, even if it no longer mattered. Maybe there was at least some resolution in that.

"It said *do not trust her*. We didn't want to put stock in some anonymous warning, but maybe we should have."

"*Do not trust her*, eh?" Gurjin echoed. "Strange thing to write about Aughra. It's not as if she misled us. What was there to trust . . . or not trust? All she did was tell us nothing."

"Someone was just trying to save us the time," Tavra said. It was the first thing she'd said since they'd left Aughra.

"So first you don't want us to read it, and now you use it as weight on your argument?" Naia retorted. "How very Silverling of you."

"Perhaps if you'd told us about it and we'd heeded its advice, we could be at the Black River by now."

Naia crossed her arms and faced Tavra full-on.

"No. We agreed to do everything we could to follow through. Sending the warning is the right thing to do. We're all in this together. Even if we can't rely on Aughra."

"Then what is your plan?" To that, no one had an answer, and Tavra flipped her hair self-importantly. "I see. Well, then might I suggest while you formulate your plan, we descend to the river. By the time we reach it, surely you'll have come up with something brilliant."

The sarcasm was so palpable, Tavra might as well have been serving it for supper. Naia leaned and grabbed Kylan's arm possessively, her grip tight and proud.

"Kylan will find something in that book. Won't you, Kylan? *Before* we reach the river. I have every faith in you!"

And with that, the Drenchen girl stomped off down the path. Kylan folded his arms around the book when Gurjin and Tavra laid eyes on him. He wasn't sure whether to be annoyed or flattered that Naia had stuck him with the pressure of coming up with their next move, and under a time limit, no less.

Tavra shrugged and tossed her cape to the side so she could sheath her sword. She gave Kylan a challenging, dubious snort.

"Better start reading," she said, then turned and followed Naia down the hill.

CHAPTER 12

They made it nearly back to the forest valley before making camp for the night. The spot Tavra picked was near a broad lake, nestled between the highlands and the wood. Through the sound of wind in the leaves and the awakening night creatures, Kylan could hear the lake, and maybe even the gurgling of a creek, one of the Black River's tributaries. Over two dozen smaller rivers and streams originated in the tall mountains and fed the river channel, or at least that's what he'd learned from the maps in the old book.

The maps were no help, though. In order to use a map, one had to have a direction, and that was what was sorely missing from the old text.

Kylan leaned against a rock. His eyes were sore from reading. To give his mind a break, he prepared his own scrolls and worked on the day's record, recalling as many details as he could before the memories faded. In his journal, the memory of the orrery could be preserved forever. Their journey there could be smoothed over. Their interaction with Aughra could be just a stumble on their path to ultimate success. All it would take were more chapters to show that this dark disappointment was not the end, but just some dimmer part in the middle. Maybe it was better that way.

No, Kylan decided mid-etching, *it is better. No* maybe*s about it.*

And so he wrote it into the diary that way to make sure that any future readers would understand it to be so. By the time the fire was lit, Aughra's domed observatory and the metal-sphered machine that filled it felt like nothing but a distant dreamfast.

Naia and Gurjin were quiet, though when talk of who would be more successful in catching their supper began, an old rivalry came back to life between them. Whatever lingering moroseness they'd had over Aughra—and the following confrontation with Tavra—quickly faded as they hiked off in opposite directions, a *bola* in Naia's hand and a spear in Gurjin's.

Kylan put away his scrolls and stared at the book, willing it to cooperate this time. He had to believe that hidden in its pages was something they could use. Something that would make their trip to Aughra worth it in the greater song of things. Trying to renew his sense of hope, he picked it up and opened it once more.

"Found anything yet? I've never seen a Gelfling read so studiously, even among those who could."

Tavra stood behind him, tying a laundering rope between two trees.

"I'll probably never be a warrior like everyone else in my clan, but I might as well hone the few skills I have." He set the book in his lap and watched the Vapra string the cord to another tree, knotting it off with practiced, dexterous hands. She tied it so quickly, it was as if there were no knot at all, yet from the weaving work, Kylan imagined the rope would stay taut and strong even in a gale.

"I didn't realize you were so skilled with knots," he said. He tried to sound friendly in the hopes the Silverling warrior might warm to him even a little. "I've heard that the Sifan clan's weaving and sailing knots are unequaled, but it seems they may have competition!"

It was a weak attempt, and he knew it. Tavra merely said, "I have many skills."

Then she unclasped her cloak and draped it over her arm, walking into the wood without any further explanation.

Kylan read, alone, as the suns began their nighttime descent. The book's topics were all jumbled together, in no particular order. One moment they would describe a recent feast shared with the village; the next, the notes described the biology of a suri-wing in graphic detail, with drawings showing all the bones and muscles and feather shafts.

Kylan paused at the words on the next page. It was another diary entry, but this time it was written in Gelfling, instead of in one of the many other languages scattered throughout the book. Most remarkably, the passage finally gave a name, and Kylan read the words hungrily:

> *Mother forgot my name today.*
> *I had to remind her: "Raunip. Raunip, Mother!"*
> *I cried, "The name you gave me!"*
> *How could she forget?*

She has been consumed with the heavens. The heavens, and the shard, buried deep underground. She will not admit that neither above nor below will heal this sickness. Only we of Thra can be the antidote; and to heal our world, we must purge it of those outsiders who have taken our heart captive.

"Raunip," Kylan whispered, placing his hand on the page as if he might dreamfast with it. "It's a pleasure to meet you."

He lost track of the pages he turned. Sometimes he read sections from beginning to end, and sometimes he skipped back and forth. In the beginning, he marked pages with leaves, but when the book began to bulge from the number of bookmarks, he realized that someday he would simply have to read cover to cover if he wanted to absorb everything it had to say.

"The song of the Heart of Thra can sing the hollow bone from the bell-bird wing."

He had become so entrenched in the book that for a time, he even forgot the reason he was reading. When he heard himself read the passage aloud, his mind cleared. It was as if he'd been listening to the book speaking for so long, only half listening, but now it had called out to him by name.

Read this, it was saying to him. *These pages are for you.*

The page showed the illustration of a *firca*, the forked flute many Gelfling carried, but this *firca* was different. A song in verse that accompanied the illustration explained how: This *firca* was crafted by Gyr the Song Teller, crafted from the forked bone of a bell-bird's wing. The song told how the legendary traveler had played on it in the Caves of Grot, deep in the mountains. As his song echoed through the endless caverns, the words to every song he knew were dream-etched across the walls. There, the book read, the Grottan Gelfling protected the songs, as well as the other lore of the Gelfling people.

Kylan didn't know what to believe at first. It seemed impossible. Dream-etching was a slow and painstaking process, and the bell-birds were creatures of fantasy, long since died out. Even Gyr had lived long, long ago—so long ago that his *firca* may well have crumbled to time. The whole thing was more likely a song romanticizing the invention of writing . . . and yet Kylan's heart stirred, as if it knew there was something more real to this story than myth.

If the *firca* was real and could truly dream-etch simply by the power of its song . . . He worried it was a false hope, but Naia had believed in him to find something, and he didn't want to let her down. It was enough that he decided to tell her.

Darkness had set in by the time Naia returned with Gurjin. They came back bearing the same game, fish caught in the lake. Kylan read and listened while they compared the size of the fish and argued over whether length or weight was more important. Finally, their hunger got the better of them, and they focused on preparing the food, Naia scaling and de-finning the fish while Gurjin made the spits. When they weren't in competition, they worked seamlessly together, and in no time the scent of blackened fish filled the air. Kylan closed the cover of the mysterious book.

"Where's Tavra?" Naia asked, circling the fire. The Vapra had not returned, and they didn't wait for her before eating, though

Gurjin moved her fish away from the fire so it wouldn't burn.

"Went to take a bath in the lake, I think. She's been gone a while... Naia, I have something to show you. I think it could be a clue to how we might send our message."

Naia looked over Kylan's shoulder and pointed at the sketch of the forked instrument. Gurjin joined them, and the three looked at the pages together.

"Is that a *firca*?" he asked.

"Yes. It was used to do a hundred dream-etchings at once in the Caves of Grot. Gyr the Song Teller did it just by playing the *firca*. The music echoed through the cave and etched the words on all the stone it touched."

"Is this a song, or truth?" Naia asked. "If it's true... Kylan, could you use such a thing to write our warning about the Skeksis? We wouldn't have to do it one message at a time, we could do so many at once. So many the Skeksis wouldn't be able to stop every one."

"I know. The book says the *firca* was left with the Grottan, in the caves. We're near there, according to this map, so I thought we might go..."

"The Grottan Gelfling?" Gurjin asked. "They still exist?"

It was a good question, and Kylan didn't have the answer. The Grottan clan were practically a myth themselves, even more reclusive than the Drenchen. At least Kylan had known Naia's clan actually existed, and where. When he'd met her in person, he hadn't been surprised to find that she was real. But the Grottan were like shadows at night. If any of their people still lived, they had not been interested in being seen or heard by other Gelfling in many trine.

He didn't want to mislead his friends. There was a very real chance the song in the book was only a song, but he also couldn't deny the gut feeling that there was something real in it. Something that could mean a victory for them. As Naia had taught him, he had to trust his gut.

"It's possible the bone *firca* doesn't actually exist, but maybe Aughra knows better. Maybe she sent the book with us for that reason . . . Or maybe it has nothing to do with Aughra. Either way, I just have the feeling that we should go. I wish I had more proof, but the feeling is all I have."

"Then we will go," Naia said readily. "I trust your instinct. Anyway, it's the only idea we have right now, and if it's real, it could be the answer we've been looking for."

Kylan nodded in relief. When Naia looked over her shoulder, then exchanged a glance with Gurjin, Kylan realized he had been so focused on the *firca* and the song of the Caves of Grot that he had missed something. Naia and Gurjin were brewing a secret, and they were about to share it with him. Naia sat beside him so she could whisper.

"Tavra might be back soon, so I'll be quick. After what Aughra told us about the Skeksis and the Mystics, I think I understand why they want Gurjin and me so badly. And even if Aughra says it won't work, I don't think they will stop coming after us. If we're all together, we're just making it easy for them. So . . . Gurjin and I think it's best that we split up. I wanted to ask what you thought."

Kaylan felt touched that she sought his opinion at all, even if he hardly knew what to say after being ambushed with their bold plan. He glanced at Gurjin, whose ears were alert and listening for Tavra's return while he sharpened his spear.

"Where would he go? Back to Stone-in-the-Wood?"

"Home to Sog," she replied. "Home, to tell my parents what's happened. He can recover fully there, and he'll be safe . . . It's far from the Castle of the Crystal. Traveling alone, the Skeksis will never find him. Especially not if he's headed south, away from Ha'rar."

If the Skeksis were following Rian's trail to the All-Maudra, they'd almost be to Ha'rar. Gurjin would be as far away as possible in Sog. There, Gurjin could rest and be healed by Maudra Laesid, their mother. He would be in the best place to avoid the Skeksis, should they pursue him.

"Are you well enough?" he asked Gurjin, raising his voice only enough to be heard over the fire.

"If I go at my own pace, yes," Gurjin replied. "I'm familiar with the Dark Wood, and I know how the Skeksis travel it. I know skekMal's trails. I may be weak, but thanks to Naia, I'm feeling much better. I might even be able to travel more quickly on my own."

"And he'll take Neech," Naia continued. "Neech can scout ahead at night, and keep watch, and hunt."

"You're right to say all this before Tavra gets back," Kylan said. "She will never agree."

"She'll have to choose between going after Rian or Gurjin, and my guess is she'll pick Rian. That is the path to Ha'rar, where she can finally be rid of us."

The last bit was sour. Kylan squeezed Naia's shoulder.

"She'll be mad we didn't have her approval, but I think you're right, and maybe she'll understand once it's done. If Gurjin can get back to Sog, then at least someone will have made contact with the Drenchen."

Gurjin and Naia nodded in unison.

"I'll leave tonight, when it's my watch," he said. He extended his hand, and Kylan took it. "It was very good to meet you, Kylan the Song Teller. I'm glad my sister met you."

Footsteps crunched in the shadows beyond the campfire. Tavra returned, silver hair drying over her shoulder, and tossed her freshly washed cloak over the line. Next to it went her sandals, tied at the laces, dripping clean with river water.

"Welcome back," said Kylan. He tried not to sound nervous, though each new secret he kept from her felt like one more fluttering unamoth inside him. Yet when he really listened to his gut, he realized it wasn't lying to Tavra that felt uncomfortable, but Tavra's presence itself. He didn't know what it was, but after Naia's remarks, he agreed something was not right with her. He hoped that when they reached Ha'rar, the All-Maudra would be able to do something. Perhaps she knew of a spell or serum that could heal what the Skeksis had done.

Tavra blinked twice at him, as if surprised he had said anything. Without even a thanks in reply, she sat on the far side of the fire and began weaving her damp hair into a braid. In the firelight, her single earring cast sparkles on her pale neck, and

Kylan wished he could find the right words to untangle whatever caused the animosity radiating from her. If only there were a song that could touch her heart, the way one had touched Rian's—but not every problem could be solved with a song. Kylan knew that more than any. For the meantime, he would just have to hope that Tavra would not be too angry when she woke the following morning and Gurjin had left without her approval.

When the fire had settled to embers, Naia took first watch, and Kylan pulled his cloak around his shoulders, facing away from the others so it wouldn't be too obvious that he was wide awake. He lay there, wondering how Tavra would react in the morning and whether or not Aughra had known about the song of the *firca* in the book. Maybe Mother Aughra was right: Perhaps the future was unchangeable, and knowing the greatest machinations of the heavens was the only way to know the truth of the present.

Or maybe Aughra was wrong, and it was right for them to take things into their own hands, to say goodbye to Gurjin in the dead of the night, betraying Tavra's trust and authority. Would she understand, or would she scold them like children? Or worse! She was the daughter of the All-Maudra, and acting against her could be interpreted as treason if Tavra were serious enough about it. No, that was extreme. Even if she were more serious and stoic than they remembered, she was still Tavra. She believed in them, and their cause.

Kylan worried himself into a doze, and only noticed he had drifted off when it was suddenly dawn. The fire was almost out, smoke sizzling in the early makings of dew, and the sky was the faintest of blues, barely visible through the trees above.

Someone knelt over him. He didn't stir, in case his motion might wake Tavra and ruin their hastily laid plan. A hand settled on his shoulder, and he heard Gurjin's dreamfasted voice in his mind.

Until we meet again, brother Kylan. Be safe.

Then the Drenchen boy was gone, with not a sound to mark his footsteps as he vanished into the wood.

CHAPTER 13

Kylan woke to the sound of Tavra and Naia arguing. He didn't think it would be possible to fall asleep again, so close to morning, but his body felt heavy and his cheek was cold where it had been pressed solid against the earth. He considered pretending to sleep until the argument had blown over. By now, Gurjin would be far away and virtually untraceable—assuming his skill in traversing the wood was as good as he claimed. Tavra, despite her anger, would be fighting a battle already lost if she were to pursue him now.

"He left this," Naia said, showing Tavra a flat stone with a dream-etching in it. Gurjin might not be literate, but he had marked it with a symbol most Gelfling knew, whether they could write or not: his clan's sigil. The sign of the Drenchen was the whiskered muski, which seemed fitting in trade, since Neech had gone with Gurjin, as they had planned. "It must mean he's going back to Sog. To my family. He'll be safe there!"

"Safe? Maybe once he reaches the swamp! But he could get lost anywhere in the wilderness, not to mention the Dark Wood. We'll never find him!"

"We don't need to find him. We know where he's gone, and that he'll be safe there. That's what's most important, don't you think? If we traveled together, the Skeksis could capture us all at once. At least now we've made it more difficult for them."

Tavra had not put her cloak back on yet, leaving her wings free to buzz in irritation. Unlike Naia's, they were translucent, rainbow colored in the morning sunlight. Kylan sat up and yawned, making a show of his awakening with a stretch.

"What're you two so worked up about?" he asked. Acting—lying?—was not a strength of his, but he knew better than to jump directly into the conversation. In fact, he'd rather not be a part of it at all, but there was little avoiding it. He was Naia's accomplice and the only other person in their party, now that Gurjin had gone.

"Gurjin's left," Naia informed him. "He's gone back to Sog, and I think it's best that he did."

"He's been brash. He'll ruin everything," Tavra muttered, but she knew it was a lost cause. "But there's no way we'll find him now. We can only hope he will make it to the place he says he will. We'll have to get him later. Now, come on, get up. We're making the Black River by nightfall, or so help me."

Naia crossed her arms and planted her feet.

"No," she said.

"Excuse me?"

"I want to reach Ha'rar, of course, but Rian's already far along on his way there. In the meantime, you're not the leader of this traveling party, and I'm tired of you treating us like children you've got to watch. Kylan found something in the book Aughra gave him, about a magic *firca* that might be able to send the message to the Gelfling. So that is where we're going. To the Caves of Grot, to look for the *firca*. Rian can address the All-Maudra himself, and we'll join him once we've done the job we promised we would do."

Tavra's wings spread in anger, a hint of red pinching her cheeks.

"*Tch!* Don't make me remind you which of us was about to be dinner to a weed, or who was nearly poisoned to death by spiders, and all that only in the last two days!"

Naia stomped her foot, not as a tantrum but as a challenge.

"We didn't ask for your help, and we'd be happy to thank you for it if you weren't being such a salty kelp-sucker about it."

"How dare you speak this way to me. My mother is the All-Maudra!"

"*Oh?* Don't forget, my mother is *also* a *maudra*—and unlike *you*, I will succeed her one day!"

Kylan swallowed quietly in the silence that followed. The tension had finally crowned, and in a way it was a relief. He wasn't happy that Naia had pulled rank on Tavra in the way she had—it certainly wasn't the most diplomatic way to assert her dominance, but it had worked. Kylan had nearly forgotten that Naia was the daughter of a *maudra*. Her mother, Laesid, might not be the All-Maudra, but it was possible that once Naia took her place, she might even hold more sway with the All-Maudra than Tavra. Kylan didn't know how far down the line Tavra was among her sisters, but the fact that she was out here in the wilderness and not in Ha'rar was a sign she was not near the top.

Kylan braced himself for a return attack. Tavra was holding

her breath. Was this impetuous, hostile Gelfling really the soldier who had looked out for them so selflessly? What had happened to her after the draining at the castle?

She finally let out the most exasperated sigh Kylan had ever heard.

"Fine," Tavra said. "We'll have it your way, Drenchen. Let's go looking for a flute that probably does not exist, and in the meantime, likely be trapped inside a mountain tunnel. But it makes no difference to me. Let's go to die straightaway!"

Naia clenched her fists, and Kylan interrupted before things got even worse.

"The Caves of Grot are on the east side of this lake, if this map is accurate. The book says Gyr left the *firca* there, with the Grottan Gelfling."

If they had Tavra's approval, then at least they might be able to get out of the confrontation with that. They should take what they could get. He looked expectantly at Naia to salvage as much peace between them all as she could, and although she puffed out her cheeks, she let the breath out and spoke calmly.

"Then we'll go. Around the lake. If the Grottan still exist, we can ask them, and tell them about the Skeksis if it seems they might believe us. If we don't see them, then we will find the *firca* ourselves."

"And if we don't find the *firca* at all?" Tavra asked. "Will you agree to abandon this fool's quest and go with me to Ha'rar?"

Kylan didn't want to think about what they might do if there was no *firca*, but it was possible. If Aughra couldn't help them, and the *firca* was a dead end as well, then perhaps it would be best to do as Tavra said and try to catch up with Rian. On top of that, he wanted Tavra's help.

"Yes. I'd agree that even if we *do* find the *firca*, we will go straight to Ha'rar after," he suggested. "So either way, Tavra, we will go north. If you give us your help, I think we will be the better for it. Help us find the *firca*, and we will depart for the capital even sooner."

He thought it was a good proposal, if not to smooth over the rough water between all of them, then at least to offer Tavra motivation to stay with them. The unspoken alternative, of course, was that Tavra left them and went to Ha'rar alone.

She started taking down the laundry line. The invincible knots melted in her hands, falling away as if they had never been tied, and for a moment she held the loop of white cord as if considering tying the two of them up and dragging them to Ha'rar.

"Let's get this over with," she said.

It was a short walk to the lake, and when they arrived, Kylan stopped to take out the book. Naia waded into the clear water, her skin turning greener as it soaked up the moisture. She gazed out over the flat water, thinking about her brother, Kylan guessed. Or thinking of Neech, whose disappearance Tavra had not noticed and probably wouldn't, as the flying eel was prone to wandering off on his own or sleeping hidden in Naia's hair during the day.

The sky was clear, the sun bright, and the pages of the old book easy to read. Kylan had marked the pages with maps, and turned to them quickly. He found north by looking at the moss on the trees, and based on the swoop of the highlands that rose up around the low lake, he resolved their position rather quickly. Through the pristine air, even the High Hill was visible, making him even more certain that he knew where they were and where they should go.

"That way," he said, pointing over the lake to the east, where the water met sheer red cliffs that went straight up into the highlands. It looked like nothing but mountainside from here, but the surface was porous and rippled, and Kylan imagined many tunnels and caves could hide within.

"Shall we walk the beach or fashion a raft, o navigator?" Tavra asked, so flat it was probably rhetorical, but Kylan answered anyway.

"I think the beach will be quicker. We're on the closer side, anyway, and making a raft will take too long."

Tavra sped off toward the beach. "Too bad we didn't bring the boat," Naia said as they set off after her.

The beach was sandy, speckled with rocks and sometimes the discarded exoskeletons of lake critters. Naia even found a large bronze fish scale and pocketed it as a souvenir. Kylan struggled with the maps, trying to decipher the scribbles and ink-blotted markings. There were times when he feared it was all made-up, just some abstract drawing by a madman of a place that only appeared to be real.

He must have been making a face, because Naia noticed and asked him what was wrong.

"I'm worried we won't find the caves," he confessed. He didn't burden her with the rest of his worries, that there would be no *firca* when they got there or that he was making this all up in an attempt to feel worthwhile.

"Well, *don't* worry," she said. "We've got you. We've got that map. And Thra knows, we've got Tavra. If it'll get us to Ha'rar quicker, she'll find those caves if it's the last thing she does."

He gave her a sideways glance.

"You're enjoying this, aren't you?"

"I'm not *not* enjoying it."

It was tense, but at least Naia was on his side. The beach curved, heading straight for the cliffs where the caves would be, according to the map. As they neared them, Kylan realized how much bigger the cliffs were. The wall of black fern-studded rock looked like it would block out the sky. The cliff's shadow fell over them, and Kylan shivered.

"She must have a lot on her mind. And she must be exhausted . . . maybe even in pain, after what the Skeksis did. I'm surprised she's still walking, and without a complaint. When she gets back to Ha'rar, she'll have to explain everything to her mother . . ."

"Don't make excuses for her," Naia said before he could go too far. "All that may be true, but none of that means she has to be so rude or mean. Hard-talk is one thing. Treating us like dirt is another. I'm done with it, so if she wants to keep taking out all her hardships on us, she better be prepared for some talk-back."

At any point, Tavra could have decided to leave them, yet she'd agreed to accompany them. That meant she cared, despite her attitude, and Kylan decided to take that as a good thing.

"I know, I know."

"Aughra could have done well to be more prepared for talk-back, too, eh?" Naia asked. Kylan chuckled, though his cheeks warmed.

"That was an accident. It just came out like that."

"I didn't know you had it in you. I liked it. Someone had to say what we were all thinking."

"I would rather she had given us some answers, or some hope. Or something. Anything."

"She did give us something—a reason to make our own way. And that book. You two seem inseparable! I was starting to get jealous."

"Who else was I supposed to spend time with while you and Gurjin were such beans on a string?"

It was half a joke, but Naia responded only to the half that wasn't for laughs.

"Kylan! Don't say that. If I had to pick between traveling with only one of you two, it would be the one who's here right now."

"Only because you're worried I might need protecting," Kylan said. Again, it was partly a tease, but it was rooted in truth, however small. "Or boat rowing."

"No," Naia said. "Because Gurjin and I always see things the same way. If the two of us always traveled together, we would never make it. When I'm with you, I have someone looking out for me from a different perspective. That's important to me."

"All right. I'll believe you."

"Promise?"

He was about to agree when Tavra called to them. They had finally reached the place where the beach ended, abruptly stopped by the cliffs. The lake's waves sloshed against the rock in the cold shadow of the cliff. Bats and whistling cave birds swooped in and out of the millions of holes that dotted the cliffside. At water level, Kylan could see Gelfling-size cave mouths. The lake seeped into them in narrow ravines, quickly lost in the thick darkness that filled the mountainside.

Tavra pointed to a place on the cliff above the nearest cave. Hidden under the drooping ferns and creeping water-ivies was a dream-etched Gelfling symbol. The animal pictograph was ancient, eroded, but unmistakable—a flap-winged hollerbat, sigil of the Grottan Gelfling clan.

CHAPTER 14

Though the nearest cave entrance was in plain sight, reaching it was still a challenge. The tunnels were made for boat access, from the looks of them—difficult to access by foot, with openings more horizontal than vertical. Yet there was a shallow ledge along the cliff that was still wide enough for a Gelfling to walk, and they followed it along the wall of rock until they could duck into the tunnel. Inside, cloaked in cool shadows, the ceiling was so low they had to crawl to keep from bumping their heads on dripping stalactites. It was a natural canal, low enough that they could have sat in a boat and rowed in comfortably.

But they didn't have a boat, and so they had to crawl along the narrow shelves on either side of the waterway. The lake waves sloshed all around them, sometimes enough that Kylan's hands and knees were completely submerged. At one point, a rogue wave washed so high over them that he was drenched up to his stomach, and he considered simply rolling into the waterway and swimming rather than continue scrabbling along the wet, slime-covered rocks.

When the book had mentioned the underwater tunnels, Kylan had not taken much note. Now, as he followed Naia on all fours, feeling the ceiling and walls close around them, he felt an unbidden tremor of panic low in his belly. He had never been in a space so enclosed, and was surprised at how afraid it made him, even though in his higher mind he knew he was in no real danger. It didn't matter either way, really. It was too late to back out now, and even if it wasn't, if he did, there would be no hope of finding whether Gyr's magic *firca* existed or not.

The uncomfortable journey was rewarded before too long. The tunnel opened, and the walkway on either side of the canal became tall enough for them to stand. Tavra muttered under her breath as she straightened and brushed dirt and algae from her wings, getting a smirk from Naia, who was perfectly at home in the mud and wet.

They walked down a long twisting tunnel. Through the center was the waterway, lit from below by glowing algae and schools of crawling freshwater anemones, each patterned in different-colored stripes and dots of light. The water was clear and deep, and Kylan decided he had been right not to try to swim. Who knew what kind of hungry creatures lived down in the pitch-dark ravine below.

The lights from the lake critters were bright enough to illuminate most of the tunnel, though the dim lighting would take some getting used to. Already, the bright daylight beyond the cave was nearly gone, as if they had entered another world that existed in permanent night.

"These are the Grottan caves, all right," Naia said. "Look, more writing."

On the walls, glittering from mineral deposits, were dream-etchings. More pictographs, but some words, too. Kylan traced them with his fingers, wondering whether these could be some of the dream-etchings left by Gyr so many ages ago.

"*May all light not true be swallowed by darkness,*" he read out loud. "How ominous. It's written like a blessing, but I can't help but feel we've been warned."

Tavra gave the writing no attention, though she was literate. Apparently skill had no correlation with interest.

"Move on. We can travel faster on foot, at least."

Though the walkway was wider, the path was by no means easy. Loose rocks were constantly moving underfoot, slippery and sharp and hard to see in the dark. Kylan thought he heard whispers, once or twice, but even if they were being watched by someone, there would be no way to know. Sometimes, when his ear was close to the rock wall, he heard a faint knocking and tapping, as if someone were drumming their finger against a distant part of the cave.

As they walked farther and farther from the outside world, the dream-etchings became more common, though often with words and characters Kylan didn't recognize. Soon the cave walls were covered in the etchings top to bottom, more full than the pages of his book. He and Naia marveled at the writing, and he pointed out some of the easier-to-read pictographs to her. Soon she started to recognize them: the symbols for the three suns and three moons; the curled, tripart character for *Thra*.

"Heart of *Thra*," Kylan read. "*Closer we, the Grottan Clan, to the Heart of Thra than . . . any other . . . The Castle of the Crystal is* days west. They must mean it figuratively."

"Every Gelfling clan believes they are closest to Thra," Tavra said. "And yet Gelfling are the only creatures on this planet who make a contest of it. It's absurd."

Kylan tried to smooth over the tension.

"We may have different founding *maudra*," he said, "but we're all Gelfling. Surely none of us are more intimate with Thra than the others."

Tavra snorted.

"Perhaps a consensus can be reached among the Gelfling clans, but that leaves many other creatures out of the equation. Being a favorite of Aughra affords one many luxuries, even if they might not be viewed that way. It is the definition of a spoiled child."

Naia rolled her eyes, though it was at Tavra's back, and the Silverling didn't see it. Kylan didn't know exactly what Tavra was getting at, but he let it alone. They were in close confines already, and the cramped space didn't need to be filled by more bickering. Silence seemed to be the best way to put out the fire, so silence it was.

The three walked on quietly, listening to the drip-dripping and drop-dropping of cave water and the faint rumble of some far-off underground river. Sometimes the air would warm, then cool, as if they were passing in and out of the shadows of trees in an open, sunny field. More likely, Kylan thought, there were springs flowing through the earth, heating the rock. In the places where it was warmer, thick blue moss grew in spongy balls, sprinkled with translucent, glowing sprouts. Where it was cooler, crawlies snaked in and out of the shadows, armored worms with hundreds of jointed legs and spiraled antennae, snacking on the stacks of shingled lichen that crowded between rock joints.

The caves seemed infinite, as if they filled all of Thra. Maybe they did. It was so different from the open plains and light forest of the Spriton land. Even the Dark Wood and the highlands were familiar, in a way, but the caves were as alien to Kylan as the surface of the Great Sun or the bottom of the ocean. He wondered whether this foreign uneasiness was how Naia had felt when she had first left the Swamp of Sog, setting foot on dry land for the first time in her life. Yet she had come through the Spriton plains and more, all the way to the Castle of the Crystal. Kylan remembered this and willed himself to be just as bold.

Outsider . . .

A gust of wind broke the still air, and Kylan thought he heard a voice, breathy like an exhale, but when the breeze passed, it left only the scent of fresh water and earth. Ahead was a wall, and he thought the tunnel had ended. Then the blockage wavered in another draft of fresh-smelling air, and he realized it was not a wall but a blanket of moss, growing from the ceiling of the tunnel all the way down, where its tips swayed in the surface of the waterway. It formed some kind of doorway, or a curtain, and the breeze that filtered through gave him hope that they had reached something magnificent that lay just on the other side.

Naia touched the curtain of moss first. It was thick, swallowing her arm as she reached in. Unlike the strangling finger-vines, this moss was gentle, some furry fronds curling away from the

Drenchen girl to let her pass. Without hesitation or looking back, Naia stepped through, and Kylan and Tavra followed soon after. It took three steps to pass fully through the soft tendrils, and Kylan gasped when he reached the other side.

The waterway split where they stood, snaking to the left and the right through the basin of an open cavern that filled the space beyond the tunnel. The dizzying ceiling soared high above into what must have been the body of the mountains. Light streamed down in columns from holes far above, just enough to illuminate the place while leaving most of it in mystery.

"It's beautiful," Kylan whispered. The word didn't do the ghostly place justice, but it was a start.

"It's empty," Tavra added, as if it couldn't be both. "And dangerous. Who knows what might live in these caves. It smells of death. Let's find the *firca* and get out of here."

Naia stepped forward to lead but stopped when a pebble skipped down from one of the walkways above. Kylan looked up and saw nothing, but then he *heard* them. Whispers, all around them, blending into one another. They grew louder, and he made out words:

Outsider. Daylighter. Silverling.

"Ghosts?" he squeaked, but Naia was less superstitious and simply asked, "Is someone there?"

Is someone there? came the whispers. Or were they echoes? *There . . . Someone is there . . . She wants to know if someone is there . . . If someone is where?*

"Someone is here."

The soft, eerie voice came from right behind them, and Kylan whirled, stumbling back into Naia. Perched above the waterway entrance they'd just passed through was a hooded figure, so close that his dangling bare feet nearly touched the top of Tavra's head before she jumped away. The Gelfling-like figure leaned forward to rest his chin on his hands, and the scant light touched his face. Where his eyes should be, Kylan saw only deep black pits.

A chill ran up his arms and neck when the whisper came again:

"What's so important it's brought daylighters all the way to the Caves of Grot?"

CHAPTER 15

"Shadowling," Tavra growled.

"Silverling," the strange Gelfling replied, with a casual but equal distaste. He hopped down, his sparkling black cloak ballooning around him. He landed silently and effortlessly among the sharp rocks and pebbles that littered the walkway.

Pulling back his hood, his skin was pale like moonlight, with silky silver hair like Tavra's, shaved on one side and falling to his shoulder on the other. Had Kylan seen him aboveground, he might have mistaken him for a Vapra—except for his eyes. With his face hidden by the shadow of his hood, Kylan had at first thought he had no eyes at all. Now he could see two, large and black, with no whites in them. It was like looking into one of the inky ponds that dappled the cave's basin floor.

He had to be Gelfling, based on the shape of his face and body, but he held himself differently. Like a river plant, Kylan thought, or maybe even an eel or fish, eerily graceful as he gazed down at them with an unreadable expression. His movements were as fluid as if he were underwater, slow and seamless.

The whispers hushed. The Grottan boy—for that's what he must have been—took his time, turning his dark gaze from one of them to the other. Tavra gripped the hilt of her sword, though

Kylan hoped she wouldn't draw it. If they were headed toward a conflict, he didn't want them to be the ones to start it.

Naia understood this, at least, and held her empty hands away from her knife. "We're here in peace. We're looking for something. We need your help. I'm Naia, from Sog, and this is Kylan of the Spriton. That's . . . Tavra."

She left out Tavra's title, which Kylan thought wise. He was not at ease with the way they were being inspected, but the Grottan's animosity toward the Vapra seemed particularly thick. Knowing that Tavra was not only a Vapra but also the All-Maudra's daughter might be too much, and much too soon.

Naia's introduction was met with an unblinking stare. Just when Kylan thought no reply was coming, the boy headed up one of the stairways that ribbed the interior wall of the cavern.

"Well, come on, then."

The voices in the cave had settled into curious murmurs as they followed their guide up the basin, weaving along the paths that rose above the still water. The stone walkways stretched between tunnels that burrowed deeper into the mountain, their undersides overgrown with moss and luminescent flowers. Kylan jumped when a school of leather-winged hollerbats burst from one roost to another, interrupting the quiet with their whistling screeches before going silent again.

Kylan looked up as they passed through the center of the cavern, losing count of the tunnel entrances and walkways. Now that the silence had been broken, he saw silhouettes of other Grottan Gelfling stepping out of the shadows, gathering in groups of twos and threes on the ledges to watch them pass. They were all ghostly, clothed in black cloaks like their guide. Only their faces, hands, and bare feet showed, slipping in and out of the shadows like starlight.

"This really is the home of the Grottan clan, then?" Naia asked their guide. "The Caves of Grot?"

"Indeed. Though we call it by its birth name: Domrak."

Kylan rolled the word in his mind, picking it apart. The meaning was there, like pips in a fruit.

"Place-in-Shadows?" he asked.

Their guide looked back with raised brows over his black eyes. Kylan told himself the eeriness of the expression was a trick of his imagination, but the way their guide had no pupils made it difficult to see which direction he was looking. Instead, it seemed he gazed at everything at once.

"A fair translation in the common tongue. Others have called it the Cave of Obscurity. Land-in-Darkness. Hole in Ground. Either way, *grot* means crypt. Though in truth, nothing has died here."

They could not argue with that. Plant and animal life was all around them, just as plentiful in the dark as it was above in the light. Voices of children echoed from deep inside the caves, laughing. The word Domrak did not just mean *place*, but *home*.

They followed the carved stairway on a long spiraling ascent. Like every other surface in the cavern, it was textured with dense dream-etchings. It was hard to make out all the shapes and letters in the dim, mixed with pictographs and symbols too eroded by time to read. Kylan caught only pieces of the countless stories inscribed—some about the cavern itself, others about Thra. Yet others described creature life, the passing of seasons, and the medicinal qualities of certain mushrooms.

Their guide turned when the stairs met a tunnel opening larger than the others. The triangular archway was carved to look like a colony of hollerbats, round bodies hanging by the feet, some with wings folded and others outstretched. The intricate carving continued along the wall and ceiling of the tunnel, lit by glowing moss that grew like fur on the stone creatures. The ground cover and other plants thickened until they completely blocked the end of the tunnel in a mass of vines and ferns. There, Kylan waited with the others while the Grottan boy stepped through, enveloped in the plants.

"Maudra Argot? Visitors . . . yes, from above . . ."

A quiet voice replied, too masked by the foliage at the entrance to be understood. After a moment, the vines rustled, and the boy poked his head out.

"She says you two can enter. The Silverling stays here."

Tavra snorted through her nose, and Kylan wished she hadn't. If they wanted to gain the trust and alliance of every clan, they would have to be respectful, even if they did not get the same respect in return. Shouldn't a daughter of the All-Maudra know better diplomacy? Huffing, she turned away and crossed her arms.

"I have no interest in paying respects to a Shadowling bat, anyway," she said, turning her nose up. "Be quick about it."

"Don't start any fights," Kylan said. "Please."

Kylan closed his eyes to keep from being poked by the leaves and tendrils as he passed through them. Though they were soft, there were so many and they grew so densely that by the time he finally exited, he was covered in leaves and spores. Naia was in the same condition, and picked a piece of greenery out of her mouth.

The Grottan *maudra*'s chamber was large enough for a dozen Gelfling to stand in, the walls smoothed by carvers so that it hardly resembled the rest of the rocky, jagged caves. The smoothing exposed thick crystal veins, which cut through the seamless wall like still lightning. The veins filled the room with a gentle light, glowing more brightly where writing was etched in narrow curving shapes. The crystal was still clear and pure, the way it was meant to be.

Seated on the stone floor, cross-legged, was an old Gelfling woman. Her wings were sheer, almost completely transparent, draped out behind her like a crystalline pool. Her eyes were black, like all the Grottan, but bore the mark of time. Her kind, wrinkled face might have seen more than one ninet—if the greater seasons even affected the Grottan clan, so deep in the earth.

She did not rise when they entered. Instead, Kylan knelt before her, and Naia followed.

"This is Naia, of the Drenchen of Sog, and Kylan, of the Spriton," their guide said. "Naia, Kylan. This is Maudra Argot, the Shadow Bender."

"An honor to meet you, Maudra," Kylan said, taking the lead. Naia had gotten them here with boldness, but the old *maudra*'s chamber begged a softer talk.

"An honor," Naia agreed.

When she spoke, Maudra Argot's voice was old and deep.

"It must be important, indeed, for daylighters to bother making the journey into the so-feared Grot. Amri here tells me you have a Vapra with you as well. Has the great Mayrin finally invited us to the Silverling capital? Ho ho hoo! Don't answer that. I know it is not true. So tell me, children, why do you stray from the daylight?"

Their journey into the caves had been so quiet under the watch of the Grottan in the main cavern, the sound of the old woman's laugh was a welcome relief. Amri, their guide, leaned against the wall behind them, hands clasped loosely at his hip.

"We're looking for a *firca*," Naia said. "One made of a special bone. Kylan?"

Kylan cleared his throat, hoping to sound as reasonable as possible in case the *firca* was nothing but a daydream. He was ready for Maudra Argot to laugh in his face and tell him the thing had never really existed, but at least then they'd know.

"It's the *firca* made by Gyr the Song Teller during the Golden Age. I read in a book that it was entrusted to the Grottan and kept here, in . . . in Domrak."

Maudra Argot thumbed the whiskers on her chin in thought and took a long time before she answered. Too long, Kylan thought, and prepared himself for the worst, before the *maudra* coughed and snapped her fingers.

"Oh yes! That. What do you want with Gyr's bone *firca*?"

"You have it here?" Kylan cried, forgetting all formality. "It's real?"

"Of course it's real. How else did you think all that dream-etching got on the walls? All of us can read here, of course, but it would have taken a whole ninet to do just half the caves the regular way. We don't have time for that. Yes, yes, the *firca* is real. It is in the Tomb. Ho ho! But I'm not going to just hand it over to you younglings without an explanation first. Why do you need it? What will you do with it? And so on."

An explanation would mean revealing what they knew about the Skeksis. What if Maudra Argot was loyal to the lords? They were so deep in the mountains, there was no way they'd escape, not if the Grottan decided to take them prisoner to hand over to the Skeksis. He didn't want to think that way, but it was what had already happened when the All-Maudra had sent Tavra after Gurjin and Rian the first time. Maudra Mera would likely not hesitate to do the same, and of course, Maudra Fara had been quick to get them out of Stone-in-the-Wood, even if she didn't turn them over directly to the Skeksis. They had no idea where the Grottan *maudra* fell on the line of allegiance, and there wasn't time to find out.

Kylan frowned. The best way to show Maudra Argot why they needed the *firca* was in dreamfast, but it had to be from Naia, who had seen the Crystal herself. Kylan's memories of what Naia had told him would not suffice. She would have to make that decision herself . . . and she did, offering her hand.

"Then dreamfast with me. I will show you what I've seen. You can decide whether it's an explanation or not."

"So you think I'll trust your memories, no matter what they are?" Maudra Argot asked, tilting her head in the other direction.

When she got a confused, uncomfortable silence in reply, she cackled again. "Ho! Don't answer that, either. I am not afraid of your dreams, little Drenchen. Show me, and we will see where they lead us."

Maudra Argot lifted her hand but did not take Naia's. It was only then that Kylan realized the *maudra* was blind. Naia caught on quietly and made the connection, grasping the old Gelfling's steady, tiny hand. Kylan watched as the two closed their eyes in unison, going still as the dreamfast began. He waited for any sign of distress from his friend, but it seemed her time with Gurjin had calmed her heart and mind, and she shared her memories with Maudra Argot in a calm communion.

Memories spoke faster than words. The dreamfast ended soon, but Kylan could tell from how Maudra Argot leaned back, putting her hands on her knees, that Naia had shared everything. The *maudra* let out a long grave *hmmmm*.

"You have the gift of dreamfast, that is for certain," she said. "Never have I seen dreams so vividly . . . It was almost as if I had my eyes back! Ho ho hoo! What a delight you are, my Drenchen daughter."

For Amri's benefit, Naia said the rest aloud.

"Kylan read about the *firca* in a book he received from Aughra. We promised we would find a way to warn all the Gelfling."

The old Gelfling tapped her chin, blind eyes pointed at the ceiling.

"The Stonewood will be first, until the forest is empty of their tales and noisy dances. Then the Spriton to the south. Perhaps they will go west next, to the Crystal Sea—perhaps north, to take the capital itself. It is only a matter of time before they come for us, I suppose, even if we are the discarded relish on the banquet tray. Ho ho hoo!"

She described an ugly future, but her chuckle was so light, it was almost the giggle of a youngling.

"Nothing but a garnish on top of a Vapra delicacy!" Amri added. The comment sent the old *maudra* into a new fit, her little body shaking with laughter. Kylan shifted uncomfortably and felt Naia do the same. It was a serious situation, but he had spent so much energy worrying—maybe there was nothing else to do but laugh. Then he thought of the Skeksis raiding his Sami Thicket, and knew he was not ready to laugh yet, even if it was out of desperation. Maybe this was wrong. Maybe the Grottan didn't care for the other clans at all—even if they did believe that the Skeksis had betrayed them.

"*Ho ho ho hooo!* Oh, don't sound so quiet. We're not making light of the situation. This old *maudra* has heard many trine come and go. Just when I think I've heard it all, the Skeksis surprise me with something new and cruel. I can't help but think Thra is telling a wicked song-for-laughs . . . Or maybe it is me who is old and mad and laughing when there are no jokes being told."

Naia kept her hands on her knees, pausing before she spoke. It seemed she didn't know how to react to the *maudra* either. Following the Drenchen path, she simply said, "Please let us take the *firca* to send the warning. I think it's most important that all the Gelfling come together against the Skeksis. We won't be able to do anything if we're at odds with one another."

"We Grottan have remained out of the affairs of the daylighters; ours was a different burden to bear, here in Domrak. But you are right. The Skeksis will never want the essence of an old *maudra* like me, but my children . . . even the lazy ones like Amri. We are all Gelfling. I'll give you the *firca*. I'll even give you Amri. He will show you to the Tomb of Relics and then go with you to Ha'rar on behalf of our oft-forgotten clan."

For the first time, Amri's voice sounded juvenile, more Kylan and Naia's age, when he protested.

"Wait! That's not fair. I don't want to be surrounded by snooty Silverlings! Maybe if they were going south . . ."

Maudra Argot had already made up her mind. She waved her hand, as if shooing gnats from a piece of fruit.

"I'll have no more of your disruptive experiments and the smelly ingredients you use for them. I know you sneak out of the caves to gather the stuff, so consider this an extended trip. Take your *maudra*'s offer, and come back when you are grown."

Then she turned away from them, picking up a pile of cloth-weaving in progress beside her. The clicking of the weaving sticks was the signal for them to leave, so Kylan and Naia rose and bowed. As they followed a red-cheeked Amri back through the vines to the tunnel, they could hear the *maudra* talking to herself.

"Damned Skeksis. Your time has come, at long last. Ho ho hoo . . ."

CHAPTER 16

"You don't have to come with us if you don't want to," Naia said as they returned to the main tunnel.

Amri held a finger to his lips with one hand, gesturing over his shoulder with the other, indicating the *maudra*'s chamber.

"Shh. She can still hear us."

Kylan scanned the tunnel for Tavra, who clearly had no desire to stand alone in the cold dark. He hoped she had not found trouble. Naia didn't seem to be worried, so he let it go, too. The Silverling was well equipped to fend for herself if need be. He just hoped she wouldn't cause any problems . . . especially as the Grottan *maudra* had agreed to help them.

They walked in silence until the tunnel opened again into the central cavern, and Kylan took a breath of air. The caves were less frightening now that they'd met with the *maudra*, but they were still caves, underground, in the dark. He wanted nothing more than to escape out the top of the cavern and find an open green field to lie in, but saying so would be rude, and they had a *firca* to find.

"You really don't have to come," Naia repeated.

"It's not that I don't want to leave," Amri replied. "I would just rather go anywhere else than Ha'rar. Eh! I suppose I should be pleased that Maudra Argot is letting me leave the cave at all. Oh well, at least I might have a chance to surprise the All-Maudra. Oh, I can't wait to see the look on her face when a Grottan appears in court!"

The burst of youthful energy surprised Kylan. Now that Amri had been released from his guard duty, he was shaking the seriousness off like a fizzgig that had come in out of the rain.

"Speaking of Silverlings. Where is your silver friend?"

Naia shrugged. "Maybe she left for Ha'rar. It's something that she has been wanting to do very much."

"Hm," Amri said. "It may not be good for her to be wandering around. Many of our people have never seen daylighters before, and if they have any opinions about the Vapra, they are bad ones. We should find her. I know a place to look."

He started farther up the cavern's perimeter walkway, and they followed. Music drifted down from above, slow and harmonic, from wind instruments Kylan couldn't identify. He kept an eye out for Tavra, but she was nowhere to be found. Maybe Naia was right, and she'd finally given up on her wards and left to pursue Rian and Ha'rar herself. Kylan felt bittersweet imagining that she might have. On the one hand, it might be a relief to be free of her relentlessly negative attitude. On the other, though, he realized he would miss her if she were gone, and worry about her suffering alone from her ordeal at the castle.

Amri guided them upward until the stairway ended at a round half chamber carved in the dream-etching-covered wall, with a fire pit dug directly into the stone floor. Three Grottan Gelfling knelt by the fire, each with a different-size reed instrument. The pipes produced the same sounds, but in different keys, and the result was a lovely adagio that warmed the otherwise dreary chamber. When they arrived, the musicians paused. They locked their black eyes on Kylan and Naia, but when they saw Amri was with them, they relaxed.

Tavra was not at the hearth. From the ledge of the chamber they could see most of the interior of the cavern. Kylan stood near the edge and scanned the walkways and stairs for her silver cloak, but saw nothing.

"Aside from the writing, this reminds me of Great Smerth, back home," Naia said, her searching relaxed as if she might prefer they didn't find Tavra at all. Amri stood by, the least interested in looking, his focus entirely on Naia.

"I've heard of the Drenchen mother-tree," he exclaimed. "Is it true it's as old and wise as Olyeka-Staba?"

Naia lit up at the chance to talk about her homeland.

"All our people can fit inside," she said. "And its heartwood echoes with the sound of music and birds during the spring festival . . . Great Smerth is old and wise. I'm not sure any tree is like the Cradle-Tree."

"In that case, I would like to visit both. Can you arrange this?"

Naia laughed, just a little brighter than usual.

They gazed down upon the cavern for long enough to know that if Tavra was walking one of the passes, she did not want to be seen. There was no sign of the Silverling anywhere. Kylan wondered where she could have gone in such a short time. Then again, he didn't know how far the caves went, or how easy they were to traverse.

"Do you all live near this cavern, or do the Grottan occupy the whole under-mountain?"

Amri tilted his head, much like Maudra Argot had.

"You daylighters really don't know much, do you?" he asked, but the question was more amused than critical. "We're a bitty people. There are thirty-seven of us, so yes, we all live near the grand chamber."

"Thirty-seven," Naia said. "At least it must be easy to hold village meetings!"

Amri laughed, a sound that was almost comedic in itself, such a bubbling, goofy noise coming out of what Kylan had originally seen as a serious, frightening creature.

"Yes! We shout into the heart of the cave, and the echoes take care of the rest. No need for gatherings when you can holler. That's what Maudra Argot says. Ahh . . . I can't imagine what it must be like to be Vapra or even Sifa, with so many Gelfling to call kin. I couldn't remember all their names. I can barely remember the names of my own cousins."

"I'm sure the All-Maudra doesn't know the names of all under her wing," Naia said. "We've been through Stone-in-the-Wood as well, a village of several hundred."

"Stone-in-the-Wood!" Amri cried. "Oh, I envy you. I've heard the peach-berry is the sweetest in this world. Why can't we go there instead of Ha'rar?"

The musicians stopped again when voices echoed in alarm.

Down below, near the base of the cavern, a small group of Grottan Gelfling clustered around a silver-and-white-clad figure. The only thing Kylan could see from so far away was that the Vapra's sword was out, shining as she brandished it at the Grottan.

"Tavra! What's she doing now?"

Naia flicked her wings, but hesitated at leaping. She hadn't actually begun gliding yet, and there were plenty of jagged, sharp spires and rocks waiting below. The three of them ran down the stairs as quickly as they could.

"Why get into a fight at a time like this?" Kylan panted.

"Who knows what's going through her head these days!"

When they reached the landing where Tavra and the others were, Kylan could see that it was not a fight—or at least, it hadn't started that way. In fact, it looked as though the Grottan were trying to help, though their words of concern were cut short by Tavra's blade.

"Get back!" the Silverling shouted. "Back away from me, all of you!"

"Tavra!" Naia shouted as they shoved their way to the front. Tavra was bleeding from the neck, using the hand that was not wielding her blade to press a cloth against the wound. The Grottan backed away, holding their hands up in peace, some fleeing the situation altogether.

"Tavra, what's going on?"

Tavra let Naia and Kylan near so they could check the wound. Amri remained with the other Grottan, easing them back and away from the angry Vapra's sword.

"One of these damned Shadowlings attacked me in the tunnel!" Tavra hissed through clenched teeth. "Ambushed me in the dark with a knife and ran off before I could pay back the favor. Come and get it, cave crawlers! Try once more to cut a daughter of the All-Maudra!"

The whispering hush swelled. *One of the All-Maudra's daughters? It makes no difference. She is Vapra. Even worse!*

"No one touched the sun-spot!" shouted one voice above the whispers, and Tavra's grip quivered, as if so thirsty to draw Grottan blood, she could barely control herself. Still, she let Kylan pull the cloth back to see the wound—a sharp blade had cut her white neck, narrowly missing her crystal earring. Blood barely flowed from the wound, and Tavra's skin felt cold to the touch, but Kylan couldn't worry about that now.

"Naia," he said. "Can you heal her?"

"I think so, but she'll need to calm down. Stop waving that sword around, for starters!"

Kylan reached out and put his hand on Tavra's, easing it down. To his surprise, she responded, lowering the blade until the tip nearly touched the rocky platform where they stood. She didn't let go of the hilt, but became still enough that Naia and Kylan were able to get her to sit.

"Can you leave us?" Kylan asked Amri and the other Grottan. "Please? We'll find you soon and figure out what's going on."

When they were alone, Kylan repeated his words.

"What's going on?"

"What's going on is that they'll murder me before we leave

these caves," Tavra growled. "These crypts will become my tomb."

"Oh, stop it," Naia said. "What were you doing in the tunnels, anyway?"

"Nothing. Did you get the *firca*?"

"Not exactly. The Grottan do have it, but it's not here. They're going to let us have it, to use it for our message. Amri is taking us to where it is. Then he's coming with us, to Ha'rar."

"Oh? My life is in danger and you're still thinking of trusting them and staying in these caves?"

Naia held her hands out near the cut. Blue *vliyaya* light grew, as it had when she had healed Gurjin. The cut was but a flesh wound compared to the battery and starvation Gurjin had endured, and in a moment it was closed and no longer in danger of draining the Vapra of her blood on top of her already-drained life essence. Kylan remembered the chill he'd felt on Tavra's skin . . . Perhaps she was doing far worse than she had been letting on. While Naia finished the healing, he gathered his courage.

"Tavra . . . are you all right?" he asked, the question coming out much meeker than he would have liked. There was no way she would respect him with a voice like that! He tried again, and it sounded better, stronger: "If you're suffering because of what happened at the castle, you can tell us . . . We want to help you."

He expected an immediate denial, but got an uneasy silence instead. Naia arched a brow as if to say *what are you doing?* but she didn't interfere.

"You've just seemed . . . different, is all," he continued. "You don't have to be strong for us. We know what you've been through.

And we're not trying to delay your return to Ha'rar—it's just that we promised to take care of our part of this."

Kylan held his breath. Any moment, he thought, Tavra's protest would begin. Before it kept him from saying the rest of what he wanted to say, he said it.

"I understand why you want to be home, and we want you to be home, too. So you can rest."

"*Tch.* You do not understand me at all."

Tavra's reply was as far from what Kylan had hoped for as it could be. The words were so cold, he hardly knew how to react. Naia was quiet, too, but from the clenched jaw and angled-back ears, he could tell she was more angry than hurt by Tavra's blunt disappointment.

"Let's just get the *firca* and be on our way," Naia said. "Kylan, go find Amri and ask if he can take us to the Tomb right now. Ask Maudra Argot if you have to. I'll wait here with Tavra."

CHAPTER 17

Kylan spotted Amri right away, waiting near the tunnel that led to the *maudra*'s chamber with a few others.

"Is she all right? We've been looking for the one who attacked her. Maudra Argot is speaking to everyone one at a time until we find who is responsible."

Kylan shook his head.

"Tavra will be fine. Naia healed her. And I don't think she'll bring the All-Maudra's wrath upon the Grottan if you help us find the *firca*. Did you say it's in a tomb?"

"Yes. The Tomb of Relics . . . It's in a cave to the north. I'll let Maudra Argot know, and we'll leave right away."

Kylan waited while Amri scampered off. The other Grottan who stood by were silent, watching him with their stoic, unreadable eyes. Their smooth and unbroken skin made it difficult for Kylan to tell whether they were elders or younglings, and since they said nothing, he had no idea what they were thinking.

"Hi," he said. The greeting was not returned, and the Grottan turned away, murmuring to themselves. If they had garnered any trust within the Grottan clan, it was dashed after Tavra's disruption. Maudra Argot had been welcoming, but only to a point. The fact was, they were outsiders in the Caves of Grot, and the Grottan loyalty would always be to their own clan, as Maudra Fara's had been to the Stonewood.

Amri returned quickly and waved Kylan back down the stairway. When they reached Naia and Tavra, the Grottan boy bowed low, showing he knew more court formalities than he had let on in the beginning. Tavra sniffed at the gesture, and only replied, "This Tomb of Relics, it is some distance from the cavern?"

"Yes," Amri agreed. "About half a day's journey, through the mountain tunnels."

"Then lead the way. I want nothing more than to be gone from this place."

Kylan realized then that this would be the last time Amri might see his home for a long time. The boy had nothing except his cloak—no shoes or weapon, no traveling pack or rations. Yet in respect of what had happened, and his *maudra*'s command, he did not balk at the idea of leaving straight away.

"Just one moment. I am going to say goodbye."

He placed his hand against the cave wall and tapped with a finger. There was no sound to the open air, but after they waited a moment, Amri pressed his ear against the rock and listened. Kylan did, too, and heard a faint rhythmic tapping, carrying strongly through the dense rock. He had heard it before but not known what it was. So that was how the Grottan could communicate through the tunnels so silently.

Without another word, Amri pointed, and the other three followed him deeper into the maze below the mountains.

Every tunnel was the same to Kylan, and the farther they got from the central Domrak cavern, the darker it got. Amri could see perfectly in the dark, thanks to his Grottan eyes. Kylan, however, walked with one hand on Naia's back, the other tracing the cold wet wall. He considered asking if they could light a torch, but figured if it had been an option, Amri would have offered it.

"Light attracts crawlies," he mentioned later, as if Kylan had been wishing for a torch so badly, his thoughts had become audible. "Lots of crawlies."

Kylan wondered what else inhabited the endless caves, but didn't ask. He didn't want Amri to answer. He had had enough of bugs and crawlies and spiders to last a lifetime. All he wanted was to find the Tomb of Relics, get the *firca*, and find the nearest tunnel back to the world above. More than once, he lost track of Tavra's footsteps behind him, but they always returned. If she would have found it easier to hold the back of his cloak as he held on to Naia's, she didn't take the opportunity.

The journey was more than uncomfortable. Kylan kept pushing down impulses of fear and panic of the dark and the closed-in areas. The others were not happy, but they didn't seem to feel trapped as he did. To make matters worse, Tavra's words rang in his mind, summoning a recurring sourness of guilt every time he recalled them. He had tried to reach out to her, but it had been at the worst time possible. The words had been jumbled and wrong, an embarrassment coming from a song teller. So, in the dark, Kylan composed a letter in his mind. One that he would write the next chance he got, something he could put care into and give to the soldier when the time was right.

After what seemed like ages, Amri stopped. He rustled about in the dark, searching for something only he could see, then said, "Yup. Stand back a bit."

Kylan heard the click of a latch, then the creak of a wood door. A rush of musty air washed over them, smelling of paper and dust and mold. Kylan could hear the echoes of wind ahead and eagerly followed when Amri invited them. The tunnel opened into a new chamber, and after shutting the door, Amri bustled about. A moment later, a soft glow lit the room, emanating from a crystal lantern he had found.

"Well, here it is," Amri said. "The Tomb of Relics."

The room was circular, with three halls and the door through which they'd entered. The walls were lined with shelves, each stacked full of scrolls and books, boxes and crates, urns and pots, jars and flasks. From where they stood, he could see that the halls that radiated from the room were made of shelves, full of more items. In the center of the room was a heavy wood table. For examining the artifacts—the relics—Kylan imagined.

"There are twelve chambers in all . . . I think," Amri said.

"You think?" Naia asked with a raised brow. The Grottan shrugged.

"I've never actually been here myself. Maudra Argot used to visit, many trine ago . . . but she's not able to make the journey frequently anymore, with her age. I asked before she left. She said the *firca* is in a wood box etched with the picture of a bell-bird."

"All right!" Naia exclaimed. Her voice seemed big in the crowded room, but Kylan welcomed the enthusiasm. "So all we have to do is find the box!"

"As if it's easy," Tavra grumbled. "Let's split up."

Without waiting for a consensus, the Silverling plucked a crystal lantern from the wall and stalked off down the passage to the right. The remaining three exchanged glances.

"It's not a bad plan," Amri admitted with a shrug.

Kylan's imagination was coming out of hiding after the confrontation with Tavra and the suffocating journey here. He had always wanted to visit Stone-in-the-Wood to read all the tablets and songs kept there, but he had never even heard of the Tomb of Relics. Now that he was here, the wealth of knowledge and lore in the place was almost overwhelming.

"Amri, what exactly is this place?" he asked. "Why does it exist? And why here, in the caves?"

"It is a place where mysterious and powerful objects are kept, so they aren't lost to time and the elements. Even Mother Aughra has come here with items for us to keep safe. My people were charged with protecting it. This place, and the Sanctuary, to the north."

"Who charged you with the responsibility? Mother Aughra?"

"No, not Aughra . . . Thra. That's how the song goes, anyway. It's been our duty since the beginning of time. It's never been any different."

Now that Amri was in a sharing mood, and Tavra had excused herself, Kylan took his chance to ask a question that had been bothering him.

"Amri, can you tell me why the Vapra and Grottan clans dislike each other so much? I thought it was just rivalry, at first—

like the Spriton and the Stonewood. But I've never seen Gelfling behave this way to one another."

Amri rubbed the back of his neck. "Heh . . . You don't know?"

"We don't know *anything* about the Grottan," Naia said. "I grew up in Sog, but even I had heard that the Grottan might as well be a myth. Whatever you and Tavra know is a secret to us swamp and plains folk."

"Tavra wouldn't have told you, I guess," Amri said. His disdain for Tavra was deflated after the attack, but he still kept a rigid back and narrowed eyes when he spoke. "The Vapra like to keep their secrets . . . You know of the Six Sisters?"

"The sisters who founded the seven clans," Naia said. "Maudra Mesabi-Nara. Maudra Ynid, of Stone-in-the-Wood. You mean them?"

"There are many songs that tell differing stories about how the clans came to be, but most agree about the Six Sisters," Kylan agreed.

"Yes. And did you ever stop to wonder how six sisters became seven clans?"

Kylan had thought on it before, but not in depth. It was easy to imagine that one of the founding sisters had formed two clans, but which two clans, and how, and why, had never seemed important. Now that they had met the Grottan clan, though, and seen both their physical similarities as well as their apparent mistrust for one another . . .

"The Grottan and the Vapra," Kylan realized out loud. "They're sister clans?"

Amri nodded. He wiped his nose on the back of his hand and shrugged.

"There are many songs that offer explanations. Every clan has their favorite version, and Maudra Argot is no different. She says that, in the beginning, Thra had seven duties to entrust to the Gelfling race. To the Dousan, the heavens: the study of the suns, moons, and stars. To the Sifan, the skies: the telling of signs and omens. To the Stonewood, the fire of the hearth: the keeping of songs and essence of our culture. To the Spriton, the foundation of the earth: the cultivation of the land and its creatures. To the Drenchen, the water of life: the care of medicine and healing. And to the Silver Sea clan, Thra entrusted the light and the shadow: the keeping of the Gelfling history, law, and records. This task was too great to be shouldered by one clan alone, and so the clan split in two. One took on the keeping of the past: our history and dark things that should be left in shadow. The other became the keeper of our future: our laws and philosophies that lead us toward the light."

"I see where this is going," Naia remarked.

"Both are important tasks. We all know there can be no light without darkness. Still, no one wants to be bonded to shadow forever! The sisters discussed it for a long time. In the end, it came to be this way: the Vapra and the Grottan. Some say we were banished. Maudra Argot says we chose to come to these dank caves, while the Vapra flit along the crystal coasts. It's hard not to feel as if we are imprisoned sometimes. But . . . I know, truly, it's not the Vapra who charged us with this. It's Thra itself."

The idea that Thra had given the Gelfling clans such duties was a new song to Kylan. Maudra Mera had passed dream-etching on to him, and some other skills, and made sure that their neighboring Podlings were cared for, and all the other creatures nearby. She had never told him that it was because the Spriton had been charged with such a thing. Kylan wondered whether she even knew it herself. Maybe it was a secret song only the Grottan knew. If it was true, then that was their charge, entrusted to them by the Heart of Thra itself.

Amri let out a big sigh and wiggled all over, as if trying to shake out a bad flavor in his mouth.

"We may not be fond of the Silverlings who look like us but are nothing like us, but it doesn't excuse what happened. I'll make it up to you all. I promise. Starting with following Tavra's example... Let's split up and find that *firca*."

CHAPTER 18

Amri procured them each a lantern to light the way. Kylan chose the hall across from the doorway, while Naia took the passage to the left, and Amri remained in the center. If all the halls were the same, then Kylan imagined Naia and Tavra were seeing the same as him: a passage lined with dusty, lichen-covered, boxed, locked, rolled, stacked, and latched items. There were so many things crammed among the shelves that it was hard to tell, especially in the lacking light, where one item ended and the next began.

The hall linked the entry chamber to another room that looked identical to the first, with three halls ahead and to the left and right. Curious, Kylan walked directly through the first room and straight ahead, where he passed another hall and entered another chamber. Down the passage to his right he saw lantern light and a figure standing near one of the shelves.

"Tavra?" he called.

"What?" replied the Silverling's voice. "Stop messing around. We've wasted enough time."

The first room gave him no success, though not for lack of trying. There were so many things crowded in every cubby that he was sure he hadn't possibly looked through everything. Yet if he followed his impulse and inspected every crate and scroll he found, it would take forever. Each artifact was unique, and wonderful, and Kylan knew he could spend his entire life in the Tomb if he lost track of his goal.

Kylan's brow was sore from squinting by the time he reached the last chamber of his row. The room was like every other, except for the avalanche of books and boxes piled against the back wall. A shelf had collapsed and littered the floor with chests, their spilled artifacts jumbled among the pieces of broken clay vessels and other debris.

"Hm... earthquake, maybe? Looks like it's time to add some new chambers to the Tomb..."

He set the lantern and his pack down on the table and turned to begin the last leg of the search when the pile at the wall moved. He yelped and jumped back, watching as a bow-backed creature rose out of the debris and let out a resounding groan. It had leathery skin, a long neck, and an oblong face. When Kylan saw its four arms pushing the rubble aside and plucking splinters from its mane, he gasped. It looked like urVa the Archer—the Mystic. Could it be?

"Mystic?" he asked, hopefully. "Are you... a Mystic?"

"Ooooof!" said the creature. It turned to him, and the light of the lantern shone on the swirling markings on its face. It had dark, intelligent eyes, and it coughed in the cloud of dust. "Gelfling? You're not Grottan... Ah! There's one."

Amri and Naia arrived, one from the back hall and one from the left.

"I heard a crash," Naia began. Then, "Who's this!"

"Oh!" cried Amri. "You're here! I forgot to mention. This is urLii. He sometimes comes down from the Sanctuary to bring items to the Tomb."

"A Mystic?" Naia gasped.

"Oh, yes," urLii said. "That is the name Aughra gave us at the division . . . Wait! You aren't Grottan, either!"

urLii the Mystic finally cleared enough of the pile to step free of it. In full view, Kylan could see he was indeed the same race as urVa, the wise archer they'd met in the Dark Wood. He had a long body, from his long face to his long, heavy tail, his skin marked where it was visible with etching-like whorls and spirals. He was clothed in a simple mantle, wrists decorated with metal cuffs and cord ties. He cleared his throat and patted his body, as if to make sure it was intact, and then drew a pair of eye-prisms from the clutter. Once they were snug on his nose, he looked at the three Gelfling more closely.

"Amri, isn't it? Your first time in the Tomb, I think. I was . . . I was . . . looking . . . for something. Can't remember what. Then the shelf . . . well, that song sings itself."

Indeed, the large shelf above their heads was broken, bent in two after years moldering away in the cave. What had happened after did not need explaining.

"Yes, urLii. This is Kylan and Naia . . . Their friend Tavra is here somewhere, too. Oh, I'm glad you're here, maybe you can help us. We're looking for something in particular . . ."

While Amri described the *firca* to urLii, as casually as with

a sibling, Kylan tried to quiet a sudden pulse of jealousy. It was a bad feeling, and he didn't like it one bit. Not only did the Grottan have access to such a trove of ancient treasure, but they knew one of the Mystics like a family friend? He sighed and tried to wave the feeling away. There was no need to be in competition with Amri, who was only doing everything he could to help them.

"Oh yes. The forked flute in the box. I believe . . . I have seen it here. Yes. It was this way, I think . . . Yes. No! This way."

urLii looked left, then right, and then left again. Then he lurched to the right, talking to himself in reassuring tones. They followed quietly.

"Why didn't you say you knew one of the Mystics?" Naia asked.

Amri tilted his head.

"Mystic? Um . . . I guess he is pretty mystical, now that you say it! urLii has taught the Grottan clan for ages. He's a master song teller, and he taught us all to dream-etch. We call him the Storyteller. Our younglings travel to the Sanctuary when they come of age to learn . . . Is that strange? Are there others like him?"

Kylan's heart ached. A friendship with one of the Mystics, those that were as wise as the Skeksis were shrewd! Yet in all his ancient knowledge, Amri didn't even know how lucky he was.

"I wish the Drenchen had a Mystic to teach us," Naia said. She sounded more amazed than envious. "I can't imagine what it would have been like if urVa had been a friend to our clan. Kylan! Perhaps you can learn from urLii. I'll bet he knows so many songs that you've never heard!"

"Probably," Kylan said, careful not to mumble. "If he can find the *firca*, that would be enough for me."

urLii was not as decisive as urVa, and got lost more than once in the chambers. As they wandered from one to the next, Kylan kept waiting for Tavra to show up, asking what they were doing and why they were wasting time.

"Yes," urLii said, planting both feet in front of a shelf that Kylan swore they'd already looked at twice. "It was here. Forked flute, crafted by Gyr from bones of the singing mountain-gong bird. Hmm . . ."

The Storyteller searched the shelves with all four long-fingered hands at once, picking up small chests and shifting things aside, looking and grumbling *hmm, hmm* the whole while. Amri tapped a finger on his chin.

"Are you sure it was here, urLii?" he asked. "Perhaps you've confused this shelf with another? They do all look the same."

"No. It was here. I know it was. Right here, beside the Sifan Charms of Zale. Gyr the Song Teller was a Sifa, you know. I keep things very organized."

Amri gave Kylan and Naia a look that said he doubted that, but urLii was convinced.

"Here was the sextant, some Nebrie hide, the charms, and then the forked flute. What do you call it? *Firca*. Right here."

"Maybe you moved it," Amri suggested gently. "Maybe it fell when you knocked over everything else in the other room. Let's just look around. I'm sure it's here somewhere."

They divided their efforts once more, but this time kept to the same room. Kylan stayed near urLii, waiting for the courage to speak to the Mystic. They worked side by side while Amri joined Naia on the other end of the room. Kylan had questions, and he wanted to hear everything the Mystic had to share, but no matter how long he waited, the courage never came. He could not ask about Gyr, or the *firca*, or even whether the Mystic race knew their Skeksis counterparts had broken the Heart of Thra. Instead they looked in silence, Kylan's lungs filling with dust as he uncovered dozens and dozens of shelves, finding nothing.

"It's not here," Naia said after a while. As usual, she said out loud what they were all thinking. They had been more thorough here than they had been in any other room. Despite his earlier disorientation, urLii did not hesitate before shaking his head.

"Oh, *where*, then?"

Tavra came in, finally making her appearance. She took one look at the Mystic standing over Kylan, simply nodding as if she had expected him to be there. In her hands, she held a small red wood box.

"It was in the room two chambers down."

"Yes—oh yes," exclaimed urLii. "That's it, in the cedar box!"

Instead of presenting it to Amri, who could have been said to be the owner of the box on behalf of his clan that protected the Tomb, or to Naia, who had been their unofficial leader through everything, Tavra brought the box to Kylan. He accepted it in both hands.

"Here's your *firca*, Song Teller," she said.

Amri and Naia joined him, Naia grabbing his arm in excitement.

"Go on," she said, "open it. Let's see the *firca* you'll use to help save our people."

Kylan looked at the box. Etched in great detail on the lid was a drawing of a bird, standing next to a grove of trees to demonstrate its fantastical size. Its head was all beak with an eye on either side, wings half-spread over a clutch of boulder-size eggs. The only thing peculiar about the etching was a character burned into the corner of the drawing, the symbol for *S*. The etching still felt warm, but then again, everything in the stuffy chambers did.

The box was not locked, giving Kylan no excuse not to open it. He placed a shaking hand on the lid, imagining what would be inside. A tiny instrument so similar to the ones he had learned to play in Sami Thicket, but so different and so powerful. Perhaps the single item that could most quickly turn the tides on the Skeksis.

Kylan opened the box. At first, his heart leaped with happiness. Just as quickly, the relief and excitement plunged into disappointment and fear. He must have made a face, because Naia squeezed his arm in worry.

"What's wrong?"

Kylan turned the box so all could see, unable to bring himself to describe it in words. Resting in the padded box was a collection of white fragments—bone, no doubt, and some still large enough to show intricate carvings. There were just enough pieces to know what it had been, and what it could never be again. All that mattered now was what it was: Gyr's bell-bird *firca*, smashed into a thousand pieces.

CHAPTER 19

They had all breathed in and out many times before urLii finally spoke.

"Well . . . it wasn't like that when I saw it last."

Kylan felt his legs give out. He sat on the dusty floor and stared at the broken *firca*. Even if they had a way to mend it, the cracks would never be completely sealed. For a wind instrument, even a small splinter meant death. In the state that the flute was in, there was no telling how many little pieces were missing. He couldn't bring himself to close the box, though staring at the remains wasn't doing them any good.

"We . . . we'll have to find another way," Naia began. Then, to Tavra, "It was like that when you found it?"

"There was a picture of a bell-bird engraved on the lid, just as the *maudra* said. I didn't bother looking inside before I brought it."

Kylan did shut the box then. urLii tapped the drawing of the bird. His hand reminded Kylan of urVa's, though where the Archer's had been callused from nocking arrows, urLii's were callused on the fingertips. From holding instruments for writing, etching and ink, Kylan thought, for they were the same hard spots he'd developed on his own hands.

"The singing mountain-gong," the Mystic said. "In the golden years and long before. Every morning when the first sun rose, its song woke the world from the highest heights. Little Aughra and all the little Gelfling, creatures big and small. It was the good-morning from Thra, from the Heart, to all."

"What happened to the birds?" Kylan asked. He wanted a story to ease him out of the harshness of the predicament. If he could imagine something—anything—maybe he could get past this.

"Died out . . . Died out after the Conjunction. Early on. They sipped from the well of the world, you know. Like flowers grow from the suns. They grew from the song of the Heart of Thra. When the song changed, even in the very beginning . . . Oh, such large and magnificent creatures cannot subsist on anything less than what gave them birth in the beginning. Old things cannot change quickly. These birds were very old, and the Conjunction very abrupt."

"I feel like things are happening even more quickly *now*," Kylan said. He set the box down before he succumbed to the urge to fling it across the room in frustration. "I feel like every time we try to accomplish something, we're too late. The Skeksis are always one step ahead of us. Stealing my friends from Sami Thicket, and every other village. How can we hope to fight against them when they already know everything we plan to do? Are they using the Crystal to see beyond the castle? Maybe that's why they haven't bothered to come after us. There's no need! They can tell that we're no threat to them at all."

Naia knelt beside him.

"Kylan, it will be fine. You couldn't have known. You tried . . . We all did."

She sounded disappointed but composed enough to set the feeling aside to encourage him. It didn't matter. Encouragement was just another kind of story, and stories weren't going to help them right now. What had happened to the *firca* had already happened, and no amount of positive thinking would fix it.

"I shouldn't have gotten my hopes up," Kylan said. "This was a foolish plan to begin with."

He sighed and stood, putting the box back on the shelf. He was determined to leave this failure in the Tomb, where maybe it could wither away and die peacefully. No need to bring it with them.

"We'd better get going to Ha'rar, as Tavra wishes. We promised."

Naia started to say something, but swallowed the words instead. No matter how it had come to this, they had indeed made a deal with the Silverling. Perhaps the All-Maudra's daughter had been right all along.

"As you said, at least now we know," Tavra said. Her voice was neutral, neither surprised nor disappointed. She didn't even seem happy to be right. She just seemed tired, void of any emotion at all, except perhaps relief that they could finally move on.

"urLii, is there anything else from the Tomb we should bring with us to Ha'rar?" Amri asked. He had been quiet until now, respectful of the quickly passing storm of emotions. In fact, Kylan realized that everyone else seemed much more calm than he felt.

Maybe he was the only one who had been so excited about the *firca*. Well, of course he was. The *firca* had been his chance to play a part, to do something that only he could do. Now that chance was gone, and they would go running back to the wings of the All-Maudra.

"No, it's mostly junk," urLii answered.

Amri rubbed his forehead.

"Right. I've heard there's a passageway to the daylight from somewhere in the Tomb. Do you know where it is?"

"No. There was a rock slide higher up, and it became difficult to access from the outside. Gelfling may be able to squeeze through the rocks, though . . . But I don't remember where it comes in. Maybe the main chamber? Or was it the west . . ."

It wasn't a direction, but it was a start. Naia took a breath and let it out, putting her hands on her hips. Amri and Tavra were already taking their cues, picking halls that would lead them in opposite directions. urLii had gotten distracted by a scroll. When it was just Naia, Kylan, and the Mystic, Naia held Kylan's shoulder and squeezed.

"Kylan, stay here if you need to. I know . . . this has been hard for you. Don't worry. We'll find another way, and it's going to be fine."

Then she took the third hall, and Kylan was left with a mumbling, possibly senile Mystic.

"Is that the fate of song tellers, then?" he asked aloud. "To go mad?"

"Hmm . . . I don't know that story, so I couldn't tell you the end of it. A Spriton, are you? A dream-stitcher?"

urLii turned so quickly, a cloud of dust blew up from the shelf nearby. He reached with his first arm, snatching a roll of cloth from one of the high shelves. In a single motion, he held the top scroll-rod and let the bottom drop. It was a Spriton tapestry, woven in the special way that Maudra Mera was known for. Kylan touched it, feeling the beginning of a dreamfast as he did. The dream was stitched into the threads, the simple vision of a field under an open blue sky. The wind smelled sweet with grass, and then it ended.

"That's nice, but it doesn't help. The *firca* is broken. I can't dream-stitch it together. Seems I really can't do much of anything."

"That is your decision to make. One can choose either to be the weaver or the woven. The singer or the song. You know?"

urLii's words reminded Kylan of urVa in their meandering abstractness. Hadn't he wanted the Mystic's wisdom only a short time ago? Now, stuck in another dead end with his hopes dashed to pieces, the words only frustrated him with their immaterial philosophy.

"No, I don't know," he said. "Maudra Mera only started to teach me dream-stitching because it was the only thing I could do. Then I ran away."

His short-tempered reply did not offend the Mystic, or if it did, he didn't show it. urLii stroked his mane in thought.

"Hmm. The only thing you could do . . . or a thing only you could do?"

The question surprised Kylan out of his mood. It was a simple turn of words, but it put things in a different light. Was that the real reason Maudra Mera had tried to teach him the ancient Spriton *vliyaya*?

Amri's voice interrupted the thought. He had found something. Kylan floundered, unsure how to express himself to the Mystic and wanting desperately to be gone from the Tomb. urLii understood and waved him away with a hand.

"Go on, then, little song teller. Go on."

"Thanks," Kylan said, and hurried to meet his friends.

The exit Amri found was buried behind carved stones, pottery, and large rough gems. Behind the intentional-looking barricade was a door. urLii did not join them, and so on their own, the four Gelfling cleared the wall. Though Tavra and Naia took on the largest obstructions, Kylan lifted his fair share of the rocks, even while bearing the weight of the pack on his shoulders.

Tavra was the last one working after the other three had taken breaks. She hauled and shoved and moved the blockages tirelessly, neither sweating nor complaining. When the doorway was finally clear, she wasted no time turning the handle and carefully opening it, bracing with her body in case the remains of the rock slide urLii had described waited on the other side.

There was nothing on the other side of the door but a tunnel and a cold draft that smelled of the surface. Kylan had almost forgotten what open air smelled like, and despite the damp scent of dirt that accompanied it, the whiff of fresh air brought images of grass and sunlight and clouds to mind.

"Let's go."

"Wait," Naia said from where she sat on one of the stones.

"Can we rest a bit? Just a moment, then I promise we'll go. That tunnel's going to be a hike, and it might be dangerous. Let's at least catch our breaths before we switch to hauling boulders in a tunnel that could collapse on us at any time."

Tavra looked over her younger companions. Kylan was willing to go if the others insisted, but from the look on Amri's face, he didn't think they would. The soldier sucked in a big impatient breath, but leaned against the wall with her arms crossed. Amri chuckled.

"You're tireless as a Landstrider," he said. "Or, as tireless as I hear Landstriders are. As you can imagine, they don't frequent the caves. Although that would be a funny sight."

"Perhaps we'll be lucky enough to see them above," Naia said. "They're amazing creatures. If we could call a few, we could probably reach Ha'rar faster than by river . . . We rode one from the Castle of the Crystal all the way to Stone-in-the-Wood in a single night. It would have taken days by foot."

"Landstriders are the patron creature of the Spriton, are they not?" Amri asked. "Kylan, could you call them for us?"

Kylan shook his head. "They avoid the highlands. Their legs aren't nimble enough for the rockies. If we ever return to the Dark Wood, or the plains, I will call them for you to meet."

"Yes! And the Drenchen—I want to meet a muski, too. I should probably start a list."

Naia sighed, her hand moving toward her shoulder where Neech was missing. She looked sad for a moment, then reassured. Neech was with Gurjin, helping him return to Sog. That was the best place he could be, in the circumstances.

"You will," she said. "Someday."

Amri stretched and leaned back. "Yes! I can't wait. My people don't keep hollerbats as familiars . . . They poop a lot."

"What about you, Tavra?" Kylan asked. "Do the Vapra keep unamoths?"

Tavra took the question as a sign that they were well enough to move on. Like a statue coming to life, she stood away from the wall where she'd been leaning, uncrossing her arms to point into the tunnel with a stern finger. One by one, they rose to their feet and obeyed. Kylan paused, looking back into the Tomb and wondering whether they should say goodbye to urLii. Amri shook his head and waved.

"He'll be fine. He won't even notice we've left."

The tunnel was well supported in the beginning. Kylan thought he saw glimpses of sunlight coming from ahead, but he had no idea how deep in the mountain they were, or even what time of day—or night—it was. He guessed it was probably just his hopeful imagination. Amri led, followed by Naia and Kylan. Tavra kept to the rear, a few steps behind Kylan, as if to make sure no one snuck away from the party again.

In the close confines of the tunnel, Kylan heard Tavra muttering to herself.

"Unamoths are only good for one thing . . ."

It was quiet, under her breath, and he wasn't sure if she knew he could hear her when she finished the thought:

". . . *eating.*"

CHAPTER 20

The tunnel ended as urLii had said it would—in a wall of large rocks and earth. The cave-in had taken place some time ago, as evidenced by the bounty of plant life growing in the displaced dirt. Kylan was happy to find some of the flora was surface-dwelling—ferns and flowers that would never have survived without daylight. That meant they were close. Indeed, slivers of light peeked through the cracks in the rocks, and when he strained his ears, he thought he could hear birds.

Amri went first, most familiar with navigating through dangerous rocks. Even if the jumble of boulders had rested this way for a long time, the wrong pressure or even sound could jar them loose and crush them. They picked their way silently and delicately, weaving through the spaces between the rocks. There was no way urLii could have made it, and in some places Kylan thought even *he* might not be able to squeeze through. With some scrapes and a lot of patience, in time they finally stumbled out of the rubble.

It was early evening. Kylan dropped his traveling pack and fell to his knees on the grass-covered ledge. They were still in the highlands but below the tree line, and the green and gold sight of the wood-filled valley and open amber sky was the most gorgeous thing he had ever seen. Naia knelt beside him, running her hands over the thick grass and leaning in to take a big breath of it.

"It's about time," Tavra said, brushing dirt from her cloak.

Amri had not stepped out of the cave mouth when they had. He stood in its shadow, hand held over his eyes, which were squinted as narrow as they could be without being closed.

"It's so bright," he said. "I've only left the caves at night before. Snuck out, I mean."

Naia frowned. "The Brothers are setting. It'll be twice as bright tomorrow during the day."

"Maybe my eyes will adjust," Amri said. He pulled the hood of his cloak on, so far that it covered most of his face. Draped in the black cloth as if he might bring the shadows of Grot with him, he emerged from the caves. Even with the hood on, he held his hands out for balance. Naia took one and put it on her shoulder.

"For now, I'll help. Maybe we can travel at night."

"We will travel at all hours to make up the time we've lost," Tavra declared. "Starting now."

Naia helped Amri. The process began awkwardly, but by the time they learned one another's strides, their steps were less clumsy, and Kylan could see that Amri's cheeks were pink where they were visible beneath his hood. Once Tavra was sure the other three were following at an acceptable pace, she periodically scouted ahead and circled back, adjusting their route without explanation. Her confidence led to their confidence, and soon enough Kylan saw the familiar black sparkle of a river in the sunset-lit valley.

"The air is so dry," Amri remarked. "And there are so many

noises! I feel like I can hear the whole world from here."

"I thought it was dry, too, when I left the swamp. You'll get used to it!"

After the suns set, Amri was able to pull his hood back. He marveled at every tree and rock, and especially was enamored with the sky. Though he could see, he kept his hand on Naia's shoulder so he could walk with his head tilted back, staring upward in awe.

"This is why I used to come to the surface. The sky! Oh, look! The Sisters!"

Kylan tried to see things as Amri saw them—new, interesting, and fresh. Perhaps exiting the caves could be seen as an ending of their chapter of failure, and the beginning of the next song that might lead to their success . . . Then again, that was what he had thought about leaving Aughra's observatory.

He remembered what urLii had said, about the weaver and the woven, but he was tired of trying to find the best in everything and exhausted from hoping and hoping and being let down. Trying to take control of his own path was more of the same, so for now he followed Tavra's lead, like a drop of water following the path of a stream. He was just a minor character in her story now, and he would do as she directed.

Late into the night, they reached a widening of the path. Tavra had gone ahead again, so she wasn't there to protest when the remaining three unanimously stopped. The landing was peaceful, blocked by the cliff on one side. The night air was thickening with moisture.

"I'm getting blisters," Amri said. It wasn't a complaint, just a fact, and he sat on a rock and rubbed his bare feet. From the depths of his cloak came a little jar of salve, and he rubbed the ointment on his feet.

"What is that?" Naia asked, wrinkling her nose. "It smells like maggots and slime!"

"Yes! Though it is some other things, too. Do you want some? It's one of my concoctions."

"No! Absolutely not."

"Let me know if you change your mind."

Amri put away the jar, though the pungent odor still clouded around him. Kylan pulled his tunic collar up to mask the scent. Despite the terrible smell, he could see that the redness and swelling on Amri's feet was already subsiding. They still had a long way to go, and it felt like it would rain soon.

"I think we should rest," Kylan said. "We agreed to go with her with no further detours, but we didn't agree to do it in one night. I don't know how she's moving at this pace, but I can't keep it up forever."

"Same here," Amri agreed.

Even Naia flopped down on a bowed tree root, adjusting her locs so her back, wings, and neck could get air. Kylan set the pack down and, feeling lighter, stretched out his arms and back.

"I'll go ahead and find her and let her know. You two rest and make a fire."

After bearing the pack for so long, traveling without it felt almost like flying. Kylan hopped over stones and roots that studded and snaked through the diagonal wood, listening for the sounds of the Silverling who had gone ahead. He was so light and agile that even a curtain of finger-vines could not catch him as he skirted the path where they dangled.

He saw a sliver of moonlight flicker on something silver through the trees and followed it. He walked candidly at first, not wanting to surprise someone who wore a sword at her hip, but when he heard voices, he stopped. The conversation was much too far away to decipher, but he could clearly hear another voice intermingling with Tavra's. Who was she talking to out here in the dark?

Kylan realized he had dropped to a crouch, hiding behind a tree. There were plenty of speaking creatures in the world, and there was no reason to believe that Tavra's conversation meant danger . . . yet every bone in Kylan's body told him to be quiet and invisible. He listened to his instincts and crept forward as silently as he could, ears straining to pick up the words.

"Forgive me, Lord. I know. We are back on track. I won't let you down."

Tavra's apology was almost a plea. From where Kylan crouched, he could only see her back, with the light from the night sky shimmering off her wings. Whoever she was speaking to was either out of sight or invisible altogether. In the darkness, Kylan could see no one else, though he heard a faint voice reply.

"You have already let us down. We took a great risk in entrusting the Drenchen boy to you, and what did you do? Lost him! We regret our trust. We regret it dearly!"

Tavra winced at the scolding as if it were the crack of a whip.

"Forgive me, my lord..."

"Are you sure they haven't found you out?"

"They've said nothing. I can sense when they dreamfast—they have not..."

"That is the only good news you've given us. You'd best keep things such."

Tavra scrambled to appease the voice, though the words she used made Kylan wonder whether it was really Tavra at all. How many secret conversations had Tavra had while on her own, ahead of them? And more importantly, with whom, and to what end?

"This body won't last, my lord. It is beginning to fail. I need a new one if I'm to continue."

"Then you should not have allowed Gelfling to waste so much time! Bahhhh... take the Spriton or the Grottan. Or kill them, if it is easier. We do not care."

"The Spriton is so weak! I would rather have the Drenchen—"

"Lay one of those prickly little legs on the Drenchen and we'll crush you ourself!"

A twig cracked under Kylan's hand when he made a fist, and Tavra turned toward the noise, though from the way her ears twisted back and forth, he could tell she couldn't see him or pinpoint his location.

"I must go. They're coming."

She put something in the folds of her cloak and straightened out of the submissive half bow she had adopted in the presence of her invisible master. She looked stern and soldier-like once again... Though after what Kylan had heard, he could hardly say she looked like *herself*. His heart beat so loudly, he was surprised she couldn't hear it, and he froze. Should he wait until she returned to the others, circle back and arrive separately so she didn't know he'd seen her? Should he confront her here? No, that was dangerous! But if he ran back to warn the others, she would surely hear him—and warn them of what? He hardly knew what he'd seen and heard. He wished for all the world he could dreamfast with Naia from so far away, but he couldn't. There was no way to get word to his friends back at the camp before Tavra would arrive.

She had nearly reached his location. In moments, she would pass by close enough to touch. urLii said one could be the weaver or the woven. Were there really only two choices? Or was there a third?

He gathered his courage and steeled himself.

I'll be both.

Just as Tavra passed, Kylan hooked one foot under a root and took a big step with the other. The intentional trip sent him stumbling right into the Silverling as she passed, toppling them both to the ground.

"Tavra!" he exclaimed. "Sorry. I came to get you, but I lost the path..."

She stood and brushed off her cloak impatiently while he took his time climbing to his feet.

"Where are the others?"

"Amri had to stop. I came to get you to let you know we're making camp back up the trail. I hope that's all right..."

"No! It's not all right. We don't have time. Where are they?"

She stormed ahead, hand on the hilt of her sword, as if she meant to threaten them into picking up the trail if she had to. Kylan trotted after her, mind spinning. He kept hearing the words she'd said into the darkness. *This body won't last. I would rather have the Drenchen.* And to say *this body* instead of *my body*. This wasn't Tavra. Whoever it was, they worked for a powerful master that wanted Naia for itself. And Rian, on whom Tavra had been fixated since she'd saved them from the blue mouth. Only one creature in all of Thra fit the profile. The Skeksis, whom they'd tried to escape, had been with them all along.

DO NOT TRUST HER.

He remembered the words on the rock, covered by spiderwebs. He had thought they meant Aughra, but now he was not so sure. Then the strange marking for *S*, on the box. Someone had been trying to warn them—but who? The only person who could have left either message had been Tavra—the very one who was spying on them.

Kylan shook the questions from his mind. He had to focus on the matter at hand. If he didn't figure out what to do soon, either the impostor would discover he had begun to notice its deceit or it would return to Naia and Amri only to put them in danger.

As if we haven't been in danger all along! No wonder the Skeksis haven't shown themselves in person—they've known where we were every step of the way!

He forced himself to calm down. It was the only way he was going to be able to fix this. Tromping through the wood as loudly as possible, so that Naia and Amri would at least hear them coming, he followed Tavra and thought. He couldn't best her in a fight. Even Naia would have trouble doing that, and in close combat, the sword would be fast and deadly.

Kylan could see the light of the campfire through the trees, and willed his mind to think harder and faster. They needed a plan—a battle strategy to bare the truth of their situation. Only then could they figure out what to do. But Kylan was not a warrior, and knew nothing of battle. That much he had to accept.

But there was no time to feel sorry for himself. He had to decide what he *was*, not what he wasn't—and what he *knew*, not what he didn't. In the last moments before they returned to the campsite, he raced to recall everything that had happened up until then, searching for any seed that might be able to grow into a solution. The song he'd made up for Rian. The blue mouth. Aughra's observatory and the destroyed *firca*. urLii's words, and the Spriton tapestry.

Then he had it, and afforded himself a taste of hope.

This would be a confrontation of a different kind.

CHAPTER 21

Naia jumped to her feet as soon as they entered the clearing. "I don't care what you think, we have to rest."

Tavra drew her sword, though the tip was lowered. Kylan wondered whether he could simply snatch it out of her grasp from where he stood, so close behind. Then what? Who knew what she was capable of, especially after being threatened so harshly by her Skeksis master. Inciting her might just be the beginning of their problems. He dashed around to stand between the two.

"Tavra. Listen. Amri needs shoes, or soon we'll have to carry him, which will surely slow us down further than if we stop for just a little while."

"It's not my fault he decided to come. If he needs shoes so badly, he can have mine."

Tavra reached down and tore the sandals from her feet, tossing them at the Grottan boy, who flinched at the gesture.

"That's really not necessary," Amri began. "Naia cut some hide from her jerkin, so . . ."

Kylan waved his hands before the argument went off course. Once it did that, there would be no stopping it. If they didn't have some element of advantage, in a fair fight it was unlikely they could best her even if it was three against one. Tavra was a well-trained soldier, had the advantage of experienced flight, and on top of that, did not tire or seem to feel pain. They would have to take her by surprise if they were going to get to the bottom of this.

"Listen. Everyone. Tavra. There's something I haven't told you."

That got their attention. He had never been so relieved to have a sword pointed at him. When Tavra spoke, her voice was so dark, it barely sounded Gelfling at all.

"What?"

Kylan put his hand into his pocket, slowly enough that it didn't set Tavra off, and withdrew a folded piece of paper. He handed it to her and explained out loud for the benefit of the others.

"I got a note from Rian. It came by swoothu, early this evening. His boat was damaged by a rock in the river, and he was waylaid. He's close by and he said he'll wait for us if we're near. I already told him we would meet him tomorrow morning."

Kylan watched Tavra look sternly at the scrap of paper. She crumpled it in her palm and tossed it into the fire, and that was when he knew for sure that this was not the All-Maudra's daughter.

Naia furrowed her brow. She was not convinced, but she didn't pick apart the story right away. He wished he could reach out to her and dreamfast all that he had seen, but to do so now in front of the impostor would be folly. He met her eyes and willed that she trust him with all of his might.

"Oh," she said in a normal tone, as if she had just remembered. "So that's what you were doing out in the wood earlier. Why didn't you tell us right away?"

Kylan tried not to react in relief. Naia was covering for him—she trusted him.

"I wasn't sure if it was true. We haven't seen any Skeksis since we left the castle, and I think that's strange. I was worried this might be a trap."

"It's not a trap," Tavra said. "The note was genuine."

"So . . . we'll wait until morning, and then meet him?" Kylan asked. "Is that all right?"

Tavra stared into the fire, free hand cupping her chin in thought. He hoped she was thinking what he wanted her to think—that this opportunity was too sweet to miss. Her master wanted Rian, and this was a way she could regain favor.

He was rewarded when she sheathed her sword.

"Yes. Fit those sandals to the Shadowling. We leave first thing in the dawn."

Then she walked just to the edge of the camp and sat against a tree. She pulled her hair over one shoulder before crossing her arms and nodding her head, seeming to fall asleep immediately.

Naia and Amri visibly relaxed, shoulders and ears drooping. Amri picked up one of the sandals that had been thrown at him, comparing the size against his foot. It was a close match.

"The cords are snapped," he said.

"Don't worry," Kylan replied. "Those are the easiest part to mend. I'll fix you up in no time. But first . . ."

He took a stick and pried the wad of flame-resistant parchment out from the fire. He brought it with him when he circled the fire, handing it to Amri in trade for the sandal, which was more of a sole with a tangle of broken cord.

"What's going on?" Naia whispered. It was hard to know whether Tavra could hear them from her distance, and Kylan hoped she could. He put the sandals in his lap and worked on fixing them. Stitching shoes and mending laces were among the many mundane tasks with which Maudra Mera had charged him as a child. While he worked, he whispered back to Naia, loud enough that he was sure Tavra would hear him.

"I don't trust Tavra." He watched the Silverling when he spoke. She did not stir. "Something about her has been all wrong since we ran into her. You remember . . . with the blue mouth?"

Naia frowned. "Of course I remember the blue mouth."

Kylan chose his words as carefully as if he were telling a song. This was the most important part of all.

"Good," he said. "Because if you remember, then you'll understand why I want to meet with Rian in private. Tonight. I don't want Tavra to get her hands on him . . . I think she's working for the Skeksis. So, tonight, when it's quiet, I'm going to sneak out and meet him and tell him. I'm going to tell him to go on to Ha'rar without us, and tell the All-Maudra that her daughter is a traitor."

Still, no response from Tavra, though something twinkled at her neck. It was her earring, bared when she had pulled her hair to the other side. From the distance and in the night, the light played tricks, but Kylan thought he saw it move on its own.

"I don't like this," Naia said. "Why you, and why do you have to go alone?"

Kylan didn't want to go alone. It was dangerous . . . but it was also necessary. Explaining why would put them at risk, and dreamfasting would draw Tavra's attention. She had told her master that she could sense it—trying it now would only lead to failure. As Kylan had to ask Naia to trust him, in the same way he now had to trust her. To understand, and to do what needed to be done.

"Remember the blue mouth?" Kylan asked. "It was good we weren't alone *then*."

Amri had been quiet, since he likely had no idea what the blue mouth was or what it had done. In the meantime, he had uncrumpled the scrap of paper Kylan had handed him, smoothing it on his lap. Kylan focused on mending the last of the broken cord, waiting for Amri's reaction. It came shortly: a glance of confusion, then the flicker of understanding.

"This is . . ."

"Here are your shoes," Kylan interrupted loudly. "All fixed. You'll need to break them in a bit, but I think they'll serve you well . . . Now, why don't we all get some sleep. I'll take first watch."

Kylan watched the fire die in quiet, holding his hands in his lap to keep from fidgeting. Though the night was the same as any other, knowing what would soon come made it seem as if he existed inside a dome of his own thoughts. His mind felt like Aughra's observatory: constantly moving, full of things.

Stay focused, he told himself. *Tell the song. It will work . . . it has to.*

When he couldn't wait any longer, he left the camp as quietly as he could. He left the pack and anything that would weigh him down. He picked his way into the wood, ears turned back to listen behind him. It was the deepest part of the night, and reminded him of the Dark Wood when he had first entered it with Naia. He had been so afraid of it then, and jumped in terror at any noise. Now, here he was, volunteering to do so again. He hoped at least if anyone told songs about him, they would remember this as a time he showed bravery, and that he had changed for the better.

Even if it's my last stand, he thought grimly.

Soon enough, he heard them: footsteps, behind him. If he hadn't been listening carefully, he would have missed them amid the rest of the sounds of the wood. Someone was following him, keeping their distance—but not too much distance, and not with too much care. He didn't bother looking back. He knew that if he looked hard enough, he would see her silver cloak and perhaps the glinting of her blade. It proved to him that she had meant it when she had called him weak, and for the first time, he smiled about it to himself.

He led her down the path, giving her opportunities in the winding trail to close the distance between them. It was a prime place to ambush unsuspecting prey, with ledges and boulders to hide behind. So far from the campfire, Kylan imagined Tavra might make up any number of excuses for why their song teller would not be returning to camp. Ways to explain his sudden disappearance were as numerous as the predators and dangers that lurked in the wood.

It wasn't until he lost track of the Silverling-impostor's footsteps that he began to feel nervous. A twinge of fear pricked his fingers and toes as he remembered that he was in real danger. He continued on his way, hoping he could make it to the spot before she found him. If he could just make it there, he had a chance. When he saw the wall of rock that ran along the trail, he let out a breath of relief and slowed.

"So this is where he is?"

Kylan turned toward Tavra's voice just as she shoved him against the cliffside with her forearm, pinning him with her body. In her other hand she held a short knife, but more wicked was the grin on her ghostly face. She did not look like Tavra. She did not look like a Gelfling at all.

"Where's Rian?" she demanded. "Tell me before I kill you, filthy Gelfling!"

"N-not here! Not yet!"

The stammer in his voice was ready and real. Her knife pricked his neck. So close, he could definitely see movement at her neck. It looked as if shadows were crawling around the purple gem that dangled from her ear. As it slowly came to life, he saw that the black tines were not shadows, but eight spindly, jointed legs.

"Then when he arrives, he'll find you dead."

She pressed in with the knife. One swift movement and she'd open his throat. She knew it as well as he, and her smile broadened.

"Think again, mud-brain!"

Kylan ducked as a wave of finger-vines crashed over the top of the ledge, lunging for Tavra. They fell on Kylan's arms and legs without a care, but when they touched the Silverling, they ensnared her, growing out from every crack to bind her in their grasp. Kylan scrambled out on all fours, letting in and out all the breaths he'd been holding while waiting for this moment.

Two figures above on the ledge waved, and he sighed.

"You all right, Kylan?" Amri called. Naia had already started the descent, climbing down the finger-vines. They were gentle where she grasped them, helping her down. In their depths, Tavra swore and cursed, and swore again, thrashing against their unbreakable grip.

"How dare you!" she cried, but the vines near her face slithered across her mouth and silenced her. It seemed the plant did not like her, either.

"You make quite a good little blue mouth berry," Naia said.

Kylan chuckled.

"Sweet and small. We make the best bait."

Amri joined them with a torch, and the three gazed up at the furious Silverling together.

"Now, tell us who you are and what you've done with Tavra," said Naia.

CHAPTER 22

It was not possible for the impostor to respond while silenced by the finger-vines, so Naia touched them and asked them to relax their grip. They did, just enough that Tavra—or whoever it really was—could spit. Now that the secret was out, any effort in pretending to be the All-Maudra's daughter was expired, and she thrashed and hissed. She was strong enough that some of the vines snapped, but dozens of new tendrils reached out in replacement.

"I am a loyal servant of the Skeksis—more loyal than you Gelfling! You Gelfling, whose entire life being is thanks to the Skeksis and their work at the castle! You should be grateful for them!"

So ensnared by the vines, only her face was visible in the torchlight, and one of her hands. The gem-like shape dangling at her ear glinted in the torchlight, swinging wildly. Its eight slender legs shone like black metal, its abdomen a deep faceted violet. It was a spider with a body that looked like a jewel, hanging from a silver thread. Kylan cursed himself for not noticing it before. He had seen it many times but had thought nothing of it. Yet there it had been, the entire time.

"Is that you? You're a spider?" he called.

"My name is Krychk!" it shrieked through Tavra's mouth.

"Don't you forget it! *Tch!* It's the name of the one who will put you and all you Gelfling in your graves!"

Naia grabbed Kylan's and Amri's arms, dreamfasting urgently.

What if it drops off of Tavra? We'll lose it in the vines!

"You better hope I don't leave this Silverling's bag of bones!" cried the spider. "Yes! I can hear your stupid dreamfasting. Spiders are so much closer to the lifeblood of Thra than you Gelfling... We hear much more that goes on in the world. So much more than your puny little thoughts."

Kylan's heart sank. Bag of bones? And their dreamfasting was useless—were they in over their heads? Krychk the crystal spider smiled wickedly with Tavra's face.

"For example, I can hear your Silverling princess now. I can hear her voice coming from inside this dead body. *My* life force is the only thing keeping her alive! So pray, little Gelfling vermin! Pray I don't leave her to die in this hollow shell."

The threat was clear: destroy the spider and doom their friend. But if they did not...

"The crystal-singers," Amri whispered. "There are stories on the walls of Domrak about how Gyr had to run them out of the caves. They sing songs in the ears of living creatures and hypnotize them."

The spider swung on its thread enough to land on Tavra's neck, alighting like a dancer on its long legs. It waved the front two as if it was laughing.

"Had to run us out. Ha! *Wanted* to! Stupid Shadowlings. *We* lived there first. *We* sang the songs of Domrak. And now we have

Domrak again. In exchange for our loyalty . . . for you, Drenchen, and your despicable brother. Yes! My people have already taken Domrak. So before you do anything brash, you ugly, vapid unamoths, think upon *that*."

"Taken Domrak . . . ," Amri whispered. "What have you done?"

"*Tch!* Gullible Gelfling! Stupid Gelfling! Didn't think twice about trust when I showed up with the brother! Didn't think twice about trusting! *Tch!* Now my people have reclaimed Domrak, and the Skeksis will have *you!*"

Amri grabbed Naia's arm, black eyes wide in fear. "We have to stop it—if they've taken Domrak—my people! Naia, Kylan—what do we do?"

The recent thrill of success was fading quickly. Kylan had been so elated that they had caught the creature parading as the All-Maudra's daughter, and that his plan had worked. Naia and Amri had understood and followed him as he'd hoped. Everything had gone according to his song, but this was an ending he had not foreseen.

Kylan's heart hammered in his chest as he tried to think of what to tell Amri. But what *could* they do? Though the spider was immobile while it used Tavra's body, it was they who were still under its control. If they made the wrong move, whatever was left of Tavra would be gone.

"What do you think, Kylan?" Naia asked, voice low and grave. She had her hand at the hilt of her dagger, past any joy born in the challenge of trapping the spider.

"It was Tavra who was trying to warn us," Kylan realized out loud. "The message on the rocks—she put it there, but the spider must have called its kin to try to hide the message. Then later . . . the symbol for S . . . and in the cave. She was trying to kill you, wasn't she? By cutting at her own neck!"

Amri cursed under his breath.

"Kylan. Naia. This spider must die. Before it tells the Skeksis what's happened. If your friend Tavra risked her own life to try to kill the spider, then that is what we must believe she is willing to sacrifice!"

"You'd kill what remains of your Silverling?" Krychk crooned. "You Gelfling are more fickle and traitorous than I thought. You betray the Skeksis and even yourselves. You deserve what's coming to you."

Though the spider's voice was taunting, its legs splayed out, latching on to Tavra's neck. In the lull of quiet that followed, while Kylan raced to conceive a plan, he heard the familiar clicking, ticking, crawling of millions of tiny legs. At first there was no sign of the creatures that were coming, but then the finger-vines twitched and jerked. The twitching became writhing, and in the torchlight Kylan saw throngs of black spiders pouring out of the cliff, biting at the vines. Tendrils fell like cut grass, squirming as they dropped, and the finger-vine thrashed in agony as it was torn apart by the swarm of black gem-bodied spiders.

Kylan waved his torch, catching the brush on fire where he could. The spiders fled from the flames, the few that were trapped closer getting stomped by Naia and Amri in his new sandals. They were easily crushed when they were singled out, one at a time, but there were thousands here and thousands more throughout the rest of the mountains and the wood.

The heavy smoke from the wet brush fire parted. Krychk, attached to Tavra's neck like a welt, stepped over the ring of fire, sword drawn. All pretenses dropped, the spider's power over the Silverling's body was like an infection, dark and encompassing. Kylan shuddered as Krychk stepped forward, crafting that unnatural smile on Tavra's pale face.

"I am glad it came to this, Gelfling. I was tired of pretending to like you."

Naia pulled her dagger in time to block the spider's first attack, an unrestrained lunge that kicked up embers and dust. Kylan and Amri fell back, unarmed, while Naia fended off the endless slashes of the Silverling's sword. She spun away in time to avoid the sword's tip across her eye. Blood dripped from her cheek where she'd been nicked, two of her locs flying loose from her head. Kylan gave Amri the torch and fumbled at his hip, finally releasing the *bola* there, but they were so close, there was no way to throw it.

"I don't want to hurt her!" Naia cried. "But I can't hold her off forever!"

She grunted in effort as Krychk's attacks came again and again. Kylan held the *bola* with two of the three stones in either hand. If it were two against one, they could probably defeat the spider, but Kylan didn't want to hurt Tavra. Yet the truth was that the spider would not tire. Tavra's body had no life force to expend.

For it to end, someone would have to die.

"I'm sorry!" he said, and swung just the loose end of the *bola*. The rock whipped in an orbit around his hand and smashed into Tavra's head. He had been aiming for the spider, but the effect was the same. The Silverling stumbled and almost went down. Naia leaped at the opportunity, cutting at Tavra's sword hand so strongly, she released her grasp. The blade dropped, and Naia tackled her, knocking her to the smoldering earth.

"*Damned Gelfling!*" Krychk screamed. "I'll have you no matter what the Skeksis say! *Drenchen!*"

The spider released Tavra and was suddenly racing up Naia's arm. Tavra's body went limp, and Naia yelped as the spider dived into her hair. Kylan dropped the *bola* and ran to her.

"No! Naia!"

"Get it off me!" Naia choked, clawing her hair and tearing at her cloak. "Quick, quick, get it off me!"

Kylan skidded to his knees beside her while Amri continued to fend off the spiders held just at bay beyond the fire. He could see the spider's black and shining body for a moment, but then it was gone. He plunged his hand into Naia's hair and grabbed it. It bit him and thrashed with its sharp legs, sending trills of nerve pain through his body, but he held on as tightly as he could.

"Gelfling! Damned Gelfling!" it screamed in its own tiny voice. Kylan could barely hear it with his ears. It seemed to sing more in the tone of the mind, saying only one thing over and over: "Damned Gelfling vermin!"

"I told you they would succeed."

The voice came from Tavra. Her eyes were open, but barely, and milky like a lake frosted over. She did not move except to close her eyes, long silver lashes brushing her cheeks. Naia shook the Silverling's shoulders, but she did not open her eyes again.

"No. Tavra! Tavra, don't go!"

Amid the thoughts that they would lose Tavra again and the pain where the spider was clawing him with its razor-like legs, Kylan felt dizzy. Naia shook Tavra and called her name again, but it felt far away. Even the spider's screams were muffled.

Someone will have to die . . .

Kylan squeezed the spider's body, feeling the sharp edges in his palm grow hot. The heat of his dream-etching burned into it, and it screamed, a high-pitched whine that registered in his brain. He thrust the spider's body against Tavra's smooth forehead. The light of the dream-etching flashed blue and white, and the wails of the spider grew so intense that the rest of its swarming brethren backed away, then receded altogether.

"No!" Krychk screeched. "No, no no! I won't lose! Not to Gelfling! Not to the Shadowlings! Not to the dirt stealers! NO!"

"Kylan—"

The light of the dream-etching died, and Kylan took his hand away. Etched into the spider's crystal abdomen was a spiraling triangular symbol, one which even Kylan did not recognize, though he was the one who had put it there. The fire around them was going out, unable to live on the lush vegetation. The throngs of spiders, seeing their champion defeated, continued a slow retreat back into the darkness.

"No, no no, nooo . . ."

This time the voice came from Tavra, weak and soft, but it was not the Silverling's voice. It was the spider's. It breathed once, with strength only enough to let out a last breath. "Damned . . . Gelfling . . ."

Then Krychk was gone, with no life left. The spider lying on Tavra's forehead pulsed with light, its gem-like body changing from the darkened violet to a lighter blue, almost silver. The symbol etched into its abdomen glowed like starlight. Now that he had his head back on, Kylan realized he did know the symbol. It was one that Maudra Mera had taught him in his first lessons in dream-stitching, but it was different—more intricate, with several flourishes and diacritics he did not recognize. He wasn't sure where the symbol had come from, except somewhere deep in his mind.

"What did you do?" Naia whispered.

Kylan shook his head. "I . . . I don't know."

"Dream-stitching," Amri said. He stood over them, holding the torch, though there were no more spiders left to hold it against. He looked down with them at the black-and-silver spider on Tavra's face, pulsing gently like a heartbeat. "That was dream-stitching *vliyaya*. I've only heard of it."

"But what did you *do*?" Naia repeated.

The spider twitched a leg, coming to life. First one leg moved, then two, then all eight curled enough to raise its crystalline body. Naia clenched her hand into a fist, ready to smash it if the need arose, but Kylan held her back. Something was different.

"Wait," he whispered.

The spider did not attempt to run, or even bite Kylan where his hand was within striking distance. It rotated one direction, then another, then spoke in a tiny, wary voice that bore no malice or rage—just hesitation, and the slow-speak of someone who had been woken from a very long, troubled dream.

"Naia? Kylan? What..."

Naia put down her fist, and Kylan let out a shaky breath. It was difficult to hear above even the quiet night, but it was unmistakable: annunciated, with the northern accent of the Vapra of Ha'rar. The spider turned, examining its legs and then tapping three of them. It let out a spider-size sigh.

"Oh, eel-feathers," it swore mildly in Tavra's tired voice. "You've really done it this time."

CHAPTER 23

"No time to gawk. We have to go back. South, into the caves."

Tavra—for that's who it was in the crystal spider's body—leaped with considerable strength onto Kylan's arm. He jumped instinctively and pushed back the urge to shout and swat her away.

It's Tavra, he told himself. *Tavra, but...*

"... but you're a spider."

Fully extended, her legs were almost the length of his fingers, but needle-thin and shining black. She easily climbed his sleeve to sit on his shoulder, where he could see eight faceted eyes in her tiny head, like miniature crystals set in the stone of a pendant. Her small voice was much more audible from there.

"And alive, thanks to you," she replied. "It's not ideal, but it doesn't matter. If we don't hurry, all of the Grottan will be gone. Krychk called upon the Skeksis using a Crystal shard when we arrived in the Caves of Grot. I tried to stop it, but I had no power over it... I've failed you, and the Gelfling, and the Grottan. Now, we must hurry, or risk even more!"

"What do we do with... with your body?"

The swarm of spiders had fled, leaving the Gelfling alone. The finger-vines twitched sadly, almost completely eaten away. Piles of smoldering leaves and damp brush smoked, and the only light came from the dying torch Amri held. Tavra's body, occupied by Krychk the spider for only a few moments before it had lost the force to stay alive, lay still on the earth, silver hair quickly losing luster. There would be no returning Tavra to her body, even if Kylan knew how to reverse the spell he'd cast. Her body had died, taking Krychk with it. Now the only place for her was trapped in the spider's tiny form.

"Leave it. There's nothing more we can do. But first, in my cloak—there is the Crystal shard from the Skeksis and a pearl. If I'm to prove my identity when we eventually reach Ha'rar, I will need the pearl amulet."

No one was eager to search the Silverling's cloak, so Kylan did it. He found the shard and the amulet, a pearl drop on a silver chain. The pearl itself was shining, white and blue, wrapped in a silver cage shaped like tiny Vapra wings. The shard was small enough to hold in his hand, black as obsidian, though he sensed a flicker of energy from deep inside it, like the sound of voices just muffled enough to be incoherent. At first he was drawn to it, wanting to peer further into it to see what waited on the other side, but Tavra pricked him with her spider feet.

"Do not look into it—destroy it, or the Skeksis will find us with it."

Taking care not to be caught by the allure of the Crystal again, Kylan placed the shard on a flat stone while Naia and Amri hefted a larger one. After exchanging a glance and a nod, they dropped the larger stone on the smaller, crushing the shard into dust and splinters, its magnetic call silenced.

The traveling pack was still back at their camp, as were some of their other things. They did not have time to bury or cremate Tavra's body, so they paid their respects quietly. Naia soothed the finger-vines and gave them thanks for their help and sacrifice. Then they left, and Kylan grabbed Tavra's sword and hoped the forest would take care of the rest, in time.

"I'm sorry," he said as they hurried back along the trail toward camp. "I didn't mean to . . . do whatever I did. I just didn't want you to die. I hope you aren't angry with me."

"I'm not angry. My body will return to Thra. When my work is done, I will join it. Until then, I have no time to worry or complain. We need to go to the tunnels north of Domrak."

Kylan almost asked about Ha'rar but remembered that had been Krychk's goal. To chase down Rian and reach the Gelfling capital, where it could then spy on the Gelfling's plans and relay them to the Skeksis. He felt as though he knew Tavra, but if all this time it had actually been Krychk they had been speaking with, traveling with, and trusting—he realized he didn't really know Tavra of Ha'rar at all.

"Are you all right?" he asked, not knowing what else to say. He tried to imagine being in her predicament, but it was impossible. There was no way to know how Tavra felt, after the terror at the castle and being a prisoner in her own mind while Krychk controlled her withered body.

Despite all that, Tavra's response was stoic and loyal.

"I will be all right when the Skeksis are stopped and our people are no longer living in their shadow."

When they reached camp, he quickly stowed the amulet in the pack and slung it over his shoulders. The weight felt familiar but not heavy. Tavra spoke in Kylan's ear, but her voice was so small that he had to relay her words to the others.

"Amri. What is the fastest way to the tunnels that connect Domrak to the Grottan Sanctuary?"

Amri's black eyes were glassy with worry. Kylan remembered when he had first heard that the Skeksis had returned to Sami Thicket—it was no better now.

"I don't know. I've never traveled there from aboveground. If we were in the tunnels, I could show you the way, but out here I have no idea."

"Kylan," Naia said. "What about the map in the book?"

"Yes, Raunip's book," Tavra agreed. While Kylan got to work finding the book and, within it, the map of the mountains and highlands, she went on to explain. "With my body drained of essence, I couldn't fight Krychk. I could see and hear . . . some times more than others. I was able to take control long enough to write the message on the stone, when the spider went ahead to relay our progress on the way to Aughra, but it stopped me before I could finish. Called its brethren to cover the markings, though it couldn't even read what I had written . . . Naia, Kylan, Amri. I'm so sorry I was unable to stop it."

The three knelt to look at Kylan's book when he found the map.

"It wasn't your fault," Naia said. "Let's agree to all be sorry and all forgiven. And then . . . move past this so we can stop them."

Kylan and Amri agreed in silence. They turned toward more important things, as Naia suggested: Raunip's book, and how to most quickly reach the Grottan Sanctuary. The page with the map was marked, and Kylan put the book down so Amri could cast the torchlight on it. He spoke for Tavra as she whispered in his ear, pointing on the map.

"The crystal spiders are an ancient race. I don't know how long they have been working with the Skeksis, or how long they have been using weak and dying hosts to spy on the Gelfling. They are not under power, like the creatures that look upon the darkened Crystal or its veins. They are loyal to the Skeksis by will."

Kylan thought of the horner they had helped Rian with, back in Stone-in-the-Wood. It had not been like other darkened creatures, instead fixated on Rian and then Naia. Hadn't Neech found a spidery snack in its deep fur? Another crystal-singer spider, using the horner as a puppet—the horner had fallen unconscious after Neech had snapped it up. Kylan shivered as Tavra went on.

"Krychk called on the Skeksis while we were in the Tomb of Relics. When it confirmed that it had destroyed the *firca*, its spider brethren took Domrak by surprise. We were already headed away and in the opposite direction. The Grottan didn't stand a chance in Domrak . . . Many fled north, toward the Sanctuary. That is the last I heard, this night when Krychk spoke to Lord skekLi through the Crystal shard."

"skekLi!" Naia exclaimed. "A Skeksis . . . Could he be urLii's other half?"

"I do not know. Krychk was in contact with many of the lords, but skekLi was its master so far as its mission to find you, Gurjin, and Rian. It was promised the Grottan caves as payment for its loyalty. Listen . . . If we hurry, and can reach the Sanctuary before the spiders that chase the fleeing Grottan, we may be able to fight back."

"How? We were nearly just defeated by spiders," Naia said. "And that was just a tiny swarm. What are we going to do in the tunnels and mountains, against many more?"

"The Sanctuary was entrusted to the Grottan for many reasons," Tavra replied. "Amri, you've heard this, haven't you?"

"I—I don't know. The Sanctuary is one of the most ancient places in all of Thra. I don't know why it was entrusted to us aside from that it was in the mountains and accessible from Domrak. urLii travels there often. He says it's to commune with the singing mountains. But . . ."

"Singing mountains?" Kylan asked. He felt a spark of hope. "In song, those are the mountains that were formed by the bell-birds."

"The same," Tavra said. "The Sanctuary was a nesting place of the bell-birds. When the spider destroyed the *firca*, I wanted to tell you that your plan was still a good one. There's still hope. It is possible that there may be bones left of the bell-birds, though they died out many trine ago. If the Sanctuary has been untouched, and protected by the Grottan, then we may yet have a chance."

"But a bone isn't the same as a *firca*," Amri said. "Even if we were to find a bone from one of the birds, it would be just a bone. It could have some power, but Gyr the Song Teller is long gone.

There's no one who knows how to make another *firca* like the bone-flute."

The Grottan was saying what Kylan was thinking. The truth was like a cold breeze, and the tiny light in Kylan's heart flickered. Gyr's *firca* was one of a kind, kept in the Tomb of Relics because of its rarity. It felt irreverent to even consider replicating such a thing—whether or not anyone was even capable of it, which was a totally separate question to consider. Even so, Naia stood as if the answer was obvious.

"Kylan can make one. So let's do it. How do we get there?"

Her words were solid, and the flame in Kylan's breast grew a little brighter. He didn't know if he could craft a flute from the bone of an extinct bird, but if it was their only hope, he would try. He pointed at the map.

"Amri, does this mean anything to you? It says the Tide Pass. It looks like an underground tributary to the Black River that comes from deep in the mountains. Is it a place we can enter to reach the Sanctuary?"

Amri looked at the map where Kylan pointed. Their location was on the western side of the mountains, flanking the Black River where it flowed in the valley below. Where the mountains and the river swerved east before straightening back toward Ha'rar, there was an inlet and a squiggly black line. It connected the Black River to a dot in the mountains that was labeled with a symbol combining the characters for *safe* and *retreat*.

From its proximity to the Domrak and the Tomb of Relics, Kylan could see how the Grottan could likely cross through the mountain tunnels with relative ease. For those outside of the caves, though, the journey was likely to be difficult, or even deadly.

"The Tide Pass is an underground river, yes, but I don't know that we will be able to travel it by foot. It's not been made for passage, even with a boat. It's just an underground channel, mostly submerged."

"We will have to take it anyway," Tavra said. "We cannot cross the mountain ridge in time, and backtracking to Domrak or even the entrance to the Tomb will take too long and also put us closer to the place where the spiders have gathered the thickest. Naia can breathe in water, and Amri can see in the dark. With their help, it may be possible for us to reach the Sanctuary before the spiders. We will have to take the risk."

"What do you think, Amri?" Naia asked. "Is it possible, or will we die for sure?"

"You and I wouldn't die for sure," he replied, but his assurance ended there. He sighed. "If the two of you are willing to come with us, and trust us, then I am willing to do what it takes to see all four of us through."

Tavra tapped her legs, touching Kylan's cheek with one of the eight. It pricked his skin, but it was gentle.

"This body is small and requires little to live. I will not be in danger . . . Kylan, it is you who has the most to fear. But it is also you whom we need the most—to make the *firca* and to use it to warn our people."

The need to depart was urgent, but the three others said nothing, letting Kylan reflect on his decision alone. It was true:

Amri was well equipped to traverse an underwater cave, and Naia had no fear of drowning. Even Tavra would likely be able to find an exit in an emergency; in fact, she might even have been light enough to skate on the surface of a still pond.

But Kylan would be blind in the Pass, half or more submerged in deep, dark cave water. He was tired of tunnels and being underground. In fact, there was nothing he wanted to avoid more than another crawl through the dark, needing help from the others just to move or breathe.

Despite her new arachnid form, he couldn't help but imagine Tavra as she once had been, touching his cheek in the same way and saying the same words. He had not been able to do anything to help his own clan, but maybe there was something that could be done for Amri's. For once, there was something only he could do, and that was what he had wanted all along.

He committed the map to memory and packed the book.

"Then what are we waiting for? To the Tide Pass we go."

CHAPTER 24

Amri found the inlet just as the sky began to lighten. Kylan wished they could stay on the surface of the world at least long enough to see the suns rise, but they had no time. He would have to believe there would be endless other chances in the future.

The inlet was barely a tunnel, just a place in the mountainside where a river flowed out of a narrow crack. In times when the water level was high, the entrance would have been invisible. Kylan stared at the inlet as he shrugged out of the travel pack and any excess clothing. The others did the same, stowing their traveling bags and extra belongings beside the pack. Kylan was reluctant to leave the book and Tavra's pearl amulet, but getting snagged on a rock or tangled in their own travel gear would mean sure death. Even Naia shed her cloak and tied back her locs, baring the gills on her neck and upper shoulders. At least if they were caught underwater, one of them would be able to attempt to rescue the others, but Kylan desperately hoped it would not come to that.

They gathered at the entrance and waded into the river where it flowed from the mountain. The water was cool, but slow moving and clear. Amri bent to sniff the faint draft coming from inside the tunnel and looked back.

"The tide will stay low for a few more days, and there are no currents here, so as long as we keep calm, there's no danger of being washed away. I'll lead. Naia should be at the rear in case of . . . Well, just in case. If we could walk it, the path would not take long, but crawling it will take longer. Remain calm, and your body will thank you for it."

"Ready?" Naia asked. It was to the group, but specifically for Kylan. He took what he hoped would not be his last breath of open air.

"After you, Amri."

The tunnel was everything Kylan had dreaded it to be. It was so dark, he might as well have been blindfolded, with none of the luminescent plant life to light the way. The floor of the riverbed dropped away quickly once they were inside the tunnel, leaving them to pull themselves along by handholds on the cave wall. In some places, the surface of the water was so high, Kylan had to tilt his head up to reach the meager sliver of air above it. When he did, he could almost kiss the ceiling of the tunnel, his ears dunked below the water, so he felt deaf as well as blind. Tavra made matters more uncomfortable by riding on the top of his head, her prickly legs tickling his face.

The going was slow. Amri navigated ahead, checking back frequently, and Naia touched Kylan's back occasionally to let him know she was there. When the tunnel seemed to end, they paused in the pocket of air. Here, there was enough air for Kylan to get his entire head above the water, but the closed-in space felt like it was closing in even further.

"There's a low area ahead," Amri said. "We'll have to swim through it."

"Should I go ahead and check it out, first?" Naia asked. Unlike how Kylan felt or how Amri sounded, she was hardly out of breath.

"You won't be able to see it. I think we should go together. Once we make sure it's clear, and see how far it is, we'll come back. Will you be all right, Kylan?"

He tried not to panic at the idea of being left alone in the dark. If something happened to them, there was no way he would be able to even backtrack out of the tunnel. There was no other choice, though. They were far enough in that, if they could make it, it would probably be faster to find the exit on the other side.

"Yes, I'm fine," he said, feeling like a liar. "I'll wait here."

Naia squeezed his shoulder. He felt the hilt of her dagger in his hand.

"Take this. We'll be back soon."

Then the water rippled and bubbled, and Kylan was alone in the dark with Tavra, who perched on his forehead. She was so light that he almost couldn't feel whether she was there at all, but then she spoke.

"We are close. I can hear the voices of the other spiders. When Naia and Amri return, we will pass through this tunnel and enter the Sanctuary . . . but I fear we are too late to warn the Grottan that fled Domrak."

"What? Then . . . what do we do?"

He felt like he was talking to himself, the dark was so thick and Tavra's voice was so small. She sounded like his conscience, disembodied and pensive.

"What we came here to do," she said. "Find a bone of the bell-bird. Perhaps we can yet save the Grottan if we could find one."

"You mean there's a chance we won't be able to save them . . . just like we couldn't save those they took in Sami Thicket."

"Don't misunderstand. Even if we're unable to save these Grottan now, if we can find the bone and you're able to make the *firca* to warn everyone, it would still be a victory. This is the beginning of war with the Skeksis . . . Lives will be lost, and sacrifices made. To endure, we must focus on the greatest good."

Kylan couldn't help but think Tavra was speaking to herself. Her brand of optimism was that of a seasoned soldier, a sort of bitter take on the constant bright hope Kylan had tried to commit himself to for so long. Even Naia's optimism came from a place of wishing for the best; Tavra's words, though not exactly comforting, were nonetheless realistic.

"You think the bone could stop the spiders?" he asked, trying to fill the silence so it didn't overwhelm him. "How?"

"The spiders are sensitive to sound, and they are close to the heart of Thra. They are an ancient race. If the bell-bird's song cannot make them submit, I know not what else might."

It was a glimpse of hope, even if it still meant they had to find one of the bones, a task that might well be impossible. Kylan listened to the dripping and the quiet sloshing of water. There was no sound of bubbles or movement in the idle waves.

"It's it been a while. Should Amri and Naia have returned?"

"It's difficult to say. The voices of the spider swarm are growing, though. We will soon be far too late, if we are not already."

Kylan put Naia's dagger in his belt and felt along the cave wall. A moving current eddied below, near his feet, where Naia and Amri had disappeared. It was his role to wait for them to check ahead—not because he was weak, really, but because they were better suited to do the job. Yet if they had run into trouble, despite how impossible it might seem for him to make the journey without their help, it was his role as well to save them if he could.

"Can you see in this dark?" he asked.

"Yes. Are you going after them?"

Her question was mostly neutral, though it had a hint of what Kylan hoped was pride, or respect, or something like that. He didn't want to. Every nerve in his body was ringing in alarm and fear, but it didn't matter. He was here, and if he was going to get out of this place, there was only one way to do it.

"Try to tell me if I'm about to die," he said.

Tavra gave a very dry chuckle.

"I will do my best."

Kylan took the biggest breath he could, and dived.

The underwater tunnel was narrow and had only one route, so at least there was no fear of losing his way. He couldn't tell whether his eyes were open or shut, pulling himself through the rocky passage with his hands. Tavra held on to him, pressing her body against his shoulder, sometimes pricking him with her legs when he neared sharp rocks or came close to the sudden twists and turns. More than once he hit his head, or shoulder, or ankle when he kicked, and he had to let the air out of his lungs slowly when he realized the saved breath was causing him to float.

There was no sign of Naia or Amri. His lungs began to burn, and his body wanted to panic, thrashing or swimming upward in search of air, but he took hold of himself and forced a steady pace. Just as he began to fear the tunnel would never end, Tavra pricked him with all eight legs, and he opened his eyes. Overhead he saw a light, and he kicked as fast as he could toward it, swimming up and up until finally he broke the surface and gasped for air.

"Be careful," Tavra hissed into his ear, in an even tinier voice than usual. "The enemy is all around us."

Kylan's lungs strained in protest as he fought to breathe as quietly as he could. Though there was light coming from above, he couldn't see. He couldn't do anything, at first, but gulp air. If the enemy were to find him now, there would be nothing he could do. His lungs were so starved for air, the most he could do was stay in the water. All he wanted was to drag himself out and onto whatever land was nearby.

When his head began to clear and his gasps calmed to shallow panting, he opened his eyes. The underwater tunnel had opened into a pool. At his back was a small waterfall coming from higher in the cavern. Though it was not very large, it was steady, and the echoing sound of it had probably masked his gasping for air.

This was in his favor, for all around him, the rocks, walls, nooks, and crannies were coated in spiderwebs. Some of the webs were elegant, glistening like silver thread, while some were so thick and gauzy, they looked like fleece laid upon the rocks. Crawling on every surface of the cave and along every web were spiders of every shape, every size, and every color. Some had long thin legs like Tavra. Some were large, squat, and furry. Some were small, like black dust, and others much larger. One spider, reclining on its hammock of netted webbing, had legs the size of Kylan's arms.

There was still no sign of Naia and Amri, and Kylan took in the cavern from his spot in the pool, submerged up to just below his nose in the hopes that his dark hair and skin would camouflage him in the dimly lit grotto. The cavern that housed the pool was far smaller than the Domrak central cavern, and he could see a single passage that trailed off on the other side. He smelled open air and could see daylight coming from that direction.

The Sanctuary, he thought. *But how will I get there? And where are Naia and Amri?*

There was no way they would have seen this and gone ahead without coming back to get him. The only answer was that they had been captured . . . or worse. Kylan looked over the spider-infested cave once more. Maybe they were hiding, or being held prisoner. Either way, he had to find them. They all had to get to the Sanctuary and find the bone, and the Grottan, if they could.

Kylan held his breath and sank into the water up to his eyes when a shadow fell against the corridor that led outside. From the feather-ornamented mantle and wickedly hooked beak, he knew what it was before it came into view: a Skeksis, in a black-and-red cloak, holding a crystal-topped staff as it came striding down the tunnel.

The spiders chittered and scurried out of the Skeksis's

way, some of the smaller ones kicked up by the many layers of ornamented and embroidered fabrics. The Skeksis held the staff out, letting the light glinting out of its crystal head illuminate the cave.

"skekLi," Tavra whispered in Kylan's ear. "The Satirist . . . The Skeksis' entertainer. Krychk's master. Be careful!"

Kylan shuddered in the water as the Skeksis Lord's gaze passed over him and stopped. He hoped that maybe the Skeksis hadn't seen him, but the gasp that followed was proof to the contrary.

"You!" called the Skeksis, jabbing in his direction with the staff.

His voice matched the one that had been speaking to Krychk through the Crystal shard. Kylan wanted to duck into the water and swim back through the terrible tunnel below, but the Skeksis strode forward so quickly and with such ferociousness that his joints locked up and he could not move. When he finally regained enough control to push away from the lip of the pool, he was too late. The Skeksis towered over him and splashed a clawed hand into the water, grabbing him and pulling him out.

"You!" he crowed again. "So you took the Spriton after all! We thought you would fail us. Yes, we did. But here we are."

What was he saying? Took the Spriton?

He thinks you are the spider, Kylan answered himself. The realization was like lightning, just another force charging through his fear-racked body. He pushed himself to look the Skeksis in the eye. Tavra, still attached to his neck, did not move. He hoped she had realized the same thing.

"Y-yes," he stammered. "My lord. The . . . the Vapra's body failed me. So I am here. I trust . . . you found the Drenchen and the Grottan?"

The Skeksis set him down with surprising care, though the carnivorous sneer still cut beneath his pointed beak. He was thinner than the other Skeksis that Kylan had seen, with a long neck and sinewy fingers. On each finger he wore a ring, and each ring was connected with a web of silver chain, decorated with dangling charms. The same chain-and-charm decorations cascaded from a three-pointed fascinator, pinned to the Skeksis's head with a pair of long narrow feathers.

"Yes. We have them in the Sanctuary. Of course, would've been better with *two* Drenchen, but . . . Come, come! We have the Grottan *maudra* as well. That is fine in trade. At least for now."

The Skeksis whirled, flourishing with his staff, and strutted out of the cavern. Kylan caught his breath. The spiders all around were quiet, twitching their mandibles while they watched him. Did they know? Could they know that he was not being controlled by Krychk? He didn't want to wait to find out, and pulled his chin up as he had seen Krychk do when in control of Tavra's body. With a forced sense of self-importance, he marched after the Skeksis toward the Sanctuary, heart fluttering with worry at what he might find there.

CHAPTER 25

Kylan followed skekLi into a passageway and toward the sound of rushing wind. Like the Grottan caves of Domrak, the walls were thick with dream-etching, but as they neared the end of the tunnel, the organic facets of rock and moss gave way to architecture of a grander scale. The dirt underfoot became brick and steps, and around them moss and other green plants prevailed—so much so that the exit was completely overgrown with brush and ferns.

skekLi pushed his way through the veil of green at the end and they emerged beyond the foliage. The space beyond took Kylan's breath away.

It was a corrie, the remains of some ancient, dried-up mountain lake. It looked as if a big hand had reached down and scooped out the rock and lifted it away. Growing from the bottom of the open corrie were a dozen giant mushrooms, with pillar-like gray stems and wide flat caps. They were enormous enough that some had structures built on top, torch circles and dream-etched stone pillars. Between the mushroom caps were a network of rope bridges, so one might wander between the caps in a peaceful labyrinth of contemplation. At the very bottom of the corrie, Kylan could make out water flowing from a deep spring,

perhaps the origin of the Black River that quenched the thirst of all the Skarith region. The air was thin and cold, and carried the sounds of bells, though none could be seen. The sounds were echoes from a distant past, and Kylan knew he had reached the Grottan Sanctuary.

Even here, the spiders crawled and spun their webs on every surface. It was not as infested as the cave, but Kylan saw that there were many other exits that pocked the interior wall of the space, and spiders were lazily spinning webs and crawling up and down the corrie walls. They were not vicious now, as they had been during the confrontation with Krychk, but they were thousands, if not millions, in number. Over time, the entire Sanctuary would become one huge spider nest. If Krychk was any indication of the spider folk's feelings, it would mean complete exile for the Gelfling from this sacred place.

skekLi proceeded down the nearest rope bridge. The ancient bridge creaked and swayed under his weight, but he went on without a care. Kylan followed, tiny parts of tiny plans flitting through his mind as he picked his way across the wood slats. If he could get Naia's knife out in time, he could cut the bridge and hope the Skeksis might fall to his death. Or would he? He realized he didn't even know if a Skeksis could be killed. They had hurt skekMal, most certainly, but the Hunter remained at large, at least enough to have stolen Spriton from Sami Thicket. And even if they could destroy skekLi, it would mean doom for his Mystic counterpart, wherever he was.

As they approached the nearest mushroom cap, Kylan pushed

back a tremor of fear. What he had mistaken for more webs clustered around a circle of pillars were actually Gelfling bodies, so wrapped in web, they were almost unrecognizable. They were mostly Grottan, and mostly unconscious, though one let out a whimper when skekLi approached.

"Yes, cry, little Gelfling. Cry because you ran right to us. Did you think we would not know where you would flee when the spiders took Domrak? Stupid Gelfling. Fled right into our arms, like children."

Kylan breathed slowly to control his impulse to cry out or flee when he saw Naia and Amri, bound to one of the pillars in thick, sticky webbing. Naia was unconscious; her head hung to the side and was dark with a big bruise and cut. Amri was awake, eyes nearly closed in pain against the growing light, but he saw Kylan. Before he could say a word, skekLi whirled, holding his staff over his head and laughing so loudly, it echoed one-hundredfold against the mountains.

"Krychk, behold! The Drenchen girl. The Gelfling Sanctuary. All the wisdom of the ages!"

skekLi let out another round of laughter, taking huge strides across the cap while holding his staff high. After trine upon trine under the open sun, the mushroom's surface was petrified and nearly stone, littered with chipped-off, fossilized fungus and shards of what Kylan realized were giant eggshells.

"And who brought it to the Emperor? ME! skekLi! Not the Hunter. Not the General. Not even skekGra the Conqueror. No, it was skekLi. The *clown*, they said. The *jester*. Ha! See what this court clown has done that not even skekMal could do! We'll see what Emperor skekSo thinks about that! HA! *HA!*"

Although Kylan knew he should fear the towering black-quilled creature—should hate it for what it had done—a tiny part of him connected with the Skeksis, and he understood. Why skekLi was so overjoyed, even in his terrible way. The connection, as repulsive as it was, gave him a handhold in the situation where he had otherwise been slipping, and he grabbed on.

"You succeeded where others failed, my lord," he said. He cursed at the quavering in his voice, pressing it out like he would wring water from a washcloth. "You did what the warriors could not do. You . . . you tricked them. Led them straight here. It was a genius plan."

"Oh, wasn't it? Yes. Yes, it was. Oh, bask in my glory, Krychk. A great victory for me means a great victory for you. Now, we must hurry. To finalize this conquest, with Rian and the other Drenchen. Ohh . . . yes, soon . . ."

Under the watch of all the spiders, Kylan could hardly glance at Amri to reassure him. He looked at Naia and hoped she would be all right. He could see that she was breathing, but she did not look well. The size of the welt on her forehead matched the crystal at the end of skekLi's staff. He hoped that she would be able to run if she were able to wake at all.

But where would they go? They were completely surrounded by spiders, and one sweep of skekLi's staff or clawed hands and they would topple over the unguarded edge of the cap. Even Naia's unpracticed wings would not slow her fall enough to save her.

Amri flicked his ear. Kylan looked furtively in the direction he gestured. Along the vertical cliffs, he saw massive tangles of shrubs and roots. At first he thought they were merely mountain-growing brambles, but the more he looked, the more he could make out other shapes. The structures were woven, a combination of large branches and sometimes what looked to be whole trees, overgrown with giant hanging moss and the broad-leafed ferns that sprouted throughout the valley. It wasn't until Kylan recognized the broken shaft of a huge feather jutting out of one of the structures that he understood. These were nests, once, though the birds that had built them had been gone for over a thousand trine.

"The bell-bird nests," Tavra whispered. "Where we might find a bone . . ."

It was a nice thought, but far from possible right now. So much could go wrong, and in very little time. Even if Kylan made a run for the nest, he'd be intercepted by spiders or skekLi. Not to mention that he'd have to leave Amri and Naia to do so. Trying to free them from the webbing would take more time than he had. Once he betrayed the fact that he was not being controlled by the crystal spider on his neck, it would be over.

He tried to think strategically, as he thought Tavra might. If he could get rid of the spiders, he might be able to at least outrun skekLi. All their weapons and supplies were in a pile where the river left the mountain. All he had with him were his wits and his quick Gelfling feet. Tavra had said the bell-bird bone could do it, but they'd never find it like this. He needed help.

"So, my little spider friend. We promised your kind the Caves of Grot. Take them, and do not forget our great generosity despite your failure. Remember this moment, when we conquered the Gelfling who infested your domain. We will call upon you soon for later matters."

That was all the Skeksis had brought him here for? To witness his gloating?

"Thank you, my lord," he began. "Might I ask one other favor of you? This Spriton body is not to my liking. I know you must bring the Drenchen back to the Emperor, but the Grottan... It is like the Vapra. Might I...?"

skekLi chuckled. "Yes, the Spriton is tiny. It makes no difference to us. Take the Grottan if you like. Its eyes may serve you better in the caves anyway."

Kylan approached Amri and began tearing the webbing away. As he did, he tried to make some work on the web that bound Naia, too. When his careless-seeming ripping and shredding jostled her, she stirred and opened her eyes.

"Kylan...?"

"Shh. Play dead. Amri, go with Tavra. Find the bone. When you cross the bridge, cut it down."

"What? But how..."

"Use a rock, a knife, one of those eggshell shards. I don't care. Just do it!"

The webbing was thick and his fingers were sore, but Kylan finally freed his friend.

"Amri and I will find the bone," Tavra said. "Good luck, Spriton."

Tavra detached from his neck and darted down his arm, leaping to Amri's shoulder, and Kylan took on his next character, the weakling Spriton the Skeksis thought he was. He yelped and fell back, putting his hand to his neck.

"No!" he cried. "What have you done?"

Amri pulled himself free of the remaining web, casting about with an unsure frown. Tavra moved to a place on his shoulder where Kylan hoped she was whispering to him. Her voice, if she was, was imperceptible to him over the echoing wind.

"Ah, yes!" Amri said suddenly. He snatched one of the sharp eggshell pieces that were scattered about, pointing it at Kylan as if to silence him. "This Grottan body is much more appealing! Stay down, puny Spriton!"

It wasn't perfect, but it would have to do. skekLi didn't seem to notice the change in attitude, much more interested in preening his robes. Amri brushed himself off and stepped toward the bridge. The motion was stilted, as if he was both reluctant to leave his friends while desperately wanting to run as far from the Skeksis as he could. It was a mixture of emotions Kylan knew well.

"Yes," Amri said again. "Well, thank you, my lord. My lord, skekLi. I will now . . . go. Back to Domrak to claim the prize . . . Goodbye."

Kylan stayed where he was, pretending to be immobile, but every muscle ready to leap when it was time. skekLi waved a dismissive claw as Amri started across the bridge.

"Stay at arms. Soon we will finish what we started."

Amri turned and bowed deeply from halfway across.

"Yes, my lord!"

Then he hurried across the bridge. Kylan watched, feeling his fingers and toes tingle as he waited. When Amri reached the far side, he attacked the ropes that secured the bridge, hacking away with the fossilized eggshell.

skekLi didn't notice what was happening until the ropes snapped. He howled as the bridge fell away, the end nearly disappearing into the depths below.

"What are you doing, you stupid spider?"

Kylan leaped to his feet, bolting across the cap to the second and only remaining bridge.

"Come and get me, Skeksis!" he cried.

skekLi shrieked as Kylan passed him, first trying to intercept him with his staff and then clambering after him as he reached the bridge. Kylan nearly toppled off as skekLi stepped foot behind him, the Skeksis's heavy, uneven weight sending the bridge into a wild swing. He fought for a handhold and continued running, skipping whole panels in his flight.

He reached the second mushroom's platform before skekLi. Two more connecting bridges waited, and he raced for the closest, drawing Naia's dagger and cut at the rope posts. skekLi's shouts and curses grew louder, and Kylan ran to the second bridge. Slicing the rope, it fell away just as the Skeksis mounted the cap, panting and growling.

"Wretched Gelfling!" he hissed. "Vile pest! How dare you run from me, your lord? I ought to make a puppet of you!"

"You're just mad I fooled you," Kylan said, backing away. There was one bridge left, but it was the one skekLi had come across. Now it was the only way off the mushroom, and they were both well aware of it. skekLi strode forward, keeping his giant mass between Kylan and the ropeway and rearing up to his full height.

"I am no fool," skekLi said.

He snapped his jaw, and Kylan jumped in spite of himself. It was hard not to imagine that sharp beak locking shut on him, those clawed hands grabbing him and ripping him apart. He gave more ground, and skekLi followed. Out of the corner of his eye, he saw movement. Amri was climbing the cliffside, nimbly and fleetly as one might expect of a cave dweller, making his way toward the biggest of the abandoned nests.

"Going to dash by again, cut that bridge, too? Eh, little pest?" skekLi chided. "Good luck. Try it and we will snatch you up and squeeze the essence out of you here and now."

skekLi swung his staff, and Kylan ducked, feeling the bangles from the end of it whistle over his head. A dark shape glimmered behind skekLi, at the end of the bridge where it reached their mushroom. When skekLi swung his staff again, his coat and cloaks flying up in swaths of crimson and ebony, Kylan saw Naia had crossed the bridge. She was waving wildly down at the other end. Soon after, Kylan heard the creaking and twanging of the bridge's ropes being cut.

skekLi sniffed the air and whirled. Naia rolled under a swing from the staff, skidding to a crouch near Kylan. skekLi cast down, letting out half of a surprised *squawk*.

They all looked below. Naia had freed herself and torn the

web from the Grottan prisoners. Even now as she joined Kylan, the Grottan used rocks and eggshells and even their teeth to sever the far end of the bridge. Before skekLi could clamber back to the other side, it fell away, stranding the three of them on the mushroom together.

skekLi hissed, thrashing his claws and whirling toward them. His head jutted out and his eyes flashed, but he did not scream. He did not shriek like an uncontrolled beast, as skekMal had. Instead, he lowered his head and growled, his voice dropping low and poisonous.

"You will regret this," he said.

The spiders that laced the inner walls were a throng of hissing, chittering, and chirping voices. Some were already pouring down the cliffs to the corrie floor. If they were able to cross the lake that lay at the bottom, it would not be long before they climbed the mushroom shaft and overran them. When that happened, there would be no escape.

But the Grottan prisoners were safe, at least for now. That had been Kylan's main goal. Now he stood with Naia, trapped on an island with an enraged Skeksis. He could only hope Amri and Tavra would find the bell-bird bone in time.

CHAPTER 26

Kylan and Naia parted, flanking skekLi instinctively. Armed with the staff, the Skeksis's reach was incredible. With the long weapon, he might even be able to sweep them both off the platform in a single move, should they be in the same place.

"We gotta get that staff," Naia said, echoing Kylan's thinking out loud. She pressed her hand to the wound on her head, wiping away some of the blood that was still seeping from it.

"Are you all right? I tried to get him away from you . . ."

"I'm fine. I'll be better once we take care of this big heap."

They had left their *bola* at the entrance to the Pass, but Naia did have Gurjin's dagger, though it seemed impossibly small compared to the looming Skeksis before them. Even if she were to strike him with it, Kylan wasn't sure how much damage it would really do. He glanced over his shoulder, dizzy from the height, and wondered whether they should try to escape instead.

"Thinking of flying?" skekLi asked. "Drenchen wings can't fly. Long drop from here, you can see that. She would be lucky if she could save herself. No way she can carry you, too."

Kylan grimaced. Even once Naia's wings had fully grown in, she would never be able to fly like Tavra had. Drenchen wings were for swimming and gliding. There would be no escape for the both of them should they jump.

skekLi's beak broke into a grin.

"Though we could then say you had fallen for each other! Ha!"

He laughed, turning his attention a smidgeon more toward Kylan. That was when Naia leaped. She made it inside the reach of skekLi's staff, ducking under it as he swung wildly toward her. His aim was bad and uncoordinated, and Kylan realized the Skeksis was not a fighter. He was large and dangerous, with the advantage of a weapon, but he was no hunter. Naia surfaced right inside the space made by his outstretched arms, then jumped, holding her fist up and clocking skekLi solidly in the bottom of his bill. His beak made a loud *CLACK* and he stumbled backward.

Kylan took the opportunity and skirted the flailing arms and thrashing staff, going for skekLi's hand. He grabbed the Skeksis by the wrist and used the only weapon left that he had—his teeth. He chomped on skekLi's hand, right where it gripped the staff. skekLi shrieked, but did not let go. The Skeksis grabbed at Kylan with his free hand and flung him away. It was only because of skekLi's lack of coordination that Kylan was able to grab hold of a ridge in the cap's surface and stop himself before he slid right off and into a long, long fall.

"Wretched Gelfling!" cried skekLi.

Kylan spit the rancid, salty taste of Skeksis skin from his mouth. Naia fell back again, on the other side of the cap, crouching and readying herself for the next attack. skekLi righted his head and hunched over again, arms wide and claws ready to grab. Kylan looked over the side of the cap.

"I don't mean to add to our troubles," he said, "but the spiders are coming."

Indeed, arachnid bodies were streaming from the walls of the corrie, trickling like streams to the lake below. As Kylan had feared, most of the spiders floated on the water, skating across it like pond-walkers toward the base of the mushroom.

"Maybe you should go," he told Naia.

"I'm not leaving you. Once Amri finds that bone, we're going to need you to use it."

"Someone else might have to!"

skekLi made a trilling, laughing noise that came out of the top of his beak and forehead. He narrowed his eyes, and the corners of his mouth turned up, baring the sharp teeth inside.

"Oh yes. The bone! The bell-bird bone from the Book of Raunip. Krychk told me of it, that you had a bone to pick. Ha! I'm sad to say, you won't find it here. Poor, stupid Gelfling. All the bones have been borne away, chewed up by ruffnaw and crawlies and time."

He stepped forward, this time with Naia in his sights.

"You know. If you came with us, Drenchen. We might consider letting your friendlings go. The Grottan. This little Spriton. If you came with us, to the castle. To the Emperor. We only need a little essence. A little, only a little. From you and your other half. In exchange, we would feed you. Care for you, as we have always cared for Gelfling. We need only a little to save our Emperor."

"Save him?" Naia asked. "You mean steal the life force from *his* other half. I won't help you do that."

skekLi's head tilted, wobbling as if his brains were rolling from side to side. He stepped forward, but when Kylan and Naia moved away, he stopped his advance.

"No, no, no. You misunderstand! Emperor skekSo is dying. So, too, his other half is dying. In a way, we are all this way . . . But with special Gelfling essence . . . we can reunite. We can save ourselves *and* our others."

Kylan didn't like skekLi's tone at all. It sounded too noble, too good to be true. Yet when he slowly lowered his staff, Naia did not attack.

"I think he's lying," Kylan warned her.

skekLi ignored him, appealing to Naia instead.

"That is what you want to do, isn't it? Drenchen? Save the others? Save the Crystal? Save Gelfling—save Thra? To do so, help us save *Skeksis*. Look! We are not mad with Gelfling. Even when it bites us. We only want Drenchen twins, for reunion. Only a little. You would spare only a little, if it might save everyone . . . wouldn't you?"

"A minute ago you were trying to kill us!"

"If all they wanted was a little of your essence," Kylan added, "then why would they have gone through such efforts to capture us? If all they wanted was a little, to save themselves and the Mystics, why not just ask?"

"Speaks around us as if we're not here," muttered skekLi. "Would Gelfling have believed us? Eh? EH? Imagine this! Skeksis comes to Drenchen village. Dressed nicely, of course. He asks if this one will come back to the castle. Sit in the chair. We've seen the chair in the Chamber of Life. Sit there, staring into the fire? Sure? Ha! Who would do that! But listen, Gelfling. Listen. Gelfling people entrusted the castle and the Crystal to the Skeksis. We keep it. We protect it. Dust the mantel, clean halls, and so on. All for free, with never thanks. So, least Gelfling could do is help the Skeksis when they can. What are two lives to all lives on Thra?"

Two spindly legs peeked over the side of the platform, and Kylan jolted back into defense. The spiders had made it to the top of the mushroom already. skekLi crowed as Kylan and Naia jumped away from the spiders that crept over the edge. Kylan cursed under his breath. Whether or not he was telling the truth, skekLi had been stalling, and they'd fallen for it.

The Skeksis chuckled to himself, gnashing his teeth.

"Gelfling waited too long. Time to make a deal is over. Now the deal is only that both Gelfling come quietly, or Spriton dies."

Kylan gulped as skekLi swung the staff so its crystal-clubbed end was pointed at him, so close, it nearly touched his nose.

"Hey! I got it!"

Amri's voice was so far away, Kylan thought maybe he had imagined it. The corrie walls bounced the words back to them, and they scanned the cliffs. Kylan finally spotted the Grottan boy high up in one of the bell-bird nests, waving. Even as the wind was caught in the tiny object in his hand, an eerie tone filled the valley. The spiders chittered, and even skekLi turned his gaze upward.

"The bone," Naia whispered. "He found the bone—now what?"

"Play it!" Kylan shouted.

"Play it? I'm no musician!"

"Just blow in it!"

"Oh!"

From so far away, Kylan could only see Amri move his hands to his face. None of the spiders moved, frozen in anticipation, one with its foreleg on the top of Kylan's foot.

A long soft note rang through the corrie. It was faint, and only one note, but it brought a chill to Kylan's spine. The spiders that were closing in on the nest where Amri perched backed away, too close to the sound of breath in the bell-bird's bone. Even the spiders on the cap trembled, whispering among themselves in hesitation and fear.

But the note did not grow louder, instead fading out as Amri lost breath. Kylan fidgeted in frustration, licking his lips. He knew if he had the bone, he could raise its song to fill the entire corrie. Amri was blowing too hard, or too soft—either way, it wasn't enough.

"It's too difficult! I don't know how!" Amri called. "I'm sorry!"

"Naia. You have to get it for me."

Naia's mouth fell open in protest, but then she yelped as a spider reached her heel. She kicked it away, tightening the grip on her dagger. skekLi's promises and stories had disarmed them for long enough, and whether or not they held any truth did not matter now.

"We'll stop him first," Naia said, pointing her blade. "Then get the bone."

"Yes. You cannot leave the little Spriton alone with the spiders and us!" skekLi said. He prodded Kylan's chest with the staff. It was sharp, but the gesture was more patronizing than meant to hurt him. Kylan felt the heat of anger growing inside him. He reached out and grabbed the end of the Skeksis's staff, holding it tight and raising it over his shoulder so its sharp end could no longer jab him.

"I'm not a hostage," he growled. "And I'm not helpless. And I'm not weak! Naia, go get the bone from Amri and bring it to me. Then I will take care of the spiders and this Skeksis liar!"

skekLi grunted, then hissed, trying to pull the staff back. Kylan held on, lifting his feet just a little so he slid easily across the surface of the cap. As long as he held on to the staff, it wasn't a danger to him. Naia watched, torn between doing what Kylan had told her to do and protecting him, as she had always done in the past. Then she sheathed the knife and turned toward Amri.

"Throw it!" she shouted.

"Are you sure?"

Kylan wrapped his arms around the staff as skekLi hoisted him into the air, shrieking and waving the thing back and forth, trying to dislodge the Gelfling attached to the end. Kylan held on, far from the Skeksis's grasp, and for the moment, he grinned. Naia saw that he was not afraid, finally turning her back completely. Under normal circumstances, that might have scared him—but now, his heart exploded with pride. Naia trusted him to take care of himself.

Naia put her hands to her mouth and shouted, "Just throw it! On three!"

skekLi changed his attack and let out a cry, slamming the staff down onto the mushroom cap. Kylan let go before it struck, landing nimbly on his feet and shielding his eyes as the end of the rod and its crystal shattered and splintered. The ringing from the crystal breaking brought up squeaks of pain from the spiders. Even skekLi halted, holding the unbroken end of his staff, beady pupils floating in the whites of his eyes.

"No!"

"One . . . two . . . three!"

Amri threw the bone. Kylan uncovered his eyes in time to watch the tiny white bone spin through the air. It fell fast, at first, but then something blue sparkled on it. A balloon of web blossomed from the bone, slowing its fall like a seedpod floating in the wind. Naia took a running leap toward the end of the cap, wings folded along her back.

"No!" skekLi cried again, but the words had no effect. Naia was in free fall, unafraid of the depth below her. The bone twirled close enough that Kylan could see it was fork shaped, much like a *firca*. As it flipped, the wind caught it in different ends, eliciting a three-part note that sent the spiders shying away.

"NO! Drenchen! I hope she drowns!" skekLi screamed.

Kylan jumped back as the Skeksis slashed at him with the splintered end of his staff. He couldn't see whether Naia had caught the bone or had opened her wings in time to keep from crashing to her death. He had to trust her, and save his own hide in the meantime. He scrambled back, snagging a piece of the crystal that had not fallen into the pit below. As the spiders darted toward him, he struck the crystal against the fossilized flesh of the mushroom cap. Its ringing sent them away, back over the edge of the cap, where they watched with their trembling legs and faceted eyes.

"She can't drown," he told skekLi. "She caught the bone. Even now, she's got hold of the bridge dangling there. Any minute she'll come over the side, and I'll have it. I'll send these spiders away with a single note. Then it will be just you and us."

"You can't know that. You can't see it. We'll kill you before she gets here!"

Kylan snatched one of the staff's splinters, stepped and threw it like a miniature spear. It made its mark, striking skekLi in the shoulder, sticking out like a pin. The Skeksis squawked and yanked it out, but Kylan threw another, and another, sticking him full of darts from his own staff.

"GRAGGGHHH!" roared skekLi. "Stop it! Stop it, Gelfling!"

"Or what?"

"Or—Or—wait! Stop it, *and*! AND! Stop it *and* we'll let you go! Eh?"

"I don't think you're in a place to negotiate!"

"Oh, really? Which one was it, said the Drenchen is coming up the bridge? Eh?"

Kylan frowned. In his confidence, he'd lost track of the location of the bridge that hung from the cap. Now he saw skekLi had taken up position there. The Skeksis crouched and held up a finger in front of a smile, plucking two more slivers from his arm.

"Listen," he cooed. "Listen!"

Kylan did. He did not like what he heard—Naia, shouting

and swearing, close but too far away.

"She's on the bridge, but the spiders are after her!" Amri shouted from his vantage above. Without the bone, he had moved from ledge to ledge, batting the spiders away with a tree branch. "Kylan, you've got to do something!"

"Here we go. Watch, Gelfling. skekLi will do something. Yes! Something kind. Spiders! Away!"

skekLi whistled sharply, and Naia's yelps calmed. skekLi leaned over the edge and reached. When he did, Kylan thought of running and kicking, sending the Skeksis over the side—but he wasn't sure he had the weight to do it and would probably just make things worse. So he waited, holding his breath, as skekLi straightened. In his hand, he held Naia by the back of the neck, lifting her up. In both hands she clutched the bone, and though skekLi shook her and shook her, she refused to release it.

"Let her go!" Kylan said.

"Oh? Now we're in a mood to bargain!"

"Don't bargain," Naia said, voice tight in her throat. "Do your thing!"

She threw the bone. skekLi tried to catch it with his other hand, but it was full with the broken staff and he missed. Kylan lunged and snatched the bone from the air. It was larger than a normal *firca*, sun-bleached white and sharp on all three ends where it had been snapped.

skekLi crowed a warning and lifted Naia higher.

"Play it and I'll dash her head on the rock!"

Naia beat at skekLi's claw with her hands.

"Do it, Kylan! He won't hurt me, he needs to bring me back to the Emperor!"

"But what if he doesn't?"

A tiny shape flashed out from within Naia's tunic, darting down skekLi's arm and flying into his face. Tavra latched on to his eye, and he screamed as she bit. She raced across his prickling head as he dropped the staff and tried to smash her with his claws. He didn't let Naia go, and she kicked and struggled against his grip.

"Do it, Kylan!"

He raised the bone and played.

The note was a thousand times stronger than when Amri had tried. It filled the corrie like wind, or water, or fire. Its reverberations circling against the walls from the pool at the bottom and all the way up to the sky. As it echoed, it reinforced itself, growing louder and louder until the mountains themselves began to sing with its song.

The spiders detached from the cap and every wall, falling like leaves. Even Tavra, in her spider body, could not withstand the sound in her sensitive spider ears, and fell from skekLi's head to lie motionless on the ground, all eight legs folded under her.

"NO!" cried skekLi, barely audible above the ringing. "I'LL KILL HER!"

Kylan took another breath and played, willing that the ancient song of the bell-bird would take its toll on the Skeksis as well. skekLi resisted, free hand pressed against the side of his head where his ear hole was, lifting Naia and making to smash her against the hardened mushroom cap with all of his strength.

Kylan's breath caught in his throat, and the note began to die. It wasn't working. The bone-flute dropped from his hands as skekLi let out a battle cry, thrusting Naia downward.

The song of the bone-flute faded, but skekLi's death thrust halted midair. A second note, then a third, vibrated through the corrie. The tones were deep. Primal. Voices, Kylan realized. As the two-tone chant sank into the walls of the cliffs, Kylan picked up the bone-flute from where he'd dropped it. He played the instrument and found the single note joined the other two with no discordance. It was the song of Thra, after all—the song that would move mountains.

skekLi dropped Naia. She fell with a gentle *thump*, then climbed to her feet and stumbled away. The Skeksis was frozen where he stood, eyes wide and pupils tiny, panting so heavily that drool dripped from his open mouth.

"Look," Naia whispered.

Kylan lowered the bone-flute and looked where she pointed. High on the edge of the corrie wall, two long-necked creatures stood. One held a tall bow, arrow nocked, though the point was lowered. There was no need to use the weapon while skekLi was held immobile by the bone-shaking song. He twitched and jerked against the power of his other half. He could do no more harm to the Gelfling, at least for now.

Maybe a Mystic could keep a Skeksis in one place . . .

Aughra's words echoed in Kylan's memory. He smiled as he recognized the long-maned oval faces of urVa and urLii, whose song filled the corrie as if it were the chamber in a seashell.

CHAPTER 27

SkekLi's breath came in and out in furious, haggard wheezes. The chanting faded, but the power of the song remained, holding the Skeksis immobile.

"This is not . . . ," skekLi began. He shot a look at Naia and Kylan, then back at his Mystic brothers. "This is not nice—not fair!"

"Let the Gelfling go," urVa called, his low voice resonating inside the corrie so it sounded as if it were coming from everywhere at once. "You are outnumbered."

Kylan edged away from him when skekLi splayed his claws, as if contemplating an attack despite his position. They might still be in danger. skekLi spat and barked a laugh.

"Or what? You'll raise that bow and run me through? And what happens to our other, eh?"

urVa stood watch while urLii began the winding descent down the corrie wall. He made the climb look easy with all four hands and his long-toed, bare feet, almost as dexterous as a spider himself. He paused on a ledge, half-hanging from the rock face, and tapped his chin. He was close enough now that his thoughtful murmur was audible.

"Hmm . . . That *would* be an interesting turn of events . . ."

"Don't say that!" Naia muttered under her breath. "Kylan, let's get Tavra and get out of here."

Kylan had never agreed with a sentiment more. skekLi's gaze latched on to him as he pocketed the bone-flute and approached Tavra, who was crumpled on the ground in a little ball of legs and crystal body. Kylan had to step in reach of the hulking Skeksis, but he refused to be afraid anymore. He gently took Tavra in his hands before returning to stand near Naia.

skekLi was spiny with anger, all the quills and feathers along his neck and the back of his head raised. His bloodshot eyes burned with hatred and vengeful excitement.

"Just wait," the Skeksis hissed. "If you think tiny spider servants are wicked. They are just the prologue. Just a test. You wait to see what skekUng is making. Big servants. Mindless, heartless servants. *Flawless* servants, with claws that could snap Gelfling in two. See what Gelfling do then, eh . . . if any are *left*."

Kylan shuddered and backed away. He didn't know what to say, so he said nothing.

As much as he might have liked to, skekLi could do nothing to stop the Grottan Gelfling from flying over on their shimmering wings. He stood by, glaring at the Mystics overhead as the Gelfling took Kylan, Naia, and Tavra away to safety. It took two Grottan girls to bear Kylan's weight, and one to keep Naia aloft. When they alighted on the far side, Kylan looked back. skekLi stood in the center of the mushroom cap behind them, quivering eyes fixed and unblinking.

"What was he talking about?" he asked. "Heartless servants?"

Naia shook her head. "I don't care. He's a liar. I say we strand him here."

Kylan let out a shiver, trying to shake the memory of the Skeksis's words and penetrating eyes. Tavra stirred, finally, straightening her legs. He placed her on his shoulder.

"He will not be stranded for long," she said, whispering even in her spider voice. "The other Skeksis will come and rescue him. He will go back to the castle and inform them of everything we have done, if he hasn't already. I don't know how much Krychk told him, or whether he's shared the information with the others—but if he hasn't, we shouldn't take any chances."

"What are you saying, that we should kill him?" Naia asked. "And urLii with him? That's not right. urLii didn't do anything wrong!"

"No one's done anything wrong," urLii corrected. He met them and the Grottan, dusting his hands of rocks and sand from his climb. "We are all doing what it is we do, what is our nature and our character. Right and wrong . . . are a terribly complex song."

"But that doesn't help us," said Naia.

Kylan held out a hand to her, hoping to calm her.

"What do we do about skekLi?" he asked urLii.

"Hmm . . . I suppose that depends on your character."

Tavra and Naia were in conflict, and it was unspoken but understood in the following quiet that they were waiting for Kylan's opinion. Amri joined them, too, out of breath and scratched up, with some spider-bite welts along his arms and legs but otherwise spry as ever.

Kylan watched skekLi, as dark and unmoving as a bad omen, still gazing at them from across the cavern expanse. The image reminded him of the shadowy cloaks of skekMal, the Hunter. The fire-eyed Skeksis that had killed his parents and tried to kill Gurjin and everyone else, without remorse. skekLi had tormented Tavra by giving her to Krychk the crystal spider, and had not only tried to kill them this day, but betrayed his own Emperor's requests in doing so. He had no loyalty even to his own kind.

urLii proposed that there was no right or wrong, but that in itself did not seem right. It wasn't wrong, either. The paradox gave him a headache.

"I don't think we should kill him," Kylan said in the end. "The Gelfling are a peaceful people. Even when we fight among ourselves. If we're to be the heroes of this song, we must show mercy, even when we're not shown mercy ourselves. The Skeksis have done terrible things to us . . . but I would rather believe that we can unite for the good of our people, not for revenge."

Naia puffed up and crossed her arms as if that settled the matter. Tavra was diplomatic, although she disagreed.

"You'd rather let him go? That is not for the good of our people."

"No. We shouldn't let him go. I think Naia's right . . . At least for now, we should keep him here, but someone will have to keep watch over him. Prevent the other Skeksis from finding him."

"Ho ho hoo . . ."

The tired laugh was familiar. Still picking bits of spiderweb from her cloak, Maudra Argot stepped forward from the small group of Grottan. Of the thirty-seven Grottan Gelfling, even fewer remained, bedraggled and afraid, some elders but mostly younglings Amri's age. They had lost the Caves of Grot as well—all in exchange for the bone-flute. Kylan's heart broke for them all, and he hoped that it was worth the sacrifice.

Amri took Maudra Argot's arm to guide her to where Kylan and Naia stood.

"This task falls to my people. The spiders took us by surprise in Domrak. They are not under the control of the Skeksis. They will not fall back just because skekLi has been defeated, nor will they stay away even if we evict them with the bone-flute. The truth is, we cannot return. The Sanctuary has caves in plenty for us. We will be the guardians of skekLi, as we have guarded the other wonderful and terrible secrets of Thra."

"I will remain here as well," urLii added. "Between the Shadowlings and myself, I believe skekLi's song has come to an end."

Maudra Argot waved an accepting hand to the Mystic. The hand latched on to Amri and shook him gently.

"Amri. I still want you to go on to Ha'rar. I won't be happy until those Silverlings in the capital welcome us to the table, and you still have quite a lot of growing to do. Ho ho hooo!"

Kylan nodded.

"We should go. We have the bone. We can make the message for all our people. We should do it as soon as we can. If skekLi has told the other Skeksis even a little, they'll be after us. Especially once they find that he failed in his plan to capture us."

"I can agree on that," Tavra replied. "Time is not yet out of our grasp. Kylan, how long will it take you to make the *firca*?"

"I don't know. I've played many, but I've never made one before . . . I can't mess it up. We only have one chance."

"I didn't see any other bones in the nest," Amri agreed. "That was the only one."

Naia gestured to the bridge that would take them to the outer walkways of the Sanctuary.

"Then let's get out of here, at least. I can't stand being here with *him*."

Kylan hoped they could find an exit that was not as difficult to navigate as the underwater tunnel, but at that moment he would brave three hundred of the dratted things if it meant escaping the ever-present gaze of skekLi.

They said their goodbyes to Maudra Argot and the remaining Grottan. Kylan lingered, watching skekLi where he was alone on the mushroom in the center of the corrie. He had not moved since they had left him, except to hunker down to a squat. His cloaks draped out from his narrow shoulders, his mantle and headdress fluttering in the constant breeze. He looked like a feathered obsidian stone, though unlike the obelisks in Stone-in-the-Wood, he would be ready to leap, to claw and bite and slash his way to freedom the moment he was given an opportunity.

urLii's cool shadow covered Kylan's shoulder.

"I would give my life to stop him from escaping," the Mystic remarked. "He is me, after all. But I do not believe it will be necessary. Even if it were, it would certainly be a dramatic moment, eh?"

urLii chuckled despite the somewhat morbid sentiment. The bell-bird bone felt immensely heavy in Kylan's pocket. They had fought so hard for it, and lost much—and he still had to craft the *firca* from it, a process which could possibly destroy it, if he did not take enough care. This was what he had wanted, though, wasn't it? Purpose did not come lightly.

"We spoke with Mother Aughra, before we came to Domrak," Kylan said. "She had no words for us. She said only time would tell. That understanding the heavens would find us in our place, I think is what she meant. If we could understand the grand song, we would be able to find our way. But . . . the Gelfling don't have time for that. We have to cut our own paths. We have to make the choice between being the weaver or the woven. The teller and the told. The singer and the song . . . But I choose to be both."

urLii scratched his chin with his slender fingers and tilted his head.

"Hmmm! Weaver *and* the woven, eh? Where did you hear such fine advice?"

Kylan smiled and sighed.

"Goodbye, urLii. I hope to meet again someday."

"We probably will not. But I will hear the song of the bell-bird again, yes . . . When light and shadows collide, under the triple suns."

The words were like poetry, and Kylan did not know what it meant. It was like a refrain to a song whose main chorus had not yet been revealed to him. He had seen similar words on the walls of urVa's hut, and even in some places in the Caves of Grot. Yet the bigger picture was still unclear. Perhaps that was the vision

Aughra was seeking. The Great Conjunction, and all it entailed.

In the meantime, Kylan bowed to urLii, and then to urVa, who remained stoic on the ridge above, bow in hand in case he should need to use it. He gave skekLi a last glance, remembering the Satirist's sinister words.

Wait to see what skekUng is making. See what Gelfling do . . . if any are left.

In his mind's eye, he saw nightmares, looming in the dark of the earth. Monsters, mindless and heartless from looking into the darkened Crystal. He wanted to believe it was just another lie—just more words meant to burrow into his mind and poison him with doubt. If they were a lie, would skekLi have mentioned skekUng by name? Which of the Skeksis was skekUng, and what was his role in the court of the Skeksis? Most importantly, what was he *making*?

The spiders were only a prologue . . .

"Look away, Kylan."

He had almost forgotten Tavra was there, crouched on his shoulder. For a moment, it was as if she were standing beside him, just out of view, resplendent in her whites and silvers, the opposite of the black tower of hatred that was skekLi. In truth, her tiny shadow did not fall beyond the folds of his cloak, and her touch was only a pinprick on his cheek instead of a comforting hand.

"Forget him for now, or you will not be able to look ahead."

He did as she suggested, turning his back on the Skeksis's piercing gaze and hurrying after his friends.

CHAPTER 28

There were many exits from the corrie, though most were overgrown and difficult to find. Amri led them along the spiraling stair ledge to one such egress, a triangular opening below where urVa stood watch. The Archer's mane danced in the wind where it was not tied back in braids and topknot, and he faced the direction of the breeze to take its scent. He had put up his bow when skekLi was confined to the open-air prison, and now leaned over to watch the Gelfling as they stopped in front of the tunnel.

"urVa! Will we see you when we come out?" Naia called.

"No. I traveled this far in search of my others, little Drenchen," he replied. "I found one, but it seems he will stay here. I must move on. We will meet again. Someday."

"Are you all right? We fought skekMal . . . I was worried we would harm you as well."

urVa shook his head. When he did, the wind blew his mane from his face, and Kylan saw a wound on his cheek and eye, in the same place where he'd struck skekMal in the Dark Wood.

"What is done is done. The suns turn."

urVa straightened, his warrior's back strong and hard. Rocks and pebbles skipped down from the ledge as he moved away from it, departing.

"If you see any of my urRu others," the Archer said in his heavy, weighted way, "tell them I seek them . . . Tell them to meet me in the valley. Farewell, little Gelfling."

They waved after him until the tip of his tail disappeared from view. Once he was gone, they pushed aside the ferns and other plants and started into what Kylan hoped would be the last tunnel he ever saw.

"urRu," Kylan breathed, trying out the word. "That must be the name of his people."

"The urRu . . . ," Amri echoed. "The urRu and the Skeksis."

Despite the familiar confines of rock and moss, though, this tunnel was short, and lit from both ends by daylight. In fact, Kylan reflected, it was almost nice. Naia took the lead, as usual, thinking out loud.

"The Skeksis live together in the castle . . . They have power there, because of the Crystal, and because they are all in one place. The Mystics are alone. We found urVa trapped in the Cradle-Tree. urLii was in the Tomb of Relics. They had power over skekLi, with their song . . . but only because he was outnumbered. If all the Skeksis were to overtake urVa alone, or urLii . . . if they all came to rescue skekLi, and only urLii was here to guard him . . ."

"But if the Skeksis come to get skekLi, they'll have to defeat urLii, right?" Amri asked. He held up two fingers in parallel. "But if they defeat urLii, then won't skekLi also be defeated? Right?"

"Either way," Kylan put in hastily, "urLii stayed behind by his own will. He seemed confident he could contain skekLi safely. We have no choice but to trust him. We have our own journey. Right?"

Naia nodded, slowly at first, and then more firmly.

"Right."

In no time, they exited the tunnel onto a moss-covered landing. The mountains here were soft and undulating, not jagged and rocky. The air was clear, blowing flurries of leaves and sometimes white and pink petals by, and Kylan thought he heard the sound of chimes. It was beautiful and gold and green, but the scene left something to be desired. Kylan frowned deeply. Their belongings were back at the entrance to Tide Pass, including the Book of Raunip, the pearl amulet, and Tavra's sword. The others were quiet, too. No one wanted to be the first to bring up the subject, but it was too important. They couldn't just leave their things, not with the journey they had ahead.

As he was about to say something, Naia let out a loud sigh that dissolved into laughter. She trotted forward through the tall serpentine grass. Sticking out of the ground cover was a long arrow shaft, decorated with a string of bells. Kylan recognized it as one of urVa's, and when they reached it, they found their traveling pack and the silver Vapra sword hidden safely in the grass.

Kylan stooped and opened the pack. They drank from the water gourd, and he found the book, turning the pages until he found those that described Gyr's *firca*. As he read passage after passage in Raunip's scrawling hand, he felt the rest of the world drift away. He forgot the caves and the spiders, swimming in the pitch-dark and holding his breath until his lungs burned. He forgot the fear when he had seen Naia's wound and worried he had lost her. He forgot skekLi, unbroken even in his defeat, and his frightening promise of what would face them in the days to come. He even forgot, just for the moment, Naia, Tavra, and Amri, as they gave him space and silence in which to work.

All he saw were the sketches of the *firca* and the hope it had to offer. It was like every other *firca* he'd ever seen or played, with one mouthpiece, which split into a fork. The pipes on either end of the fork were carved with three finger holes, one for each finger when held properly in two hands. *Firca* were made out of many materials, each with a slightly different voice. Most were carved from a single piece of wood, though many were made from forked reeds. The Sifa were even known to make theirs from the prongs of welhorn shells, and their *firca*'s voices came with the ghostly roars of ocean waves. The *firca* was the most common Gelfling instrument, and perhaps one of the simplest, yet the many materials used in its creation also made it one of the most varied. It could play single notes as well as harmonies, while still being small enough to dangle around one's neck.

Kylan took out the bell-bird bone and laid it on the open pages of the book. It was already forked, a bit bigger than a standard wooden Spriton *firca*, but in one unbroken piece. They were lucky that Amri had been able to find the thing—fortunate that not only were there any bones left at all, but that the one Amri had found was in the perfect shape. A single bone might have worked as a pipe, but Kylan wondered whether it would not have had the same impact. He remembered joining urVa and urLii's song with the *firca*. The third part had given the song power, though he suspected it was the urRu's connection with skekLi that had been mostly responsible for holding him.

No, a pipe or flute would not have been the same. The *firca* was special. It could play two notes at once, leaving room for a third. What that third voice was, Kylan didn't know, but he felt instinctively that it had to do with the legend of the bell-bird. The birds that sang and the mountains sang back. Perhaps, if the bell-birds sang with two notes, it was Thra itself that sang the third part. Perhaps the *firca* was so valued by the Gelfling because it left a place for the very voice of Thra.

Kylan picked up the bone and turned it around, inspecting it from every angle. He did not even have tools to sand or carve with. The location of the finger holes had to be precise as well, or their tones would not play in harmony. If he had been asked no more than a trine ago how he might craft the *firca* that could well change the fate of the Gelfling, without any tools and from an ancient bone, he would have laughed. Now there was no time to laugh. He had to do it here, and now, and with what he had. He had no other choice.

He knew that if he hesitated too long, he might lose his courage, so he took a breath and ran his thumb along one of the flute ends of the fork. He willed the heat of dream-etching, just in the surface of his thumb. As the blue light shone, fine white smoke rose from where he touched. The vibration of the etching heat made the bone sing in a high, resonant key.

He had to work slowly and with great care. In the end, he lifted his thumb and looked. The edge where he had etched was smooth, as if beveled with a sharp knife by a practiced whittler. It was pure and white, as the rest of the bone, and no longer jagged where it had broken from the rest of the remains. It was hot to the touch, but cooling, and he let out a breath. It was possible, then. He could do this.

It took all afternoon and into the evening. By the time he heard Naia return with her catch for dinner, Kylan's forehead and the hair at the nape of his neck were slick with sweat, his brow sore from bunching in concentration. When he felt a hand on his shoulder, gently squeezing to get his attention, he let out a little laugh and looked up.

"What do you think?" he asked.

Naia looked over his shoulder, and he opened his hands. Lying in his lap was a white *firca*, sculpted and smoothed to the finest detail. He hardly remembered making it, or at least, he recalled none of the moments. As his head cleared from the focus, he realized he had gone into a kind of trance. His fingers were blistered and sore, but the product of his dedication was perfect, as if he had transformed the bell-bird bone into the instrument it had always been meant to be.

"It's beautiful," Naia said.

Tavra, perched on Naia's shoulder, traveled down her arm to get a closer look.

"Indeed," she said. "I wish I still had Gelfling ears to hear you play it."

It was bittersweet. He didn't dare play it so close to her; it had paralyzed her when it had been just a bone. It was sad, but there was nothing he could do about it now.

"I'm still sorry. If I hadn't trapped you in that spider's body..."

"If you hadn't, I would be dead. And I would not have had the chance to see the two of you succeed as you have. For this, I am only grateful . . . Stop berating yourself for doing the things your heart calls you to do. Now! You'd best eat after your hard work these past days. I'm sure Naia agrees."

Naia's stomach rumbled.

"I am pretty predictable," she agreed.

Kylan joined them at the fire. Naia had caught several fish, and Amri had them roasting directly in the fire so their scales blackened and smoked. He had put a paste on it from one of his mysterious bottles, though luckily this one smelled much better than the salve he'd used on his feet. Naia leaned and whispered, "I told him I'd let him cook. I'm sorry in advance."

"I may have trouble seeing in the daylight, but my hearing is impeccable," said Amri.

Whether or not it was intentional, the blackened fish was salty and filling, with a satisfying flavor that reminded Kylan of mushrooms and berries.

After supper, while they sat around the fire, he found some cord and hung the bone *firca* from his neck. It was now his most precious possession. He refused to lose it.

"So, I have a question," Naia said in between licking her fingers. She tossed the skewer into the fire and watched it crackle and pop. "When you made your plan to corner the crystal spider, you gave Tavra a note. Whatever was written on it fooled the spider. I want to know what it said!"

Kylan felt his cheeks warm, though he knew no one could see

the blush in the dancing light of the fire.

"Oh. It doesn't matter..."

"I have it right here!"

As if by magic, the piece of paper appeared in Amri's hand, smoothed and folded as it had been the evening Kylan had given it to her. He reached for it to take it back and get rid of it before anyone else read it, but Amri jumped away with it.

"*Dear Tavra,*" he began to read. Kylan interrupted in a hurry, hoping to drown out Amri's reading.

"I guessed that whatever was controlling Tavra couldn't read. That it couldn't read the note on the rock wall, so it had the spiders try to conceal the message—"

"*... I write to you on behalf of Naia, and Gurjin, and those others whom you have helped since leaving Ha'rar on an errand for the All-Maudra...*"

"—I had to test it, so I used—"

"*I know it must be very difficult for you, having been betrayed by the Skeksis in the most painful ways. I wanted to let you know that we all care for you and that, should you need us...*"

"So I used what I had on hand..."

But there was no stopping Amri, so Kylan put his face in his hands and waited for it to end. Amri stood before Tavra, Naia, and all the stars and moons above, reading for all to hear:

"*... simply call on us. For especially I admire your courage and your loyalty to all that is good and right, and even if I'm unable to put these sentiments into words to say to you directly, I wanted at least to give to you this promise in words that stay. Your friend, Kylan.*"

It was very quiet after that. Kylan counted to nine before looking up to see if the coast was clear. Undoubtedly proud of himself, Amri folded the note back up and put it in his pocket, sitting back down beside Naia. With night's dark around them, his eyes were open wide and bright, shining with laughter. Naia was grinning, too.

"I hope one day you'll write me something as sticky-sweet as that," she teased. "I'd learn to read just so I could read it. Every night, before I went to bed!"

Kylan patted his cheeks, trying to cool his embarrassment.

"Listen. I—I was trying to tell her in person, but I couldn't get it right. So I wrote it down. When I saw Krychk talking to the Skeksis, I had . . . I had to make sure it wasn't Tavra, before we trapped her. Tavra can read, but it seemed like Krychk couldn't. I knew that if she didn't react . . . to that note . . ."

"That I was not myself," Tavra finally spoke up, from her current place on a rock near the fire. Her little sapphire body shone, the dream-stitching symbol that had bound her soul to the spider's body glowing softly. "A clever plan. I am glad it succeeded."

"When he showed it to me, I knew something was wrong," Amri added, nodding with self-important pride. "There's no way a Silverling princess would be illiterate."

Naia's smile hadn't faded. She leaned her chin on her hand and grinned, but it was soft and happy.

"And now here we are, with the *firca*. Gurjin will arrive in Sog soon . . . and Rian must be almost to Ha'rar. I'm so glad we will be able to meet him there and have good news to tell. Even if there is some not-so-good news as well."

Tavra waved a foreleg. Despite his conviction that she would have reacted to his letter had she been able to decipher it at the time, the All-Maudra's daughter showed no reaction now. Kylan wasn't sure which he preferred.

"That is the price of success," she said simply. "And there are more prices to be paid. We can only hope that in the end, we will have riches enough to exchange for our freedom from the Skeksis and the situation in which they've placed our people."

Kylan was glad of the shift in words, even if it was to something so serious. At least, for the time being, he could offer something positive and encouraging. For once, he could point out a bright star to guide them, if only for a short while.

"Tomorrow I will play the *firca*," he said. "urLii reminded me of something in the Tomb of Relics. Dream-stitching. Binding a dreamfast, or the thoughts of the mind, to writing. Not all the Gelfling race can read, so I've been thinking. We can't just write a message with the *firca*, no matter how large or widespread. Only some would be able to read it, and that includes the Skeksis."

"So you'll bind a message in dreamfast?" Amri asked. His teasing face became serious and he clenched his hands into excited fists. "That's brilliant! Then the Skeksis won't be able to decipher it, even if they catch one of the notes!"

"They'll surely be able to guess what it says, if it's written at a time like this," Naia said. "I can't read, but if I were a Skeksis and saw something like that, I would assume it was a warning to the Gelfling people. Will that really make a difference?"

Kylan shook his head.

"I'll disguise it. I'll use a symbol that means something else, but when a Gelfling hand touches it, the dreamfast will happen. Maudra Mera began to teach me, but I left Sami Thicket before I mastered it. I always thought she only taught me because I was bad at other things. But I think I did it to Tavra. I stitched the dream of her mind to the spider's body."

It wasn't a strong enough statement to pull the pensive mood from the air, so Kylan reassured himself and gathered the words he wanted to say. There was only one way to succeed, and it was to take control of his destiny.

"I will deliver the message that begins our fight against the Skeksis."

That night, they slept under the stars. Kylan watched their slow spinning and listened to the warm wind in the grass. For the first time in a long time, he felt like he would be able to sleep in peace. He rested his hands on the *firca*, over his heart. Though he wanted nothing more than to play it, he waited. He would wait until tomorrow, and until then, save the anticipation and longing. It would make the final song that much more powerful.

A blade of grass moved to the side near his cheek. It was the only sign that Tavra had joined him, silently picking her way across the tips of the grass as he might hop along the pathway stones in Sami Thicket. She said nothing, balancing on the stalk of a grassflower like a tiny, delicate acrobat.

He waited for her to speak, but she didn't. There was simply a shared quiet—an acceptance—and then she left, not one word spoken.

CHAPTER 29

In the morning, Kylan took care to let the others sleep as he left for the nearby hillside. More of the pink petals flitted by, and as one landed on his tunic, he remembered seeing one similar, all the way back in Stone-in-the-Wood. The wind had carried it there, and the water of the Black River, and then to all of Thra.

That was how he wanted his message to be carried. And so up he trudged, striding over the bowed grass and clusters of flowers, until he found the tree that was the source of the petals drifting across the mountainside.

The tree was tall and handsome, gnarled like an elder's hand with many knots and joints and ankles. Its leaves were filled with blossoms in peach and pink and red. When the wind blew through it, the petals released in flurries, flying out over the Dark Wood and, he hoped, across the rest of Thra. So dense were the flowers and leaves that even after a strong gust, it never seemed it would ever run dry. This was the tree that he would sing to with the bone *firca*.

He sat before the tree and placed his hands on the flute. In every dream of the previous night, it had called to him; in every dream he'd felt bonded to it, as if he belonged to it and it to him. It was as if the spirit of the bell-bird was inviting him to bring its song to life after so many ages of silence.

Now, finally, he lifted the instrument to his lips, and without thinking, began to play.

He lost himself in the song. The sound of the *firca* was perfect, its tone in a key Kylan could not quite identify. When he played, it was as if the very dome of the sky sang back to him, as if the mountains themselves were coming to life and humming in harmony. He closed his eyes and brought up memories while he played: the journey that had brought him here, and the hardships and joys that had followed. He remembered skekMal, the Castle of the Crystal. Naia and Gurjin, and Tavra the All-Maudra's daughter. He called upon the memories of what Naia had told him, what she had seen in the castle—what Rian had seen, too. Though he could not project their dreams into his, he could remember what he had felt, and remember that he had known the truth. He recalled the fear that had struck them beyond the Tomb of Relics, the fight with Krychk the crystal spider. With a little tremble, he brought into his mind the terrible black eyes of skekLi, and his forewarning words about what was to come.

When the song finally ended, his lips and fingers were numb. His mind both spun and was blank, like the endless rushing of water in a fall. When he looked up at the leaves and petals of the tree, his vision throbbed. It looked as though the tree was glowing blue, each leaf and petal inscribed with a sacred symbol: a circle enclosed in a triangle, enclosed in a final circle. This was the dream-stitching: a dream that would stay. Their message to the Gelfling people.

His friends had joined him while he had been playing. Even Tavra was there, alert from her post on Naia's shoulder. The song had not harmed her, as it had when he had played it against the spiders in the Sanctuary. He did not know how long they had been listening, but both Naia's and Amri's cheeks were streaked with tears.

"That was . . . ," Naia began, but did not finish. A rustling of wind washed up the mountainside toward them, and Amri gestured at it excitedly.

"Here it comes—here it comes—there they go!"

The gust hit the tree and sent the leaves and petals soaring. They spiraled away in a glittering dance, carried by the wind and flying off into the valley. Thousands more waited on the tree's great boughs to be blown away; even the trunk of the tree had been marked with the dream, Kylan hoped to its very core. Every new leaf and blossom would bear the message.

He put his hand on the tree's whorled bark and thanked it. Its branches swayed in the wild wind as if waving them on, and so, song sung, the four headed back. In a daze, Kylan said little, shouldering the traveling pack as the others took up their own belongings.

"Do you think it will work?" Amri asked.

Kylan didn't know how to answer that question, but Tavra did.

"It has already worked, so far as we can control it," she said. "What people do with the information, once they receive it, will be up to them. All that remains now is to hope my mother may be able to do something more once we bring the truth to her."

The reality of what Kylan had done struck him as he saw another petal float by. Soon all the Gelfling of the Skarith region would know what the Skeksis had done, and where their missing brothers and sisters had gone. There would no longer be a false peace between the Gelfling and the strange, cruel lords within the Castle of the Crystal. By the end of the day, the first messages would already be delivered. Questions would be asked. Some might reject the message, even after having received it. He hoped there would be a call to unite, but he had already seen that fear could cause division, as it had with Maudra Fara in Stone-in-the-Wood.

Sides would be taken. The All-Maudra would be put in the middle . . . and eventually, the Skeksis would respond, one way or another.

"We better get going," he said.

Walking single file, they began their journey down the mountains to the valley, toward the Black River. It had been their destination for so long that reaching it seemed like an impossible daydream. But as the trees parted in the wind, they saw its mighty sparkle, and Kylan knew that they would reach it before long. After that, Ha'rar awaited them on the coast of the Silver Sea.

Until then, Naia led their group with Tavra as a guide on her shoulder. Amri took the rear, bearing the Silverling's sword. Kylan dug Raunip's book from his traveling pack, searching for the last page he had cornered. Finding it, he read while he walked between the other two, claiming his place in the middle.

GLOSSARY

bell-bird: An ancient, extinct bird whose bones and beaks are said to resonate with Thra's song.

bola: A Y-shaped length of knotted rope with stones tied to each of the three ends. Used as a weapon, the *bola* can be swung or thrown, enabling the wielder to ensnare prey.

daeydoim: Six-legged desert-dwelling creatures with large dorsal scales and broad hooves. Frequently domesticated by desert nomads.

firca: A Y-shaped Gelfling wind instrument, played with both hands. It was Gyr the Song Teller's legendary instrument of choice.

fizzgig: A small furry carnivore native to the Dark Wood. Sometimes kept as a pet.

Grot: A cavern deep in the eastern mountains, rumored to be the home of the mysterious Grottan Gelfling clan.

hooyim: One of the many colorful leaping fish species that migrate in large schools along the northern Sifan coasts. Often called the jewels of the sea.

Landstrider: Long-legged hooved beasts common to the Spriton plains.

maudra: Literally "mother." The matriarch and wise woman of a Gelfling clan.

maudren: Literally "those of the mother." The family of a Gelfling *maudra*.

merkeep: A delicious tuber. It is a traditional food of the Stonewood Gelfling.

muski: Flying quilled eels endemic to the Swamp of Sog. Babies are very small, but adults never stop growing. The oldest known muski was said to be as wide as the Black River.

ninet: One of nine orbital seasons caused by the configuration of the three suns. Arcs in which Thra is farthest from the suns are winter ninets; arcs in which Thra is nearest are summer ninets. Each ninet lasts approximately one hundred trine.

swoothu: Flying beetlefur creatures with strange sleeping patterns. Many act as couriers for the Gelfling clans in exchange for food and shelter.

ta: A hot beverage made by mixing boiling water and spices.

Three Brothers: Thra's three suns: the Great Sun, the Rose Sun, and the Dying Sun.

Three Sisters: Thra's three moons: the Blue Moon, the Pearl Moon, and the Hidden Moon.

trine: The orbital period of Thra moving around the Great Sun, roughly equivalent to an Earth year.

unamoth: A large-winged pearly white insect that sheds its skin once every unum.

unum: The time for Thra's largest moon to circle Thra once, roughly equivalent to an Earth month.

vliya: Literally "blue fire." Gelfling life essence.

vliyaya: Literally "flame of the blue fire." Gelfling mystic arts.

APPENDIX

The Gelfling Clans

VAPRA

Sigil animal: Unamoth
Maudra: Mayrin, the All-Maudra

The Vapra clan was an industrious race with white hair, fair skin, and gossamer-winged women. Considered the oldest of the Gelfling clans, the Vapra resided in cliffside villages along the northern coasts, making their capital in Ha'rar. The Vapra's *maudra*, Mayrin, doubled as All-Maudra, matriarch leader of all the Gelfling clans. Vapra were skilled at camouflage; their *vliyaya* focused on light-changing magic, allowing them to become nearly invisible.

STONEWOOD

Sigil animal: Fizzgig
Maudra: Fara, the Rock Singer

This clan was a proud and ancient people who dwelled on the fertile lands near and within the Dark Wood. They made their main home in Stone-in-the-Wood, the historical home of Jarra-Jen. Many Stonewood Gelfling were valuable guards at the Castle of the Crystal. They were farmers and cobblers and makers of tools. They were inventive, but pastoral; like their sigil animal, they were peaceful but fierce when threatened.

SPRITON

Sigil animal: Landstrider

Maudra: Mera, the Dream Stitcher

Age-old rivals of the Stonewood clan, the Spriton were a warrior race inhabiting the rolling fields south of the Dark Wood. With such bountiful land to raise crops and family, this clan's territory spread to cover the valley in several villages. Counted among the most fierce fighters of the Gelfling race, the Spriton were often called upon to serve as soldiers for the Skeksis Lords and guards at the Castle of the Crystal.

SIFA

Sigil animal: Hooyim

Maudra: Gem-Eyed Ethri

Found in coastal villages along the Silver Sea, the Sifa were skilled fishermen and sailors, but very superstitious. Explorers by nature, the Sifa were competent in battle—but they truly excelled at survival. Sifan *vliyaya* focused Gelfling luck magic into inanimate objects; Sifan charms enchanted with different spells were highly desired by travelers, craftsmen, and warriors of all clans.

DOUSAN

Sigil animal: Daeydoim

Maudra: Seethi, the Skin Painter

This clan made their settlements on sandships—amazing constructs of bone and crystal that navigated the Crystal Sea like ocean vessels. Resilient even within the arid climate of the desert, the Dousan thrived. Their culture was shrouded and unsettlingly quiet, their language made of whispers and gestures, their life stories told in the intricate magic tattoos painting their bodies.

DRENCHEN
Sigil animal: Muski
Maudra: Laesid, the Blue Stone Healer

The Drenchen clan was a race of amphibious Gelfling who lived in the overgrown Swamp of Sog, deep in the southernmost reaches of the Skarith region. Sturdier and taller than the rest of their race, the Drenchen were powerful in combat, but generally preferred to keep to themselves. Though one of the smallest Gelfling clans, the Drenchen had the largest sense of clan pride; they were loyal to one another, but remained as distant from other clans as possible.

GROTTAN
Sigil animal: Hollerbat
Maudra: Argot, the Shadow Bender

A mysterious, secretive breed who dwelled in perpetual darkness in the Caves of Grot. Generations in the shadows left them with an extreme sensitivity to light—and solid black eyes that could see in the dark and large ears to make out even the faintest of echoes. The Grottan clan was said to number less than three dozen Gelfling, and their life span was said to be unheard of, lasting three to four times as long as other Gelfling.